Guest Boy

Book I

Light Piercing Water Trilogy

by Djelloul Marbrook

Mira Publishing House CIC.
PO BOX 312
Leeds LS16 0FN
West Yorkshire
England
www.MiraPublishing.com

Light Piercing Water - Trilogy
I. Guest Boy
By Djelloul Marbrook
ISBN: 978-1-908509-06-2
First published in Great Britain 2012 by Mira Publishing House CIC.

Printed and bound by CPI Group (UK) Ltd, Croydon, CR0 4YY

A full CIP record for this book is available from the British Library.
A full CIP record for this book is available from the Library of Congress.

For David C. Wayland
1940 - 2012

Weep and say your farewells,
for the treacherous wind
has got the better of us
and driven our ship
into the world's farthermost ocean!

The Last Voyage of Sindbad the Sailor
Tales from the Thousand and One Nights
(N.J. Dawood translation))

Part I

Djelloul Marbrook

1

For dying ships and dead sailors he wishes a fine descent to the bottom of things. It's one of the few wishes left in him. Ships and their sailors mostly go ugly, and an hour out of Elizabeth, New Jersey, *Delos Victory* sounds like she knows it.

The new Verrazano Bridge throws a shadowy net over her as she pushes towards the sun groaning with a bellyache of Brown & Sharpe dies.

The new men elbow each other, seeing their bosun stowing the thick dock lines in long loops alongside them. They're used to orders, not help.

His name is Bo Cavalieri, Bo for bosun. He moves like champagne fume, tall, a hawk's face, black hair streaked with gray. His green eyes catch available light like a camera set wide-open. It's January 1967. Bo's thirty-six. He's been in the merchant marine for twelve years. Before that he served five years in the Navy as a frogman and boatswain's mate.

Some of the older seamen have sailed with him before. They know they'll leave the ship with his sketches of them. They like him but can't remember a thing he ever said to them, not even a command. His silence reeks of death. Sometimes divers who've seen their deaths hear angels approach at the plink of the angelus accompanied by the sound of falling crystal. That's what he hears when he dives and when he draws. Shipmates file his sketches in their underwear and visit them to think about who they are. Hare-lipped Marco Salazar over there has been wondering for years why Bo drew his face in red chalk and then inked his name like crumbling mortar. He grins at him like a conspirator in the gloom of the rope locker.

Bo usually sails as second mate or navigator, but if the ship's going to the right place he'll sign on as bosun or even able seaman. This morning he's in the rope locker and not the chart room because *Delos* is headed for Glasgow and he wants to find somebody in Scotland.

As *Delos* shrugs off the bridge and waddles out of New York Bay, Bo feels like blackening his face and honing his seven-inch frogman's knife. He's seen old charts that say beyond here be dragons, but he's never thought of them this close to shore. He feels the acrid purpose that fills the air before an ambush. He goes down below and puts on his old khaki deck jacket with *USS Leyte CVA-32,* Deck Division, stenciled on the back.

Abel Portman & Son in Glasgow goes belly up before *Delos* clears Montauk Light. Hardly missing a beat, Brown & Sharpe in Rhode Island orders her to take the groaning dies to Hamburg, spoiling Bo's plan to play detective in Edinburgh.

~

The sun hauls down a carnelian sky with it, signalling new weather. Coming back from a walk along the Hamburg wharves, he kicks his white canvas sea bag under his rack, slaps cold water on his face from a fungal sink, and heads aft to the galley for a mug of coffee. Then, strolling up towards the forecastle, he surveys the steam winch with professional glumness, picking at the rust. Hal Carmody, the radio officer, comes up behind him.

"Some kinda bad news, Bo." He hands him a yellow paper.
AmirCavalieri/Sandro died last July/Ulrike.

Carmody clamps his shoulder and offers him a silver flask. He swigs and nods. Carmody leaves him with the flask. Last July.

Ulrike Theiss, his mother, took her sweet time to notify him his stepfather had dead. His mind slips back to Korea. He's nineteen.

~

—*Darken ship*. In the Navy he piped that command from the quarterdeck a thousand times. He hears the bosun's pipe and sees the lume of the battle group fade, and in a while a memory appears. Pusan, Sophie's Bar. He's sitting next to Fred Dietrich, a big doughy gunnery chief whose hobby is playing bagpipes miserably. He has a note from Sandro Cavalieri in his jumper pocket. "Dear Isadore, your father is very proud of you."

No signature. No Isadore either. Isadore, Sandro's son, a talented sculptor, died at twenty-five of tuberculosis before they learned how to beat it.

Bo, Sandro's stepson, has just received the Navy's Silver Star, occasioning Sandro's confusion. It's the only letter he ever got from Sandro, in spite of all his own letters to Sandro. He spots himself in the blue mirror behind a forest of bottles and salutes. "Here's to you, Isadore." His gesture piques the curiosity of the young hooker at the end of the bar. She likes his looks but prefers officers. Overcoming her scruples, she approaches him with her head cocked to one side.

"You funny-man-sailor. You like fun?"

He looks her over, trying to figure out how loaded he is and how much change he has in his sock.

"What's your name, sailor?"

"Isadore. My name's Isadore."

"That's not a sailor name, I call you Joe, okay Joe?"

He waves his finger in front of her piquant face.

"Soldiers are Joe. Sailors are Earl. Call me Earl, ole Earl."

"Okay, Oil, I call you Oil."

"Thas the stuff, Suzy. Call me Ole Oil the sailorman."

It isn't hard to read her mind, so he just falls into his drunk swabbie routine, drapes a long arm over her shoulder and gives her left tit a chuck. Then he turns back, eyes Dietrich, peels off a Lincoln while Suzy studies his wad intently and says, "Hey, Sophie, buy my grandfather here a beer."

"See ya later, Oil," his grandfather says.

"Well, I hope ya found yer son, Sandro," he says as he swings his long legs into his berth.

~

In the bloody plate-glass windows of the Reeperbahn he watches himself shop for sex. Unless you are very young you look for kinks. Bandy legs, lascivious mouths, sly eyes, anything to raise the snake.

In this melancholy grace, he happens on the boy Lakhdar Ali Wahab and the girl Ute-Britt Broghammer.

Lakhdar, a Moroccan busboy and dishwasher, is lion-eyed, edgily sculpted, sick in love with pale, fey Ute-Britt, the barmaid.

At first Bo thinks he returns nightly to Armin Steegemueller's rathskeller because his sketchbook intrigues the boy, because the boy himself can draw and wants Bo's friendship, but after a while he knows he returns to see if Ute-Britt returns Lakhdar's love.

He doesn't tell Lakhdar his name is Amir. The boy would surely recognize a fellow Saracen. Only later does he regret this stinginess. Now he draws Ute-Britt as if he can draw her to the boy. It's harder than overseeing deck work by the lummoxes who work for Hapag-Lloyd on rust humps like the *Delos*.

Keen as he is, it never occurs to him Ute-Britt, an adept flirt, treats him like somebody's grandfather because she respects the nature of his night work.

Lakhdar she knows she has; what she wants is this stranger's approval. Lakhdar, her thrall, who's despised in her homeland, has won an austere, commanding friend who admires him. Knowing this obsesses her.

Lakhdar is beneath her, beneath everyone, and she loves him, but not because of that. It nearly drives her to play for Bo, to see if she can, and thereby to share Lakhdar.

She and Bo share a secret, Lakhdar's great soul. She's a slave to defeated men, cunning in their unaccustomed servitude. Her small rebellion is to edge her love for the boy toward the man. She knows, that way, whatever Bo's response, she will lose what she's afraid to own.

This stasis Bo understands, but not her acuity.

In his sketches her austere beauty startles her. She looks like paintings she has seen—Memlings, Bosches—and it feels like too great a responsibility. Her fragility eludes Bo. This failure of intuition—no, this failure to act on his intuition—will haunt him decades later when he can recall her only by drawing Lakhdar from memory.

His trial of the girl—she is depicted in his sketchbook as shadowed chalk severity where it could have been purity of line—ends abruptly one night when returning to his table from the toilet, he sees Ute-Britt slip from around the bar and caress the boy's tired face as he sits on a barrel outside the galley.

Bo sighs like God on the seventh day. He orders a celebratory schnapps, bolts it and walks out into the curdled morning rain in his yellow slicker and Navy watch cap, his sketchpad stiffening his back behind a broad black belt.

Two blocks down toward the docks a topiary redhead bobbing on precariously long legs stalls him with a hectoring stare. He responds by staring at her crotch. She smiles dirtily.

"Sailor, you just like to look? Okay, I give you a lot to look at."

She holds out her palm.

But he knows he has scared her. Bent seamen regularly cut Hamburg's sisters. So when his face crinkles into a wholehearted smile she feels reprieved.

He puts his arm around her and clasps her sharp hip, propelling them to wherever she'll go.

"So what is it, sailor?"

"Bo."

"Gerda."

"Could we be like children learning about it, Gerda?"

His German is Preusse Deutsche as if spoken by a stammerer.

"If I vud be an actress vud I be a whore?"

He takes his arm back. "Appreciate your honesty." He walks off.

"Bo! I like vhut you said, but also it pisses me off because my feet hurt. This is not maybe something I need, but ve could try. Also you're not an actor either."

"Gerda." He savors her name from maybe eleven or twelve feet off. Then, walking back to her, "Thanks. So we'll try."

"You have some little girl in mind. Tell me about her."

"Dacia, her name was Dacia."

"Ach, foreign names I like so much! Gerda, it sounds like something a client left in my throat."

She swoops down into his face.

"You cry, Bo? You cry?"

~

Weybrandt Gundersen is a hotel freak. A chief mate's cabin, even on a paint-glued hogback like *Delos,* is adequate, but his paycheck enables him to indulge. Bo walks like a sick cat when drunk, with pompous dignity. He leaves the hotels to Gundersen and picks his way back to his fo'c's'l. Gundersen is a man who goes to sea. Bo is a seaman.

Laid up in Hamburg, Gundersen acts like a buddy hot for your kid sister or like a man fending off cobras with rubbing alcohol, a trick he heard about in India. Now, a bit vaguely, not knowing why, Bo dislikes his friend and mentor.

"You think hootch'll work on those snakes, Gundy?"

The chief mate stands by the gangway in a stiff east wind, the troublemaker wind. He looks at Bo as if he doesn't know him.

"Fuck you then, I'm gonna get drunk." Bo walks past him down the gangplank and heads for Armin's.

When Gundersen gets there, his blond flattop stunk up with bay rum, Bo has made sketches of half a dozen drunks, left them to contemplate their likenesses and shoved off.

Bo knew the big flathead would show up and he's sick of him. He's sick of *Delos* and her ailments, of her hypochondriac dipshit Greek captain, of her maggoty chow and dog-ass crew.

All Ute-Britt likes about Gundersen is his friendship with Bo.

When he hands her a Hapag-Lloyd envelope on his way to the crapper she slips it between dirty glasses and continues on her way to Lakhdar's pantry. She sets down the tray, turns her back to the boy and reads. There are ten American twenty-dollar bills in it and a loopy note: "Chief Gundy begs the pleasure of your company tonight."

Sucking her pinkie reminds her to think. It's a lot more than the big girls in the red plate glass windows make in a night, but something howls from her navel down.

She needs to brush her teeth, wash her hair, rinse her eyes. She feels Lakhdar looking. She turns and chucks her chin at him belligerently.

Lakhdar looks away. She clenches both his shoulders from behind, shakes him violently and runs, knowing how he's misread her look. How far will two hundred Americans go? Can Lakhdar buy a falafel wagon with them? He won't take them. Can they make a run for it? Where? What's a little ass? Who'll know? She wouldn't call the flathead a shit, but he isn't the other one either.

In her back alley room he grinds the girl pestle to mortar, stinking of Macanuto cigars and schnapps, calling her baby and grunting "shit" when he comes. She watches herself ride him in the window. She thinks she looks like a Sonneberg doll whose face somebody's greasy thumb has rubbed off.

That morning no bath has ever seemed so useless.

When the two-hundred-dollar American leaves she considers weeping. She wets her hands and slicks down the wispy hair at her temples. Then, remembering he likes to sketch those wisps, she grabs a towel and rubs them dry and free. She hikes her boobs in the heels of her palms—they're as high and quince-tart as boobs get—and looks at her startled face, startled because it isn't the boy she's thinking about, it's the man.

She's not an innocent, but she lacks what it takes to take in the size of the night. German girls of her generation don't confuse sex with cosmic issues. Soiled panties you can scrub, but the feeling that she's soiled Lakhdar's friend ambushes her. She dips a finger in a dead beer and smudges one of Bo's sketches, staring at him defiantly.

~

In the morning she sends herself back to her own class by shaving her armpits and legs.

While she's doing this thing disdained by her grander sisters Lakhdar strings the hemp rope Armin keeps for his dumbwaiter over a rafter in his attic and hangs himself.

When he kicks aside the chair under him he too thinks of Bo Cavalieri, his friend.

Only thinking of Bo makes him sad.

"The Arab boy, I'm sorry, Bo, he hung himself. The police have him."

Armin Steegemueller, who'd served in the SS Liebstandarte Adolph Hitler and rues his life, wipes his face with his apron and pours Bo a Dinkel/Acker pilsner.

"He was a good boy."

Bo stares at him.

"Ask the girl," Armin says.

It hardly ever occurs to Bo that he is half German, but now he says in Ulrike Theiss's precise Prussian, "Ask the girl what?"

Armin grins to hear his own language spoken slowly but well.

"A woman is a war, Yankee—a man could live without both of them, trust me."

Bo is inclined not to trust anyone who asks to be trusted, but service in the Liebstandarte Adolph Hitler entitles a man to philosophize about war if not women.

"Don't mistake me, I liked him. I will bury him. So he was not a Christian. So what? You think this is a Christian nation?"

Bo clasps the soldier's shoulder as he rises.

"I'll take him home."

"Where'd you get your German, Bo? It's, it's from over . . . "

"Stettin, ja. It's my mother's country. I am half German and half Arab."

"In this crazy world you cannot even be sure you belong to the human race, is that not so?"

He hasn't let go Armin's shoulder. He squeezes it.

"You belong, Armin, you belong."

"Ja, well then God help us both, but me I don't think he will."

"To dispose of such a body they will kiss your American ass. They will even kiss your Arab ass."

He draws a map on a napkin to get Bo to the police station.

"Your mother is German?"

"Ja, Ulrike Theiss von Stettin."

"Ulrike Theiss, a frog name it's not. She was a good mother, Bo?"

"Auf weidersehn, Krieger."

~

Sometime after ten p.m., August 12th, he comes to Lakhdar's attic in Kaltenheiserstrasse. The stairwell smells of lamb marga. The Moroccan emigrés, like swamp gas, waver and part to let him pass. The police haven't bothered to seal Lakhdar's room. The overpainted pea-green door is ajar and a sulfurous gibbous moon stares into the single gable.

The blue super-giant Sirius in Canis Major is eighty-seven thousand light-years from here and dense enough to make our mountains seem like fluff. Its white dwarf companion, according to the daft Stamos Vafiadi, the itinerant Greek navigator who taught him rudimentary navigation, is going nova, causing much upheaval in Ursa Major. It's part of the end of the Piscean era, Stamos told him.

Consider that, not this, Cavalieri.

Moonlight chalks the room. When he sees the rope's shadow he drapes his forearms on his knees, sits, and looks up. It's not a noose but an ugly knot that must have brought a wretched death.

Morgue, embassy, cops, Lufthansa—he jots tasks in a pocket sketchbook. Papers—find out where Lakhdar came from.

The moonlight scours his mind. He remembers gashing his leg with a strip of sheet metal in the bosun's locker and dousing it with xylol. The remembrance of that pain, pure and focused, is better than this. The floor planks are enameled black, their cracks were painstakingly filled with epoxied sawdust, not something the landlord of such a warren would do. Had the guest-boy done it? What an interesting trick for an Arab boy to pick up. The boy had been observant, like himself, curious about little things. He nods his bosun's approval.

Bedroll cinched. A small square wooden table stripped and clear-varnished makes him smile. Under one of two chairs the green Holy Koran and a black Lutheran Bible lie side by side. He swallows hard.

No cooking facility or bath. A Bedouin encampment in an infidel land. Then he notices the roof. That's what it was—not a ceiling—high, full of angled beams, joists, slats, all painted a South Atlantic green that required savvy mixing. Perhaps the boy was trying to remember the sea off Essaouira. Suspended from a crown post is a five-foot white cardboard bottle-nosed whale, the savviest cetacean in the deep.

Lakhdar's rope begins with three turns around a beam about a foot from the whale's belly. Bo rubs his eyebrows with his left forefinger and thumb. This needs Arab women ululating eerily: you, you, you. You, not Bo Cavalieri.

The girl stands hip-slung against the door frame, leg sinister up on point. He has studied her before, savored her oval face redolent of Jeanne Hébuterne, Amadeo Modigliani's ill-starred mistress. But her eyes and the say of her face always elude him, not because her body, he now sees, captivates him but because her face is uninhabited. Now it is inhabited. There. The eyes he knows to be blue are discs of the moon—of Artemis, dispassionate, arresting. Her tow hair is drawn aside to the sort of muscled braid men long to finger. The straight mouth calls him. Her lower jaw extrudes, truculent, quivering. An aberrant current runs in her upper lip.

She is after all a vulnerable child, perhaps even a sister who's done her brother to death.

Ute-Britt Broghammer never interested him as (his shipmates would say) a fuck, owing to that jaw and her sidewinding gaze, provocative in some women, but disquieting in her.

Now he remembers that he too at her age was unable to look at the other half of his kind for fear his soiled thoughts would betray him. Can he tell her now that the dirt of such thoughts is good soil?

He signals her to enter. She sits beside him.

He tries to remember how her English is and can't. He tries to speak and chokes. In time she rests her head on his shoulder and he smells lily of the valley. He pushes down sobs and she puts her left hand on his heart.

When he stops she gets up and crosses a corner of the room and retrieves a little black folio from a cupboard.

Charcoal and pencil, Ute-Britt and Bo, sketch after sketch. Bo is art-wise, almost scholarly, and he's never seen such fondness in an artist, such liking: Bo drawing, Ute-Britt drying a glass. How pure the boy had been.

Bo thinks of the young Parmigianino copying Correggio.

Now Ute-Britt offers some measure of her English. She touches his forearm to have his eyes, points to the folio and then to her head: Lakhdar had executed these from memory.

It amazes Bo. He wants to say, Have you any idea how hard, how unusual it is to do that?

But he closes his eyes and shakes his head, and she understands. The work is spare and inspired.

She closes his hands on the folio. They are hers to give. It's a perfect gesture and he feels for an instant in love with her himself.

Only many years later does it seem surpassingly odd and beautiful to him that no thought of Gundersen intruded on that dirge—and he chooses to think that this owed as much to Ute-Britt Broghammer as to himself.

They sit with their eyes lowered to the shadow of the rope as it sweeps the wall, shaken by passing trucks. After what seems hours Bo rises, pulls a rigging knife from his pants pocket and cuts down the rope.

Then he does a ritual, seamanly thing—he parts the three strands of the rope and backsplices them into the standing part of the rope, undoing in this way the instrument, the bight of Lakhdar's death. He carefully shaves ends of the interwoven strands to smarten this crown knot.

Then, unable to abandon a discipline, he feels for the lay of the line, its wont. He coils it and hangs it on a finial of the chair astride Lakhdar's books.

This silent liturgy Ute-Britt will recall at every exquisite angle in her life until inevitably it's the only thing she clearly remembers of Lakhdar, until it commandeers her secret climaxes and her prayers. Or is it Bo? She will grow to like the question more than the memory. And one day, sixteen years from now, kissing her son Tariq's head, she'll say to the part in his hair, "And nothing else ever happened to me." Then they'll watch the sun at Grossenbrode breach the Baltic.

He turns out Lakhdar's camouflage bedroll and settles his long bones with his arms beside him. Ute-Britt comes and stands by his left hand. She studies it. It has named her. It knows her. And Lakhdar. It has shown them things they didn't see in themselves. She picks up the stole of his arm and wraps herself in it as she slides into the bedroll.

He breathes the night air through her hair and it is analgesic. Down through the draw of her frock a lucent nipple rises, back-lit by the moon, and he feels the exaltation of the helmsman bringing a stern around to wear a crossed sea.

They lie there mute, alert, until morning, when Lakhdar truly dies.

2

The sun bleeds in the cranes like a heart in a surgeon's hand, the kraut pilot postures like Himmler, the belligerent tugs want gelt for showing up too early. The harbor's a pain in the ass. Anything he has to think about too long is a pain in the ass. Actually it's a pain in the harrowed track over his left sacroiliac where his father laid him open the night before he left Oppdal for good. Trouble is just shit happening.

Brandt Gundersen feels like a man who has gotten even. But even for what? Damned if he knows. He pronged the girl, and judging by Bo's second day of absence his old friend too. He tries various formulations in his head. One he likes: if Ute-Britt had been a Tamil urchin and Lakhdar a Norwegian cabin boy . . . shit, I would've boffed her just the same. I'm a liberal prick. Doesn't Bo know that?

~

Nowadays the National Oceanic and Atmospheric Administration likes to hear from sailors about slam-down winds that pipe up improbably. They're called dry squalls and we don't know much about them.

Gundersen, standing at the rail of *Delos* rail that morning, is considering a dry squall between himself and Bo. Men don't like to miss other men.

Mad as he is at himself and Bo, he turns red and tries to rub it right out of his face as he remembers something about Bo Cavalieri that turns him into a fool when he thinks of it.

They had been nursing the old *Transmontana* through her melodramatic death throes.

They needed a release valve for the repairs, so they bumbled over to the old Phoenician port of Malaga. It wasn't unusual to run into seamen they knew. If you'd had a few, you greeted them like buddies, but it was hard to take some of them sober. When they sat down in the Alcazar Cafe they found themselves next to Farris Pipes and Win Favor—two British officers they knew—and they guffawed. Pipes and Favor were both notorious cocksmen, forever cuckolding each other.

There's not much difference between hilarity and God's own truth when you're snockered and next morning it doesn't mean a rat's ass. Gundersen and Bo had already had a few before they encountered the cocksmen.

Gundersen waved them over and soon the plummy mates and the Yank cousins were having a high old time until the subject turned inevitably to skirts. Pipes and Favor resumed their dong-walloping.

Gundersen watched Bo doing his usual Doberman snarl after downing a shot. Cavalieri stood up, planted some green under a glass for the waitress, and said, "Hey, why don't you two cunts just fuck each other and spare us the crap?" Then he strode off.

Gundy's gut was heaving so hard it was banging the table. He looked helplessly from Pipes to Favor, Favor to Pipes, and their indignant looks just made him laugh harder. It set him off for years to come whenever Cavalieri did the Doberman. It never occurred to him Cavalieri's perceptivity might be as deadly as it was comical.

That was then.

Now Bo's perceptivity is turned on him. Fuck him. So what if you can count on him to risk his life for you, all that means is how little he values life.

So whuddid I do? In fairness to Weybrandt Gundersen, he despises rhetorical questions. He knows, for example, to be big and blond helps. Maybe not on a Greek ship, but who likes Greek ships? He's as foreign as a Martian in his heart. In that heart he's a wog.

Doesn't their foreignness make them brothers?

So just what did Weybrandt Gundersen do to his friend Bo Cavalieri? To Bo, his foreign brother? And now Cavalieri has betrayed him, leaving him without a navigator in a foreign port. How can he do a thing like that, leaving him to shoulder what he fears most—more responsibility than he wants?

"You know I don't speak Nor-vayjun, Chief." It's Carmody, the Cockney radio officer, a wry little roach who always looks like it's hard to talk above the static.

"Chief shit! I may be the fuckin' captain and navigator and cook for all I know."

"The Geek and the Eye-talian fucked off, did they then?"

"Get outta my face before I piss you over the side, you little Limey cunt hair!"

The radio officer swallows and vanishes.

There are things you can do something about. There are things you can do little about. There are things you can do nothing about.

And there are things you're too tired to do anything about. If you know that, you're half old and half smart and damned sure grown up.

What did I do? you ask.

You got born without proper papers and it's been a hassle with immigration ever since.

It's not because he fucked little Broghammer that he knows Cavalieri won't show. He and Bo are never hot for the same women. But everything's fucked. Who made Bo Cavalieri God?

Djelloul Marbrook

His body is like a two-hundred-and-forty-pound German shepherd. He's gotta feed it by the sack, turn around and it shits in a corner, gotta run it to keep it goin'. And that's all he's doing, running the schweinhundt to keep it going.

Damn, I'm tired! Just a flathead seaman . . . what, he wants I should be the mother of God? Christ! I paid her and stuffed her, I didn't rape her, I didn't knock her around, where the hell's he been all his life?

He keeps scanning the dock hopelessly. It's ridiculous for him to think Bo Cavalieri jumped ship because his buddy banged a barmaid.

He's heartbroken and would puke if anybody told him so.

I'm gonna be dead before I retire, that's what the wife says anyway.

Krazy Kafigidikis the captain musta got himself laid or cut or both. Now the port agent remembers: Gundersen's got captain's papers. One pissed-off, sack-of-shit captain with no navigator and no chief mate.

But maybe *Delos* isn't so bad off. Yesterday she had a chief mate, a navigator and no captain. He wants to shove off. He's always liked the engines' scat—*are-we-ready?* *'course-we're-ready*—under the deck plates.

But he has to point out to the lunkhead agent that he has no navigator, and he has to go back to Steegemueller's and not go back there, and he has to rip *Delos* out of this Sodom even if he'd rather take out his own appendix.

Is Gundersen the one thing he sure as hell never wanted to be, a captain, because Bo Cavalieri acts like he's entitled to act the way he does?

Entitled? I'll tell him who's entitled. Like how he first met Cavalieri. You wanna talk entitled, I'll tell you what I'm entitled to. Like a little goddam loyalty.

Bo had walked into the Masters Mates and Pilots union office in Brooklyn like he had an invitation.

The port captain looked up and said, "Do I know you?"

"No sir," he said, "my name's Cavalieri. I want to ship third mate."

"So?"

"I'm a bosun, lotsa sea time. I passed the Coast Guard test. I got my papers."

"Call for an appointment next time you're in port, we'll see what we got."

"You got jobs, what you don't have is third mates good as me."

"We got jobs when I say we got jobs. Unless I missed something, the only thing you got is balls, or maybe you're stupid. You stupid?"

"I'm smart enough to know there's guys kissed a lotta ass and pulled a lotta strings to get jobs they don't rate. I'm smart enough to know there's a whole bunch of people's cousins out there. All I'm asking for is an even break."

"Suckers get breaks, the rest of us play the game. Play the game, who knows, maybe next time I see ya I'll remember ya."

The two captains and Gunderson, a chief mate, worked for different companies, but what they were doing that morning was exactly what this ornery bosun was talking about, filling jobs with assholes who knew somebody.

I was standin' by the window, Gunderson recalls, *sort of payin' attention and not payin' attention. I liked the guy's style, but he was up against a greaseball who sold jobs for a living, and I guess when he realized it was hopeless he just stitched his mouth up zigzag and swung around to leave, but somethin' stopped him*

Djelloul Marbrook

and when he faced around again he threw somethin' down on Greaseball Conway's desk. The three of us looked down at it. Conway looked up at me so I picked it up. I did a hitch in the Navy just before the Korean War so I knew what Cavalieri threw down was a Silver Star. Navy thinks pretty hard on this one, you gotta do a lot more'n kiss ass for it.

I looked up at Cavalieri—didn't do no good at all to look at Conway.

I nodded. He looked back at me with that green look always makes me think of the South Atlantic.

Conway took it from me and handed it to Bo.

I guess he figured he had no choice except to back up Kollewicz. "The Marines like heroes, try the Marines."

I'd had about enough of Conway.

"I'm down a mate, I'm gonna need a pier-head jump," I said. "Sail at 1500 hours. Transmontana. Pier 22. Get your ass down there, I'll take you up to see the captain."

He shook my hand.

"You better not fuck me over," I told him.

'What's your name, Chief?"

"Brandt Gundersen."

He nodded and walked out with the Silver Star in his fist and his sea bag on his left shoulder.

That's how we met. You couldn't have asked for a better third mate. He hated it. Lifeboat drills, all that shit he knew shipping bosun. What he really wanted was navigator, that's the second mate. We didn't get to be friends right off. Truth is I liked him but I figured I was a whole lot stupider than him. I think he kept on shippin' with me 'cuz the chief mate could let him play around in the chart room and try out what he knew.

Bo was a natural leader. The bosun and deckhands knew he knew their jobs cold. But he didn't act like he'd risen above them.

He'd bear a hand with them, usually giving an order at the moment he began to do the work. Fact is you couldn't say Bo Cavalieri gave orders. What he did was say somethin' like, We better ready the winch now, or, Let's see if these davits work. Or he'd just hand-sign to the crew. You have to use hand signs at sea in a blow or from a distance when you don't want the horn to confuse some other sound you're wanting to hear, but Bo made the hand signs kind of funny. Most often the crew would smile, which to tell you the truth is pretty rare. He could use hand signs better than most mates.

Could've been a bad thing. Lots of captains and chiefs don't like an officer popular with the crew, makes them jittery.

But I never saw a captain who couldn't see the virtue of having Cavalieri aboard, not even Krazy Kafigidikis.

~

Delos steams by 1100 hours not because Weybrandt Gundersen has sorted the paperwork or hung the decision to sail without a navigator on the agent or set his mind straight about anything— she sails because of what he and Bo Cavalieri share: they don't wait for any ship to come in, their lives are spent taking ships out, they have no thought that any living soul owes them anything.

3

Ceuta numbers some seventy thousand people. They're cowed by Generalissimo Francisco Franco, disordered by the unremitting dry mistral and the incessant growling of big black Dutch salvage tugs churning their diesels as they wait for distress signals from the sea.

Like all seamen, Bo despises these buzzard-salvors fattening on misfortune. He's eyeing them morosely as Peter Tomlinson's ship arrives.

He's dipping a four-sided green cigar in a pint of calvados, sitting on the Calle Muelle Canonero Dato, his back to Lakhdar Ali Wahab's native land. Almost due north is the Berber marauder Tariq's mountain, Djebel el Tariq (Gibraltar). Out in the worried dark the green eye of some kind of vessel stands about three hundred yards at eleven o'clock, not low, not high, probably a luxury yacht. Twin diesels, so she has range. He bites off the end of his cigar, lights it and nips at his pint, watching. When the wharf lights hit her freeboard he makes out a handsomely fitted engineering-white work ship, a surveyor maybe, some hundred and forty feet at her boot line.

He chucks up his pea-coat collar.

"Bear a hand, mate, will you?"

A tall man wearing a British Navy duffel coat stands at the starboard bow with a heaving line in his hands. She's coming in too fast. She should be backing hard in short bursts to break her thrust. But instead she's steaming in neutral, out of control. The northeasterly wind will bash her against the dock right-angling about twenty yards to Bo's right unless he catches the line on the first throw and warps it around a piling so the ship can be stalled and sprung around. It's piss-poor ship handling.

He takes off fast, motioning the Brit to heave the line as he runs—"Stupid son of a bitch, lock the line down!"—it's a fair heave and he catches it running, turning it around the next piling with a towboat hitch. He looks to see if Cheerio-and-all-that has lost a hand or foot, but he's locked the line down on the bow's Samson post and the ship is stalling.

Doing her transmission no good, the helmsman finally gets her stern swinging leeward toward the quay. Bo walks back and catches a stern line, locks it down on a bollard and walks forward to take a permanent bow line. She's certainly no yacht. She's a steel Romsdal North Sea trawler. He's seen the Hagen yard at Hjelset, Norway, where she was built. He figures she carries at least twenty thousand gallons of fuel and has enormous range for her size. He heard her right too, she does have twin diesels, probably seven hundred and fifty horsepower each, but one shaft and screw, not an easy vessel to handle, not like a twin-screw yacht that can be horsed around by opposing screws. She carries a staysail just aft of her boat deck. She's littered with small boats. He likes her salty look and walks down past the Union Jack on her stern to resume his somber dock watch. He has a notion to see the sun come up over what once was an Arab lake, and he sort of likes the little Spanish flag flapping from a bridge tree halyard and the cumbrous jack harrumphing on its staff.

"Peter Tomlinson, mate. Don't happen to speak English, I suppose?"

"You put her at risk, Peter Tomlinson."

Bo looks up into the blue eyes of a tall man about Bo's age whose left shoulder has a pronounced list.

"May I have a swig?"

Bo hands him the bottle.

"Ah, that's good. Praise God the froggies do a few things right. Don't suppose you could spare a Cuban?"

Bo pulls out a cigar and hands it to him.

"And a light? You have me at a disadvantage."

Bo laughs.

"It's not your only disadvantage, Tomlinson. You need a ship handler. Romsdal makes serious ships. I'm Bo Cavalieri."

"A good night's sleep will do for now. Cavalieri? Mmm, an Italo-Yank. Bo. Yes? How'd that happen then?"

"People call me Bo."

"For?"

"Bosun."

"I see. That explains it. You're a seaman. Well, of course. Off a Yank ship then?"

He sits down beside Bo and takes another pull of calvados.

"If the pay's okay and the route's right she can fly a Canopian flag for all I care."

"Sorry?"

"Canopus, a navstar. It's damn bright. Also an old Egyptian port."

"Excuse me, Bo, how many bosuns know ancient history?"

"Not many Arab Italians, I guess."

"Arab Italians? I missed something."

"Yeah, I'm half Arab. Amir Cavalieri. That's my Christian name, you could say."

They chuckle amiably. Tomlinson peers over at Bo's profile. "It seems to me you might be a bit darker."

"Oh ye English, ye have angels' faces, but what is in your hearts."

"Yes, well, what is in this Englishman's heart is impatience with evasiveness, Cavalieri."

Bo turns and smiles.

"Arab and German actually, and American by way of my mother. My stepfather was Sicilian-American. I'm a bosun and a second mate. Second mates navigate. Happy?"

"Content, yes. You're okay, Cavalieri."

"Yeah, well, I'll tell ya, Tomlinson, I'm not sitting on a dock in Ceuta waiting for John Bull to say so—and you wouldn't have, would you, if you didn't have some reservations."

"Yes, you really are okay, Cavalieri, I can see that."

"It's you I don't know about, not that it makes a flying fuck."

He's snockered and, having at first been set to like Tomlinson, he decides he doesn't. The guy's seductive and snide.

"You will, Bo. You will know about me, that is. Come aboard tomorrow, today I mean. Later today. When you're sober and I'm myself."

"Who've ya been?"

"Cut some slack, man! Englishmen often get off to bad starts, don't you know?"

"Look, Tomlinson, I don't like you, I don't give a shit about your ship. I want my fucking calvados back. Now is that uncouth Yank enough for ya?"

Tomlinson stands up so he can look down.

"So's your mother, Yank. I think we're going to be friends, I'd like us to be anyway."

Bo is shut up in the worst of his nature and sits there hunched like a black-crowned night heron. "Hey, Brit, I'm not anybody's specimen. The natives have always been restless but what with quinine and a preference for sub-species poontang you prigs just never noticed." Tomlinson studies him from a distance and then walks back to him. "You've suffered some incalculable loss, navigator, and I may have the coordinates the stars want to put in your way. Think on it. Good morning."

He hands the calvados back to Bo, mutters *kew* for thank you, and leaves.

Not a bad exit. Bo takes his bottle without a glance at Tomlinson, sets it between his thighs, pulls up another Cuban from his watch shirt and lights up. He's fucking odd as I am.

He remembers the nobility of Ute-Britt's profile, settles on his back and plies the morning stars.

~

Next door the hooded wolf Ferhat and the helmeted bear Fernand have recently torn out each other's throats to fanatics' applause. The blazing white cities and towns of Algeria are flagged with blood, their children wired with plastique. He has a name that belongs there, also to Morocco behind him, but unbelonging's in his blood. Algeria is the playground of the wanton children who made him. No one will accompany him back there when he dies. No, the Veterans Administration will plant him somewhere well above latitude 35 north on which he was born.

Maybe he should not have brought Lakhdar home, but he just could not imagine the boy resting in a grave among Gundersens, Broghammers or Steegemuellers. He knows he has sung this dirge as much for himself as for the boy—and for Ute-Britt, who doesn't know now what to do but later will send letters to Lakhdar in Oued Zem, where the Yank sailor buried him.

Bo has buried himself and is free to enjoy all the benefits of the dead. He can be anybody. This benefit he derives from not having found a single soul to say he'd known Lakhdar Ali Wahab. The boy had a name, a birth certificate, a birthplace, but nobody knew him. The more he wandered around Oued Zem asking questions the angrier he got. And when he was done with anger, he felt desperate. It could be himself in el-Kantara. It was himself, and now he had to live out the boy's life.

With the grating French of his prep school and college years, he spoke to the incredulous police, to a caid who treated him as mad, and to anyone else who seemed accessible. Only an old marabout was interested: Lamdjed Ben Bou Amama.

"My name is . . . " The old man's name called up someone else. "Bou Amama, he drove the French mad," he told the old man. In the eighteen-eighties along the Algerian-Moroccan border the shaykh Bou Amama had for a time halted France's empire-building.

"Yes, yes," the old man said smilingly, "Bou Amama was my great-grandfather."

Lamdjed Ben Bou Amama was charmed by this foreigner's knowledge of a piece of Maghreb history. He stared civilly at Bo's face. They were sitting cross-legged, as the marabout had gestured him to do. After some while he touched the side of Bo's face.

"Inte Arab?"

Bo nodded. His raptor's nose had given him up. He still had not told the old man his name.

But now he told him Lakhdar's story. Now the story had a resting place. He completed it by asking if the old man would help him find a burial place and someone to make a Muslim prayer.

"Some men are drawn to the djenoun," the old man said, "because . . ." he pinched the flesh of his wrinkled arm and brought away closed thumb and forefinger, by which Bo knew he meant some men have some djenoun blood in them. The djenoun, netherworld creatures, populate Arab folklore and account for all things awry and fey.

Years later he'll wonder what the old man might have said if he'd shown him a drawing of Ute-Britt Broghammer. But he was always content he hadn't.

It was his turn to stare at Lamdjed Ben Bou Amama.

He had no question to ask, but he wasn't surprised when the

marabout reached over to pinch his arm and show him djenoun blood. He smiled and nodded.

"About my friend Lakhdar . . . "

The marabout waved both palms sideways.

~

Soon after dawn a boy came to fetch Bo and led him to the burial place. The marabout was directing two young men as they prepared a shallow grave. Lakhdar, wrapped in white muslin, had been borne from the Italian undertaker's. The point of a white woolen burnoose closed at his head.

Lakhdar was truly home. The undertaker had not questioned the marabout, the marabout had not asked for money, and the three Arabs were reverent.

The marabout prayed in Arabic.

Bo knew the Anglican order for burial at sea and said it.

He sat with Lakhdar all day in that yard outside Oued Zem listening to a muezzin's calls to prayer, to the bells of camels, the tinkle of women's laughter as they stomped soapy clothing by a stream, the wind. When the wind rose he pulled his watch sweater up over his head and sat there headless. In the flash that is North African dusk the caretaker returned and reached into the black hole that was Bo for his head and patted it. In this way Bo buried himself and started north to rejoin the cetaceans.

~

He ought to be ashamed of his behavior towards Tomlinson, but profit lives simply in the next damned thing to do. Which means, on October second, shower, shave, eat and consider heading for Peter Tomlinson's ship, *Morgaine,* named after Morgan le Fay, King Arthur's sorceress sister.

Coordinates were the magic words. The Englishman used

them metaphysically. Bo believes in them. There are places where they cross, places like Manhattan, rich in happenstance, encounters, incidents, recognitions. You can hear the coordinates hum in Manhattan. He knows they're his reason for sailing. A man who speaks of coordinates under fire has grace and is worth knowing.

~

Profanity serves seamen well. Bo is partial to southernisms, from the many Texans and Cajuns who slip like oil to the sea. It makes no never mind, he tells himself as he dresses, what the fuck he wears. He's an officer, yeah, when he ships as one, but he also ships as able seaman and bosun. So he puts on brown corduroys and a Navy turtleneck and quits the sleazy Al Mamoumya looking like a bruise, black hair spuming from an unruly cowlick behind his left eye.

Three pretty boys are scrubbing *Morgaine*. It's too hot to do it. She fumes with resentment. In white trousers and T-shirts they look more like unseeded Balliol tennis players than seamen. The boys need their beauty sleep.

One of those women who look the same age too long sees him first. She's throwing her long black hair over the stern rail. Seamen, used to women's exhibitionism, instinctively tie it to peddling. She's not good at it. Arching to and fro, massaging her scalp, she works at hooking up the boys' heads to their crotches. Bo stands about ten feet from the gangway thinking of King Arthur's dangerous sister. He likes the ship but isn't sure a fairy name is wise. A fey ship? That's new. A fairy crew? Maybe not a good idea but damn sure funny.

Something about the woman disconcerts him. Maybe it's only that he prefers noticing to being noticed. There are women who affect unawareness of their beauty but succeed only in calling attention to themselves. There are women, like this one, who love their beauty and reward men with a smile for acknowledging it. Society condescends to give them decent marks. The ancients would have done better by them. But this woman, regarding the lanky stranger, offers no easy rewards for him. He looks too appraisingly. One of the boys, looking like a rugby version of T.E. Lawrence, approaches.

"May I help you?"

Bo doubts it, but he studies the fellow.

"I say, we're not hiring."

"Wogs?"

"Please?"

"Peter Tomlinson. I'm looking for him. He expects me."

"Shall I tell him who's calling?"

"Cavalieri. Bo Cavalieri."

"Sorry?"

"Are you? Give it a try. I'd do it for you."

The boy ducks and blushes gorgeously. Bo smiles and nods encouragingly.

The woman, glossing her hair with her towel, moves within earshot of this exchange and likes it.

The boy disappears down below and in less than a minute Tomlinson comes careening down the gangway locking his knees dangerously at each slat. He moves as if the surface of everything were foam rubber, his forearms paralleling the ground. Where he'd looked scurvy in the dock light he now looks alarmingly blond.

"Bo!"

He turns to the woman. "This is the man who saved us last night, Moira. I'm happy to see you, Bo."

He offers his hand. Bo takes it firmly and briefly.

"Do you like her? The ship—as you haven't met Moira yet."

His smile is artless.

"Why's her dive flag up?"

"The boys are practicing. That's what we do, Bo, dive."

For what? is the logical question, but Bo's lifelong proclivity is to circle bait with a whale's dour eye.

"You see, Moira, he is not going to ask. The best men have restraint, the others can't be trusted." Her face is the single blow of a diamond cutter's hand, treacherously austere, brightly sexual.

You see, Moira, Tomlinson says, but Bo doesn't think she sees a damn thing and tells her so with a stare that combs her pubic hairs.

"Bo Cavalieri, Moira Sayre, my companion."

"Bo."

She offers a cool hand. He holds it longer than she intends to lend it, but it's clear to her he's hostile.

Tomlinson enjoys not missing such things.

"You must come and fondle *Morgaine*'s body parts, Bo," Tomlinson says.

"I'd think twice before I'd fondle any Morgaine."

Moira smiles, showing no teeth.

"For an unsuperstitious man you picked a strange name for your ship," Bo says. "Or was it her name when you bought her?"

"I had her built, Bo. I named her. I imagine the Norwegians at Romsdal took it for an ordinary English name. What makes you think I'm not superstitious?"

"A man who talks of fondling Morgan le Fay's body parts is apt to lose some of his own, don't you think?"

Bo decides that Peter Tomlinson is determined to lose some of his body parts. If he hasn't already. That means he would be reckless with others' parts. He now finds something to like in Sayre: she just stares, as Morgan likely would have stared. Who knows, the sister may have known her brother in every sense better than his chroniclers. Did Tomlinson know Moira when he named his ship? He smiles to himself.

Noticing, Moira smiles: confederates. She's found something besides his animus to like in Bo. Birds of a feather, she decides, secret humorists. They have to be. How else can she rummage in his head so easily? A cunning head, like her own.

~

In *Morgaine*'s blaze-white engine room Bo cranks her diesels by crossing the starter solenoid's poles.

"You need an on-line starter switch down here."

He can see it hasn't dawned on the owner the engines can be started below. It suggests a broad spectrum of ignorance.

"They're not calibrated. I heard it when you were coming in last night."

He looks them over critically. Not more than five or six years old, but unkempt—grease-caked, brittle-hosed, stains showing maladjustments, nothing double-clamped, no off-line fuel filters, no nameplates, no signs of experience and savvy. "Better get them surveyed or it'll get dicey for you in the wrong place."

"Can you recommend someone in Ceuta, Bo?"

He snuffs the engines.

"Take her over to La Spezia to Ruggieri's. It's a good, small yard. The Greek tycoons haven't found it, so the prices are fair."

"Yes, well, that gets us to a point, Bo. Um, would you take us there? As I understand it, you don't need a master's papers for a private vessel. Or do you have a ship? I'll make it worth your while. How''d you come to be in Ceuta anyway?"

"God, Peter, give the man a chance to sort himself, will you? He always does that. He's really decided what your answer is, you see. I hate this, Peter . . . it's bullying really."

Bo smiles at her. "What is my answer?"

"He thinks you will say no and then he'll win you over."

"We could talk," Bo says.

"Over lunch then, shall we?" Tomlinson asks.

Bo nods. Food to sop up that calvados seems a good plan.

"I'd like to back her off and turn her around," he says. "Then we could eat, if that's okay."

"The fairy sister is yours, I'll muster her crew."

"Uh no, I'd like to check them out too. Where's the captain?"

"Charles Arnot, the mate, is our acting skipper, Bo. I fired the captain in Lisbon, some altercation or other, I forget."

"You do not," Moira says. "He was dipping."

"Dipping?"

"Dipping, Bo. I'm not penurious, I swear."

"Oh, stealing you mean."

"Peter hates unpleasantness."

Peter motions them along toward the bridge.

Bo caresses the telegraph. He unhooks the speaker mike and huffs into it.

"Testing, testing one-two-three. Charlie Arnot to the bridge, please."

Tomlinson grins. He motions Moira to stand off.

"Bo Cavalieri, Charlie," Bo says when the mate appears. He had been prompt.

"We're going to turn her so I can see how she handles. Would you mind giving me a hand?"

There is no sulk in this young man. If anything he looks relieved. Bo likes his face and his body language, square and accessible. He seems eager, interested. He nods at Bo shyly.

"How many crewmen?"

"Six plus the cook, Fergie McKechnie."

"Who's the engineer?"

"Um, that's a problem. The captain was the only one who

knew very much. Semmes—he's the one who met you on the dock
—he does simple things, but I don't know what he can do without
the captain."

"That's a problem. Well, call all hands up. You give the
orders. I'll just stand by till we slip the lines, okay? Stow the dive
flag. It's not a test. Relax."

Arnot responds with a nod.

Tomlinson likes this style. It agrees with his own sense of
going about things. The Yank knows how to handle men. No
martinet like Carther Wirthlin. Dipping hadn't been Tomlinson's
reason for dumping Wirthlin. His chickenshit had been taking the
fun out of things.

Bo checks the wind. Southerly, it will ease *Morgaine* off her
quay, so he'll bring her in the other way around if the wind holds.
He starts the engines consecutively, revs them, slows them down
to idle, then puts them in gear against the dock lines. He winces.
They're asthmatic.

"Charlie . . . Charlie or Charles?"

Arnot smiles gratefully, clear that Bo is not stung by being
corrected. Tomlinson never gave him a choice.

"Charles, actually."

"Charles, check the oil, will you? Not just the sticks, though
—smell it, see if it's rancid, sour. Tell me if it's yellow." He
continues shipping *Morgaine* against her lines, listening to the
engines. "Smells funny," Charles announces, coming back up.
"Yellow too."

"There enough?" Charles nods.

"We'll change it and the filters when we tie up. Away the
spring."

Charles Arnot, newly dignified, speaks the order into the
mike, liking this unfamiliar command jargon.

"Stern lines away."

Bo walks out onto the starboard wing to see how *Morgaine's* crew handles the lines. They'll lose a leg or a hand if somebody doesn't train them.

When they're through with their antics he swings *Morgaine's* stern.

"Okay, sir, let go the bow," he tells Charles, noting the young man has figured out what is wanted and gone forward to man the bow line.

He backs *Morgaine* off smartly. The wheel feels slack. "Hydraulics need work," he says. "I guess I can adjust them. If the cable sheaths are shot, we'll have to replace them. It can't wait."

"Is that a yes, Bo? You'll take us to La Spezia?"

Bo doesn't answer. He doesn't know. He hadn't meant his words to spell yes. "You got any papers, Charles?"

"Unh, unh."

"You ought to get them. You know enough."

Charles Arnot beams.

"Take the wheel, Charles."

"Do we have a course, Captain?"

"Nah, just don't hit anything big."

Moira Sayre snorts. She's been on *Morgaine* for two years and this is the first time she feels anybody knows what the hell to do next.

Bo starts groping the bridge spaces, touching instruments, nosing out lockers. Tomlinson is a gadget freak.

As Bo gropes the bridge he becomes uneasy. Why had he been so goddamned surly with Tomlinson, a man who obviously likes him? Not that you're obliged to like whoever likes you. You're not my fuckin' father, you know! That's what he'd wanted to say several times since meeting this prescient Englishman. Is that weird or what, to say nothing of their being next door to his real father's home? He's looking right over toward Algeria as

Morgaine comes about. Fucking Ulrike! Now that sounds right—his anger, her fucking around, him being the result.

He's furious. He's executing this dipshit little maneuver furious. Feeling the admiration of three strangers, feeling furious. Coming across as laid back but damn-sure out of control.

Ulrike is like Morgan le Fay. Better watch out what you think about her or she'll turn you into a dildo.

He slows the engines as if they can slow his brain. He wears what Gundersen calls his Doberman snarl.

~

"What does UDT mean, Bo?"

He feels something like a cat's tongue on the hair of his forearm.

"Why is the frog wearing a beret?" Moira touches his biceps. He remembers the night he got the cockamamie tattoo in Yokosuka.

"Underwater demolition team, U.S. Navy," Tomlinson says. "The Yanks call it a flat hat, I believe. Our friend is a frogman, Moira."

"Was," Bo said.

"A diver? Really?" she says.

"The very best," Tomlinson says.

Feeling merchandised, Bo pulls the mike. "All hands, prepare to lower the cockboat. Repeat. All hands, prepare to lower the cockboat."

"Am I a hand? Moira asks. "Of course Peter is a hand. He loves rigmarole."

Bo has no idea why he's doing this.

Charles pokes his straw head in from the starboard wing. "The cockboat, Captain?"

"Yeah, the tender. Port davits midship."

Charles is embarrassed. "We've never done it."

Bo smiles reassuringly.

"All hands, belay that last word. Return to your work stations. Have you ever had a lifeboat drill, Charles?"

"No."

"Well, it's a good idea. Sailors usually can't swim. Do they know the difference between the cockboat and the lifeboats? The crew, I mean."

"The dinghies, you mean?"

"Yeah, I guess. See, names don't matter much long as we all agree on them. We do have to know what we're talking about. Could save a life."

Charles Arnot smiles and goes.

"I think it's love," Moira says.

Bo wheels around. "He wants to learn. You owe him that."

"Of course we do, Bo," Peter Tomlinson says. "That's why we must have you aboard."

"I'm a merchant seaman. I like to navigate, not command. I don't dive, except for hull checks."

"Hull checks?"

"Damage, electrolysis, through-hull corrosion, limpet mines."

"Bo,"—Peter has decided to call him Bo in view of their prickly relationship—"I think perhaps you and I must talk privately. I think you must quite justifiably have the impression this is a frivolous undertaking. It's not and it'll be up to me to convince you."

"You've got a lot of technology on board, stuff I can't even begin to identify, and you've got a crew that can't tell one boat from another. Charles tells me they don't even know what the staysail's for. Everybody has to work a ship this size, even the cook. You'll get into trouble otherwise. You're in trouble now."

"Does that include me, Bo?" Moira asks.

Djelloul Marbrook

Thinking wrongly she means work, not trouble, he answers, "If you intend to help Peter with whatever he's doing, better stop walking around in a bathing suit and bear a hand."

"A man of a few mean words, Mr. Bo Cavalieri. Perhaps you'll teach me what it is then to bear a hand?"

He decides he prefers his archness in J. Arthur Rank movies. Except for the lowliest of them, he prefers Brits where their characteristic verbal savagery can be contained. He looks at Peter and wags his head. No go.

The Englishman is crushed. He prefers people who interest him to getting laid. He guesses there is much Bo Cavalieri prefers to getting laid.

"Moira, dear Moira, wisdom comes unbidden at times when one reserves one's mouth for eating."

Well, Peter is sure as hell better than a drunk-ass Greek captain who'd gotten his seafaring papers from his wife's uncle.

Thing is, what would a tony Brit posing as a twat be doing taking this B-movie guano off George Sanders here? Bait, jerkwater, remember what you do with bait? Circle it till the fisherman has a heat stroke. You said it, you being Amir, Bo's interlocutor. He's talked to himself since early childhood—profane, hieratic, loving, cynical, but somehow never hateful—and he's never been able to decide which side he's on, which voice is his.

He backs the engines one third.

"Stand by, fore and aft!"

Three or four Ceuta layabouts give the deckhands the come-on to chuck them lines.

"Wait for the command. Never mind the dockhands. Away the bow line. Away the aft spring. Now the stern line. Pay it out! Pay it out!"

He shakes his head, aggrieved. A cloven-hoofed lot.

He glances around the bridge. Moira Sayre has gone. She overplayed her hand and knew it.

Djelloul Marbrook

4

"I'm a man of obsessions, Bo," Tomlinson says when they're alone, "and the means to indulge them."

Bo gives him a did-I-ask look.

"Does it amuse you?"

"I'd call it a dangerous vocation. Danger's what I avoid. That's my obsession."

"Yes, well, a man who has lived dangerously can afford the luxury of such an opinion, Bo. He's had his pleasures, indulged his vices, you see."

"Yeah, if pleasure's a pop I can see where you'd say that."

"Oh no, Bo, his pleasures define a man. You know who you are. I have no idea who I am. The son of a successful property developer who had the instincts of a moray eel, the grandson of a buccaneering distiller." He pauses. "I am not a ne'er-do-well. I write. Successfully. Books about routes. You're a navigator, they might actually interest you. O'Sullivan's march to the Shannon, the Mughal trek to the south, the Arab incursions into Provence—now that would interest you, wouldn't it?"

Tomlinson finally ekes some spontaneity from Bo.

"Ever study the Arabs' encounters with the Vikings at sea?"

"No. Tell me about them. Perhaps we could collaborate on a book. It sounds just right for public school lads."

Tomlinson swells to this opening. Cavalieri has now finally offered something of himself.

"Scared the crap outta each other." To celebrate he offers the Englishman a Cuban. They light up.

Tomlinson looks like a wet puppy. He tugs a silver flask out of his hip pocket and offers Bo a pull. Bo swigs and winces.

Tomlinson hunkers heels to ass in a corner of the bridge.

Bo hand-springs himself onto a sideboard and takes another nip and asks, "What is this stuff?"

"Laphroaig, an Islay Scotch whisky. It's smoky, rather like a church, don't you think? Um, the Vikings?"

"Big long boats, heavy timber, clinker-built, tough as hell. Good for inshore work but not that bad in blue water. They were square-rigged, didn't have much sail area, so they were easy to handle but limited. Fine in a following wind, but you couldn't turn them into a wind. They were sort of infantry platforms for a bunch of big sick giants—that's how the Arabs saw them anyway. The Arabs were primarily horsemen and sailors, but they got booted outta naval history by Europeans. That's still happening. So the Arabs showed up on a heel, moving fast and going to wind'ard when they had to. The Vikings saw them as stringy devils with coals for eyes. The stringy devils maneuvered the dragon boats into serious trouble as soon as they encountered them. They'd seen plenty of galleys slopping around on their lake, the Med, and they knew damned well they could do a whole lot of damage in a calm but not much in the north Atlantic."

He smiles and takes another swig. "The Vikings figured the Arab sail-masters were magicians. They thought they saw them conjuring up the wind, but what they were seeing was the beauty of the lateen rig. The lateen rig is the mother of modern sailing ships. Snobby prigs in their Limey yawls owe a helluva lot to the dusky wogs."

Pain streaks Tomlinson's face. He looks like a child whose enthusiasm has been quashed by a mentor turned bully.

"I'm sorry, Peter," Bo says. "That sorta popped out."

Tomlinson smiles wanly.

"Well, the Arabs would point up and let those big yeti have a shot of Greek fire—we're still not sure what Greek fire is, tar maybe—then they'd duke it out. I don't know how hot the Arabs were for hand-to-hand fighting with the Vikings, but it wasn't long before the Vikings were busting their swords on Damascus and Toledo steel and swearing they'd met the Devil's minions. The Arabs were just as sure they'd met true djenouns. They had a high old time measuring each others' testosterone."

Peter lassos Bo's words in lifesavers of smoke. As a writer, he savors its possibilities. He feels rewarded for his trouble drawing Bo out.

"Marvelous story," he says. "I'd love to write it. Can their encounters be charted, d'you think?"

"Dunno. They wrote about each other. Arab coins have been found on Viking wreck sites in Scandinavia, the Upper Volga, even in the Black Sea. It'd take research, a lot of research."

"That's what I do, Bo. I'm good. Really."

"I thought you obsessed."

"It really has to be an obsession, otherwise you slip up, you do sloppy work, go off half-cocked. For example, one would have to know exactly what the Arabs and the Vikings wrote about their encounters, reports back home, poetry, and the like. There must have been an oral tradition. And do we know how those ships were built? What sort of wood, that kind of thing. You see?"

He can't read Bo's look. "Oh, I see, you were thinking of Moira, of that sort of obsession."

"I was just flapping my mouth. I don't know what I was thinking, Peter. The sickness of the oyster is the pearl, right?"

Bo thinks his remark disarming, but Tomlinson looks pole-axed.

"What a very odd man you are, Bo! Pearls are exactly what I'm about, you see. I intended to reconstruct the Arab pearl trade. I got the idea from the book about the Mughals. The Arabs made great fortunes selling Omani pearls to the Mughal court. I wanted to dive on their sunken dhows off Muscat and Oman. I wanted to know how they did it. They're still doing it, you know. I wanted to know which of the trade routes they charted, the pirates they encountered, all of it. I already know a great deal. I can tell pearls, sort of, but I don't know the lore that attached their value to them. I've got to study the dhows. Those lateen-rigged dhows, Bo. Not only today's—yes, I do want to see them built too—but the wrecks down there in that heavenly ooze, the sediment. The sediment keeps them. The Mediterranean is well oxygenated; that's bad for wrecks because it entertains toredo borers, the great wreck-killers. Someday, Bo, we're going to be able to dive deep in the Sea of Marmara and the Black Sea, where there's little oxygen. Then we'll rewrite history, because there are Scythian, Crimean, Achaean, Viking, Arab and Roman ships down there laden with surprises. I'm going to Oman. I've got permission. The Arabs don't call their ships dhows, did you know that? It's too general— they have booms, baghalas, zarooks, xebecs. I need to know more than Alan Villiers."

"There are plenty of dhows," Bo says. "They put diesels in them. That's how they trade with Iran. They hate each other, of course, the Arabs and Persians, but business is business."

"You know Arab history then?"

"Some. I minored in it, I forget why."

"Of course. A Yank with an Arab name is bound to have been curious."

"You said you were interested in the pearl trade. Meaning you aren't anymore?"

"I am. Still. But I have the obsessive's insistence on seeing the fifth side of a four-sided thing. So it turns out actually that it all depends on what the pearl is. I was reading . . . well, I was reading everything I could get my hands on. That quite naturally led me to UNESCO. You'd be amazed what UNESCO publishes. Look, I know *Morgaine* strikes you as a mess, what with us hardly knowing a youyou from a canot pneumatique, but I'm really quite methodical, in certain things that is. But we really needed to talk about Moira, didn't we?"

Bo stonewalls.

"Moira is the impediment. I'm sure you see that even if you don't want to talk about her behind her back. I respect that, of course. Well, it isn't just Moira, Bo, it's Moira and me, the chemistry, and you can't see yourself in the formula, can you? So I wonder if you would let me get off the pearl thing for a moment, because everything's of a piece, isn't it. We can agree about that, can't we?"

It dawns on Bo that nobody has ever made such a concerted effort to reach him. Peter Tomlinson is naked. Bo wants to salute his courage but doesn't know how. He springs off the sideboard, walks across the bridge and takes the flask from Peter.

"I'm not as hard-assed as I seem. I'm listening, Peter. I hear you."

"Are you a religious man, Bo?"

"I might be if God told me where he was between 1933 and 1945."

"Mm, yes, run for the exits, wouldn't we? I think you're profoundly religious. Trouble is you can't figure out why God or his mother stopped talking to you, can you?"

"Something to do with masturbation."

"I'm not giving up, Bo. I'm going to keep on prattling till I say something you like enough to take us diving."

"It's Miss Sayre, you're right about that." He'd been calling her Moira but now a serious discussion of her behind her back seemed at least to require the sop of her surname.

"She's got a grand compulsion to be offended by me."

"She's got a grand compulsion to be offended by everyone!" He takes Bo's shoulders and says, "You're not wrong, but you are misreading her. Look, I'm an English prig—isn't that what you said?—so I have an ingrained habit of deflating uncomfortable remarks with humor. I know what's going on. She likes you, so she punches out your lights. Didn't you ever dip the pigtail of the little missy you liked best in the inkwell? It's all so clear to me, but you don't get it because of her face."

"Her face?"

"Yes, it's the face of someone condescending to be human. There's nowhere to rest your eyes on it. That face will not harbor human trespass. Forget the face, just look at the rest of her."

"That's not such good advice, Peter. It's very bad advice. Especially if you're right."

"Yes, I take your meaning. But she is entirely devoted to this voyage. She has to deal with that face, too. Can you see that? It's not like a swimsuit she put on after deciding whether to show her navel or not. Not at all. She must wear it and deal with people— like yourself, Bo—who are always misreading it. Haven't you ever encountered men and women who have the face of God? Immediately we want to sleep with them, we want to humiliate them, and finally we want to crucify them. We want everything from them at once. They're cursed. We'd like to resurrect them just to crucify them all over again. They can't even die properly for us."

Accustomed to picking his way deftly among the stars, Bo's a poor navigator in human affairs. He can't readily abandon an emotional course and even when he's prepared to, his brain mucks up the message he is trying to send to his tongue.

He starts to make a point and recklessly perseveres even though Peter's remarks have blasted him and decided him to stay.

"Peter, I do remember the world before the Bic pen. But when we refuse to defer to civility we're terrorists of a sort, and I've had them. I know a terrorist when I see one. They rely on you not to throw the table over. They're counting on you being stuck in the old order."

"You've been one in fact, haven't you?"

"Remember the prig and hear me out. Terrorists don't belong anywhere, much less on a ship. She's out of control. She's the sort of person who, if I were sitting alone in the Ziegfeld, would walk right over to me and say, You're sitting in my chair."

"Yes, and you'd sit there and stare at her twat till it itched."

Bo screws up his face and squirms. Peter had aimed right for his boiler room.

"There's a party discipline you seem to ignore, Bo. She does want to get things done. You might say I'm a commissar. I can control her."

"Oh no. If you could she wouldn't be your obsession. She's not crew. She's plastique. I know plastique. Look, the Reds, the Germans, the Scandinavians all sail with women. I approve. I'd ship with a woman captain, but your friend's an accident waiting to happen. And it'll happen between you and me, which is a damn fine reason to part as friends now."

"I should be offended, don't you think?"

"Shouldn't doesn't count. You're not, are you?"

"You're the least offensive of men, Cavalieri, in spite of your best efforts. Moira is crew, treat her that way. And don't mix your metaphors. It's distasteful. Plastique is not an accident waiting to happen, as you and I both know. I am not unacquainted with it. God knows where you have used it. Korea, I imagine. My own experience was in Oman."

Bo has wanted off this course for several minutes so he seizes the opening. "Oman?"

"Artists Rifles Regiment, SAS, in the service of that old tyrant Said bin Taimur who could not have enough enemies to suit him. He took a liking to me and I've been waiting for us to put Moira properly to work so we could discuss the sultan and Muscat and Oman and a world of things which I think you will very much like, Bo."

"I'll take you to La Spezia, then we'll see."

5

On the first day after Bo muscles his sea bag aboard, as the three of them slug coffee on the bridge, he brings out the relevant Navy Hydrographic Office and Admiralty charts from the chart room and spreads them over the chart table.

"The mind can't stand a dogleg of any kind," he says. "It naturally wants to straighten things out."

"I'm not convinced," Moira says. "I have known minds to never encounter a twist that didn't infatuate them."

"He's talking about navigation, Moira," Peter says. "A dogleg is a bend. It could be in a course line or a river or a way a navigator chooses to get from one datum to another."

"Oh, is that what we're talking about, Bo?"

She likes having to swim in his sea-green eyes, she even likes her panic.

Peter laughs. "He's not going to play your game, Moira."

"Or yours either, it seems," she says.

Bo searches their faces. Charles Arnot, who'd come up to the bridge while they were talking, looks hungry for more. Moira responds with her hands, making a dogleg in the air.

"We lay in our courses in the mind of God with a watery ink," Peter muses. "We live in the mind of God, our earth in the cosmos, the cosmos God's very mind at work, so that all we do, all this laying in of courses, is merely God thinking."

"And just what is God feeling, Peter? That is, how does one discern what God feels or when She is feeling it?" says Moira, smiling.

Charles, worrying about how Bo takes this blather, looks at his watch, pumps his fist in the air to signify something he forgot to do, and leaves.

~

In the next few days Bo begins drilling the crew. It's less risky than drilling them under way. He finds that Mortenson and the other two divers, Dieter Benedikt and Colin Semmes, are skilled photographers but lousy sailors and worse, prima donnas. Wirthlin had apparently not bothered to put them to work. Charles, being younger, is afraid to order them about.

"The way it looks to me, everybody has to turn to, including the boss and Miss Sayre," he tells them, "otherwise some of us'll be half dead when we get to the dive sites and you won't have the kind of ship or crew you need to be safe down there. Does that make sense?"

"Jah, it makes sense," Benedikt says, "for you maybe, but ve dive, ve don't swab decks. Does that make sense, Yank?"

"Yes, it makes sense, Benedikt," he says in Ulrike's Baltic German, "on a ship that can afford the luxury. It's up to you. Think it over, I'm not going anywhere."

Semmes, Benedikt and Mortenson sulk and skulk for a day or two. Then Charles Arnot reports to Bo that Mortenson is back aft chipping and painting the stern rail. "I guess I'm the mate, have I got it right, Captain?"

"When we're alone it's Bo, Charles. You got it right, the mate's in charge of ship's work. You set the priorities. A posted order of the day's not a bad thing, if it is a little chickenshit. If I have a priority I'll tell you. Don't let anyone carve out a fiefdom. You've got to know what everyone's doing and how it's done. When it comes to diving, somebody other than the divers has to check out their gear, I don't care how pissy they get."

Next day Semmes and Benedikt amble up to the foredeck early. "What's up then?" Semmes says.

"I need to make sure every davit works. If you find one that doesn't, chip the paint, Xylol the sludge, grease it and repaint it carefully. Break out the inflatables, inflate them and make sure they're okay. Don't hesitate to ask for help."

He studies them as he speaks because, if they're going to be trouble, he wants to know it. Semmes nods amiably enough. Benedikt withholds until he hears Bo say ask for help. Then he thaws and strides off to work.

Bo drills them relentlessly. Fire drills, boat drills, damage control drills, engine failure drills, emergency power drills, emergency steering drills, sun fixes, moon fixes, Saturn fixes, and any other means he can devise to convey to them that *Morgaine* needs more than underway maintenance—she needs a crew prepared to respond by reflex to emergencies.

Within a few days everyone is following Bo's habit of touching winches, davits, rails, instruments, inviting them to confide their ailments. He logs what these fittings and instruments and machines tell him and he tells Charles Arnot that each watch must read the log.

Moira's role is to commune with others' belongings. She's the shadow behind the principal dancers. Seeming less busy, she's actually busier than anybody. She examines the few books Bo carries in his sea bag and sets out in his cabin. She examines his sea bag, his documents, his tidy estate. It's her business.

On the fiddled shelf over his berth she finds a copy of the great theosophist work by Ibn al Arabi, *Al-Futuhat al-Makkiyya* (The Meccan Revelations). The worn leatherbound book had been privately printed in Arabic and English in eighteen-eighty-four by a British scholar. It's inscribed, "For Bo, his own parent and better off for it." The illegible signature looks feminine. She also finds

Dutton's *American Practical Navigator,* the definitive work taught to Annapolis midshipmen, the *Nautical Almanac,* and the *H.O. 249 Sight Reduction Tables for Navigation.* Then she sees E.M. Forster's *Howard's End.* She's heard of the *Futuhat* and read Forster. The rest is arcana.

Before leaving—it's a hunch—she reaches under his mattress and fishes out two sketchbooks. The first, black and laced up, strikes her as a professional's. The other, a spiral pad, is smaller but thicker. In the first sketchbook she sees scenes from Armin Steegemueller's rathskeller, and some portraits of Lakhdar—what a face! What's this? A series of sketches of a startlingly fair girl carrying a tray of beer steins over her head, wiping a bar, tying her apron behind her. Is this the girl with the illegible hand? No, this child wouldn't have the *Futuhat* in her keep, would she? If so, what a precocious child! She cocks her head to listen to her better self. I will not think her a child. She is a young woman. Does she reflect Bo's taste in women? Hello, who's this then? This man has suffered. She's found Armin. Who did these sketches? Bo? There are no names, no dates.

She's sitting cross-legged on the cabin floor by the time she opens the second pad. Here's a different artist, more innocent and yet more involved. There are marvelously detailed cornices and trolls and gargoyles, gewgaws and gimcracks, hands holding glasses, a forest of bottles, an ankle, a dumbwaiter laden with food, mere wisps of hair, and, finally, the most poignant faces she's ever seen. This artist bears no grudges, has no notions, grinds no axes and draws as if it's all he's born to do. He doesn't make these pochades, she thinks, as many Impressionist artists did, to reward friends, but to remind himself that he still has something to live for.

Here's a lovely mystery. Nameless sketchbooks. No captions, no signatures. Have they a common denominator? She closes her eyes and sits listening to the steel horses part the sea. Then it comes to her—the faces are Germanic, the solemn girl, the ravaged man, even the heft of the inanimate objects. Having studied at the Courtauld Institute, Moira knows a great deal about art. The first sketchbook is informed by Goya and Daumier and haunted by Parmigianino. Its genius is in the sure-handed intelligence of its sorrow. But the second book comes from another world, one more fluid.

How to say it? A challenge. Well, you can mat and frame the first book of sketches and show them in a Bauhaus museum, something by Gropius, or some neoclassical heap. But the second book . . . Venice maybe, Istanbul?—her mind will not rest— Granada! Yes, these drawings are Andalusian.

Moira does not think she is a snoop—or worse. She is an operative. To know someone, to really know someone, you have to be brave, take risks. That's the only way to break free of the game to become what you can become. That she has broken a man's seal means nothing to her.

How she will use what she's learned means everything. A person's secrets are inviolate to her once she knows them, but she'll go to almost any length to know them. His secrets are safer with her than with himself.

She knows many men of action whose secrets she doesn't hanker to know. Carther Wirthlin is a man of action. So is Peter. Wirthlin is a bully and cheat. Peter commands by charm and a genuine concern for others. Bo doesn't give a damn. She doesn't need to know why, she needs only to touch him.

As a result of her foray into Bo's moveable domain she knows but doesn't know how she knows that she will say to him, You've been wounded, and when you're wounded you don't think straight. She believes things will come clear if she just keeps probing and arranging.

She knows something now that could bind Bo to Peter. They share an interest in mystical Islam. Then there are the drawings, if he drew them. Drawings offer advantages over photographs to archaeologists and in any event are valuable.

Considering all she has found she possesses the raw material of synchronicity. But synchronicity to be genuine must not be jam-fitted. If she'd been able to pick his brain as she rifled his cabin she might have encountered his notion that coordinates cross in certain places and times for good or ill.

Knowing nothing of navigation, she knows that Bo reads *American Practical Navigator* and uses tidy Admiralty charts as well as blowsy HO charts. That's bound to say something about him. He's something of a syncretist; whatever else she'll consider later. And then there's E.M. Forster. Why *Howard's End* with its discreet female protagonist Margaret Schlegel? She assumes he reads the navigation book, but she can't assume he reads *Futuhat* or Forster or draws sketches.

She's found a treasure better to her than anything she can dredge up from the world's bottoms. There are no customs snafus, no taxes, no danger of theft or chicanery. The men can dive in bells and suits and bring up treasures and get the bends, but Moira dives deeper and brings up better, and she knows its value is in not sharing it with anyone. She's the gods' own thief. She knows herself to bear far greater gifts than her sexuality.

Peter's role is to record their doings. He writes the playbook, and he is, as only Moira knows, astute and penetrating. One day out, he begins a new diary:

The Twentieth Century is the human psyche pulled inside out —precipices, crevices, towering seas, assassins, muggers, torturers, ozone holes, cancers—and in it Ulysses ventures unbidden, hidden, unsung.

More than muscle, wit and courage, he needs antibiotic grace.

Our new friend Cavalieri inflames the exhibitionist itch in those around him. Pretending not to focus on him, they show off in his peripheral field of vision, talk too loudly, unwittingly exiling him. They speak enticingly, waking the auslander in him.

But unhappily for them his antibiotic grace immunizes him. They're pissed. They keep it up. They redouble their efforts. But he's otherwhere and some few of them would gladly heave up on rocks to know whether he's aware or unaware. And even if they could know that, they will never know how costly this grace is to him.

~

When Moira reads these entries—their compact is that Peter should be blind to her reading his diaries—she tags herself as the exhibitionist. She is antagonized and excited. But on reflection she wonders if Peter means himself.

She has failed for a long time to notice: while Peter's speech is rather formal what he writes is conversational and rid of cliché. If she'd noticed that she'd have seen his books disappoint his gift.

6

Moira tiptoes around in her dealings with Bo, careful not to betray her investigations. She's by nature and profession a snoop. The way to betray herself is to show her exhilaration. It will flush her cheeks or tickle her upper lip, and then he'll know that she knows more about him than he knows and he'll be gone without a trace.

"How'd you become a diver, Bo?"

"You'd think I was an Aquarian instead of a Leo. I came by my profession early. I came wrapped in a caul. You know, the remnant of the amniotic sac. It never occurred to me I couldn't swim."

"Sailors used to pay high prices for that blue veil, Bo. They thought it brought them luck. Did it bring you luck?"

"I don't believe in luck."

"I think you do." She fingers aside his silver anchor cross inlaid with turquoise to grasp a gold coin bearing the moon-struck face of Alexander the Great. "Sailors thought he kept them safe." She feathers the face of the demi-god with her middle finger.

Chitchat with Peter is one thing. With Moira it's dishonest. They have business.

He asks, "Do you have any children?"

"I'm reckless, but I'm not that reckless. The whole idea of getting fucked is banal. Some anthropoid with an engorged appendage expecting me to be grateful for having my liver rearranged!" She looks at him expectantly.

He considers Oman. "That's it?"

"Is it significant?"

She's lost the thread of the conversation. So has he, she sees. But he's sweating between the nose and lip. "Would you like to be a pair of my panties, Bo?"

"All the more so, Moira, seeing how secret your garden must be."

"Jesus, you are the damnedest man, Cavalieri! I can't unnerve you."

"You can pretty well make book on that, Sayre."

"Well, are you going to play the game or not?"

"I'm playing, you just ain't listening. Somewhere along the line I lost the notion—ditched it, really—that my function is to stuff cunts. I don't see where I have to put my finger in the dike."

"Dike? Oh what marvelous fun you are, Cavalieri!"

"I mean, hell, there's so much going on there it's like counting stars. You can't do it. A seaman has a hard time finding a woman who can think of something to do besides getting down to the big issue."

"You'd have a hard time finding her if you weren't a seaman, Bo. Does this mean you're going to like me? And exactly where is this *there* where so much is going on?"

He sets the pads of his fingers firmly on her pubis and stares into her eyes. "There. Yes, it's rather like a constellation. One must be very brave to voyage there. Braver in fact than Miss Moira Sayre."

It's her turn to stare back and when she does she sees sorrow in his eyes, deep as her own sorrow, and for the first time her constellation welcomes an alien voyager.

"Even if you're not going to like me, I shall like you, Bo."

"I like your courage."

"Ummm."

She runs her hand down his face thoughtfully, leaving her netherworld unguarded.

People are far from the sum of their data. Collectibles imprison the mind. Collectors are prisoners. Moira never met a collector she liked. Bo has yet to encounter the issue.

I hear the man think. I've never heard anyone think, not even Peter. It's not that I'm attuned or that I anticipate his thoughts. I hear him think! I must show him what I am. He wants to be a pair of my panties. Considering how we started out, I can hardly believe he said it.

But he did. And I would have known if he hadn't said so. I would have heard him think it. This is a great responsibility, and I'm not up to it, but I must find a way to be, because it only comes once in a lifetime, I'm sure.

~

"You said their design cumbered the Viking galleys, Bo," Peter says.

Bo shakes himself like a wet dog and answers.

"Clinker-built longboats with canoe rudders. Yes. They could reach eleven knots. They had shallow drafts, maybe three feet, so they were good for raiding. They were cleat-lashed, so they were flexible. Fine sea boats, good rowing boats. Much better than the Roman ships. But the Vikings weren't as mechanical as the Arabs. The Arabs thought a lot about rigging, how to put up vast sail areas on booms and gaffs. You're right, of course, their design did cumber them. There's nothing like a lateen rig on the open sea. Some Arab ships could easily make two hundred and eighty miles in a day. Still do, across the Arabian Sea, down the East African coast."

Bo speaks from *Morgaine*'s wheel in the Ligurian Sea. He's holding her wheel in his left hand while leaning forward to mark the location of the Santa Lucia Bank at his starboard on a compact little Admiralty chart on the control console in front of him.

Tomlinson hesitates to pursue his point, so much has he liked this discourse on shipbuilding. He basks in his discovery that his new friend shares his taste for arcana.

"Have you heard of the Skerki Bank?"

"About fifty nautical miles northeast of the Gulf of Tunis. Treacherous."

"Yes. I think there was a trade route between Carthage and Ostia, the port of Rome, and I think it crossed the Skerki Bank. The bank is shallow. About twenty miles north of it there are fields of amphora, maybe a half mile down, richer than the fields off Toulon, maybe even richer than the Antonisos fields in the Aegean. This route is unknown. I've been thinking about a book."

"But you're not interested in crocks?"

"No, I told you I was interested in routes. Decades of marine archaeology have convinced us that the ancients hugged the shores. I think they were too entrepreneurial for that. The Romans were better sailors than most people think. They ventured far out of sight of land and I want to prove it."

7

This is the heyday of Philippe Tailliez and George Bass, pioneers of marine archaeology. Peter knows them but is not of their ilk. He has no wish, with meter poles and lifting balloons, to bring up amphorae with their vintners' seals, kraters, lekanis, hydrias, pelikes, kylixes, alabastrons, mosaic stones, faience and amber.

Unlike Lord Elgin and Heinrich Schliemann, he reveres the sanctity of place. Born to wealth, he doesn't crave it but knows how to steward it, as Bo found out at Ruggieri's yard in La Spezia where Peter spared no expense to make *Morgaine* well found but studied invoices with Hasidic fervor. There's a practical side to Peter's reverence: he knows the time has not yet come when the sea's profoundest secrets will be wrested without mangling them. The technology does not exist. Unlike Alan Villiers, an intrepid seaman as well as author, Peter is devoted solely to turning out the hoards of his mind in handsome books.

At Skerki Bank he knows he'll find evidence of a lively trade between Carthage and the Port of Rome, Ostia. More important, he'll show that Roman triremes didn't invariably hug the shores, as believed. It's a modest ambition: it will make a small book. The Romans, dragooned to naval prowess by the spectacular conquests of Sulla and Pompey, could never be proven to be maligned seamen. Their detractors wronged them deftly, making them out to be adequate seamen. Truly maligned were the Arabs, Malays and Chinese, magnificent seamen written out of marine history by westerners. The Arabs had been doubly maligned by the West's childish affection for the legendary Sindbad, as if he had been singular in his visits to Sind and Cathay. History could ignore the real Arab sailors as long as Disney embraced Sindbad. Captain Villiers had fired Peter's imagination, telling him what great seamen the Arabs had been, still were, and sharing with him the priceless story of Achmed ibn Madjid, the Arab sailing master. Madjid took Dom Vasco da Gama on his famed twenty-three-day voyage from East Africa to India, a voyage cauterized from Western history by the much-huffed-on coal of Vasco's fame. It was Villiers who inspired Peter to popularize arcana, specifically the Villiers story of Vasco's encounter with Achmed at Malindi on the East African coast.

Let me show you something marvelous, Vasco said to the famous Arab navigator. With this device called an astrolabe I shall take my ships to Sind. You've heard of Sind?

Indeed, said Achmed, and if you wish I shall tell you about it, for I have been there often. Indeed I have prayed at the Prophet's mosque in Calicat. Shall I tell you about Cathay? Or perhaps the Japons? And as for your little gewgaw, he told the ruthless Vasco, it is quite primitive—let me show you my kamal.

This is Peter's defining story. Far from envying Villiers for popularizing it, he relishes it. He knows there are many such stories and he intends to tell some of them.

~

They move their base from La Spezia, not to Palermo, which makes sense, but to Camarina on the belly of Sicily. It was off Camarina in the republican period that combat and a fierce storm sank some two hundred and fifty Roman and Carthaginian ships where they lay in the shallow Golfo di Gela, making it an even richer cache than the Grand Conglouee off Marseilles. As they pick their way down through the Stretto di Messina across which Italy tries eternally to punt Sicily over to the Arabs, Bo remarks that it makes better sense to operate out of Palermo. Peter responds that Roman wrecks from the time of Trajan and Hadrian, imperial Rome's high-water mark, had yielded giallo antico at Camarina. Giallo antico, he explains, is marble from Chemtou in Algeria. There's very little yellow marble left at Djebel Chemtou, Peter says, "so we are quite privileged, you see."

Bo's defenses drop. Tomlinson is guileless. Bo doesn't know it, but he's signing on for the long haul.

Moira has passed along the intelligence that Bo is probably an artist. Peter knows her too well to ask how she knows. "I need a photographer, which I have in Moira," he announces after they drop anchor at Camarina, "and now I need an artist." The sun rises over the sea, shouldering Malta aside. "Ah, Alexander's shield!" Peter exclaims.

So the Romans might have imagined, so mystically they revered the Macedonian conqueror. Peter mines Bo's eyes for an answer. Moira is there, smiling as if she were merely an audience.

"It'll mean more pay," Bo says. Actually he doesn't give a damn about the pay, he simply likes the game. He's never made a penny from his drawings, doesn't even sign them, so it's a bit of a kick.

"Of course," Peter says. "As I presume the utes had no need of underwater scriveners, I'll show you some interesting underwater writing gear, but actually I think you'll find yourself doing most of it from memory. I see you have something of an eye for dingbats . . . "

Peter would babble on entertainingly, but he notices Bo smiling at Moira and he knows why. "The utes, dear," he explains without missing a beat, "are UDT men, not, as you might have thought, a native American tribe. Did I ever tell you," he says to Bo, "about the Antikythera computer?"

Bo smiles like a favored child.

"They recovered this mysterious machine from a wreck site off the island of Antikythera in 1901. They assumed that it was an ancient sextant. It had a four-year dial, a differential, a crank handle, wheel circles and axes, gear teeth, an entire gear train! Can you imagine it? It was better, oh much better than having found Haroun al-Rachid's warrior robots or his deciduous coin tree. It was flabbergasting. Still is, but not for the reasons they thought. It turns out that it's some kind of computer, perhaps an ancient enigma machine, and since it was found on a merchant-man, it's quite likely there were others. I want to write about such things. Did you know the Phoenicians circumnavigated Africa? Vasco didn't know that. Did you know their forebears were the Canaanites of Biblical infamy?"

The fact that Bo never told them that he makes sketches goes unmentioned. Being frisked by Moira confers a reciprocal right that excites him.

Their work at Skerki Bank, now avoided by deep-draft ships and any ship freighted to her Plimsoll mark, gives Bo time to think. He starts with recent events.

Getting to Skerki Bank hadn't gone smoothly. After leaving Camarina Bo had gone below to familiarize himself with the writing implements Peter showed him. He fell asleep with them heaving on his chest and he woke up a few minutes later hearing something he didn't like. The passage of a ship over deep water sounds different from her passage over shallows. The quicksands off North Africa, called Syrtes in the Aeneid, are infamous and Bo is quite familiar with them. He didn't like *Morgaine*'s belly howl.

When he reached the bridge he found what he feared. Dieter Benedikt had relieved Charles Arnot and altered *Morgaine*'s due west course to Isola di Pentelleria, the Italian military base guarding the eastern approach to the Strait of Sicily, to take them across the Adventure Bank to Skerki Bank as the crow flies. Like most veteran Mediterranean navigators, Bo knew Adventure Bank. He knew that even with local knowledge it was dangerous. He checked the log to see if Charles had superseded the course he'd laid in before turning over the watch to Benedikt. Even Benedikt hadn't changed it, he'd just ignored it. Bo stuck the Admiralty chart in front of Benedikt. "If you want to change a course, ask whoever laid it in. The Adventure Bank is shallow and we have no pilot on board."

"We're not a merchant-man, Captain. We have only a twelve-foot draft. I was saving us money. Isn't that what you do for the Greeks?"

"There are some twelve-foot waters in there, but that's not the point"—he was going to make a point, but he disliked Benedikt so much he changed his mind—"the point is what I say goes."

Benedikt locked the wheel to the iron mike, the gyro pilot, and turned to size Bo up. Bo signaled him to come and get it. Benedikt considered it, then decided this mischling would probably not fight him honorably.

"Take a break, I'll take the wheel," Bo said.

~

"Dieter's not in *Morgaine's* graces, you know, so you'll have to get rid of him before she does, unless you'd like to make *Morgaine* a little sacrifice."

She had been standing out on the starboard weather deck and now leaned into the pilothouse. Given their apparent wind and a twelve-knot northwesterly, he didn't think she could have heard, so she must have interpreted body language.

"Have you read *The White Goddess?*"

"No."

"Well, you ought to. You are one of her servants. You may read my copy if you like."

He nodded. He liked hearing Moira and Peter speak. He felt like their patient. The doctors had given up. They had left him to Moira's and Peter's potions and spells. They were healing him of Gundersen, of Kaltenheisserstrasse and Oued Zem.

"You know what we are, Bo?" She was going to tell him. He waited. "I don't know what we are, but I know we're in a state of amnesiac disgrace. We all know much more than we admit. But that's not our disgrace. Our disgrace is that we've denied it for so long that we really have forgotten. We know that we change shape, fly, hear each other think, but we pretend that we forget and after a while we do forget. As if this weren't bad enough, along comes Herr Doktor Sigmund Freud, with his cancerous fixations, to institutionalize our disgrace by insisting we are grandiose megalomaniacs when we seek to shake off our amnesia."

He had been marking a course line while handling the wheel. He had taken up the powerful seven-by-fifty Zeiss binoculars he often wore and had focused on a pair of Italian corvettes off Pantelleria. Then he realized Moira wasn't going to continue.

"How did we suffer this amnesia?" he asked.

"I want to say we suffered it struggling down the birth canal, damaged by the navigational hazards erected by our mothers' ambivalence, but I know people who came easily and were welcomed with great love—and yet they're not unusual."

He finished his course line and idly scanned the corvettes.

"I'm going to take my amnesiac disgrace down to the galley for some coffee," she said.

~

They sled over Skerki Bank like cloud-bound children over a swimming hole. Bo and Moira Sayre, their two-hose regulators hooked up to twin air tanks, amass hours, then days ghosting over fields of amphora suspended by trapezes. They're trying to decide where to set up their divers-down buoy flags. There's no need for helmet diving. Aqua Lungs are adequate in these shallows.

He knows the rapture of the deep, narcosis; this is the rapture of the about-to-be-born. Only when practicing tae kwon do has he known anything like it.

~

He thinks of her remark about our lost powers as their shadows cross the debris fields of imperial galleys. She takes her left hand off her tow bar and signals him as he thinks a proper Nereid might, an hermetic signal. A fancy slips through his brain's baleen and is being digested: she, more than their ship, is left-handed. He embroiders this fancy: Morgaine was wronged by the great Arthur. The fabulists, even the ones masked as historians who shoved Arab and Chinese seamanship off the table, would not have hesitated to trifle with the tale. Now he entertains the notion of seeing if *Morgaine* backs to port, her side sinister. Vessels favor one side when backing, just as people back off a position distinctively. He seems to remember she had backed to the left at Ceuta.

~

Peter is envisioning a modest book about the Carthage-Ostia connection. He wishes only to remark that the Romans hadn't been as timorous at the helm as thought and that the marble quarries at Djebel Chemtou, the vineyards and granaries of the northern Sahel, indeed all the treasures and riches of Dido, played an important role in Roman culture. When Cato said, as he did ad nauseam, *Carthago delenda est*—Carthage must be destroyed—he took it for granted that Rome's legions would buccaneer and did not intend to plow with salt the entire Tell of North Africa. Peter had written far more ambitiously of the Silk Road, the Spice

Road, the Arab monsoon trade, the Viking-Varangian Routes, Achaeans plying the Black Sea, and now he proposes to write about Omani pearls and the Mughal Court. His custom, because Moira is a skilled photographer as well as marine archaeologist, is to use her photographs, drawings adapted from them and lush and fanciful cartography to illustrate his books.

But now he and Moira are delighted by Bo's drawings, redolent of the Baroque perfectionist Carlo Dolci—red and black chalk on paper, pencil with red chalk, pen and ink, ballpoint, charcoal, and pencils of different numbers.

Not only is this talent a bonus, but he draws their researches from memory—their shadows haunting fields of amphorae, the sorting of gear on deck, the ablutions of divers and their angels.

So far no devils. So elegant and pure are his lines that his employers, who know a great deal about art, refrain from speaking of his work so as not to break the spell. They don't know, couldn't know, that he's celebrating his friendship with them by using color for the first time. True, it's a modest polychromatic sortie, but for Bo it's an indulgence. Bo can be to him what the artists McBey and Kennington had been to T.E. Lawrence, Peter hopes. Perhaps he'll produce a book of Bo's drawings, but for the moment what intrigues him more than the drawings is that Bo hasn't questioned how they knew he draws.

This fortuity of employing a draftsman-captain enables them to finish up at Skerki Bank in only six weeks. They've disturbed nothing, at least not enough to irk the archaeologists waiting in the wings to emerge in the 1970s and then revolutionize marine exploration.

They've pilfered nothing, although they've found much to tempt an Elgin or Schliemann. Moira, who has never troubled to learn navigation, not even dead reckoning, charts the wreck sites precisely and, with Bo supervising, marks his big HO charts correspondingly.

Years later Peter will give them to George Bass, the brilliant explorer of the Trojan wrecks off ancient Halicarnassus in Turkey.

Peter, feverishly jotting down the details for which his books are justly respected, prolongs their stay over Skerki Bank because he dreads Bo's leaving. Peter doesn't know, hasn't noticed, how Moira and Bo are getting on, and he thinks he ought to let well enough (if that's what it is) alone. It does occur to him—he is not the man to miss such things—that Bo has drawn every crew member, even Benedikt, but he's drawn only Moira's hands and her shadow. He has begun to like Bo so much he's run out of banter. In his admiration he begins to emulate the seaman's taciturnity, and this bemuses him.

One night as they make coffee and sandwiches in the galley while Bo works in the chart room topside, Peter says, "Do you think it's the Prussian or the Bedouin that's taciturn?" and Moira answers, "I suppose a chatty Prussian or Bedouin is possible . . . " This sort of camaraderie binds them. They're helplessly addicted to each other's powers of observation.

"You know," Peter says, "he's like the Egyptians, he draws what he knows, not what he sees." Moira slices a few tomatoes before she says, "He told me he feels malaise in museums because he's invaded the artist's privacy, intruded upon a sexual moment."

"Not the subject's?"

"He feels the artist has already done that. He's responsible only for his own intrusion."

"The corollary is that he feels the artist is still at work. Why sexual, by the way?"

"Well, I think, I'm not sure, that he thinks painting is sexual."

"So he steers clear of it?"

"Well, not quite. We must be thankful for that."

"Yes. I do remember that impossibly Teutonic sylph you

showed me in his sketchbook. Just the sort of thing to titillate Lewis Carroll."

"No! I don't agree at all, Peter. First of all, I doubt it's Bo's work. I don't know how he came by it, it's too innocent to be his. Our friend's not innocent. Whoever drew that girl was wild about her. There are some drawings of her which I know Bo did— they're dispassionate."

"We should encourage this talent, Moira."

"I think we should think twice and yet again as to what we encourage in him, because I never met a man whose balance is so precariously tuned. Remember this, Peter, the three of us are engaged in diving for the past. That's not an accident. To do it and not succumb to the bends or sharks or fouled lines or shifting debris, we need our angels."

They'd struggled under Malta in the teeth of an east wind, the kind that rips off awnings and torments eucalyptus in Algiers and reminds the pieds-noirs that their fancy about "French air" on the high plains outside Algiers during its stupefying summers is only that, a fancy. For a man who has never visited his native land, Bo knows a great deal about it and thinks of it often as he transits the Mediterranean. He knows, for example, that the coast and high plains, the Tell, experience leaden rains.

~

Topside on the bridge Bo takes the wheel and Charles Arnot transcribes what Bo has plotted on the big roll-up U.S. Navy charts to the handier Admiralty charts. This teaching practice has been routine.

Moira and Peter come along the starboard Africa-side deck into the pilothouse. Peter looks about with his binoculars. Moira noses around the controls and modulates the marine radio. Then, Peter first, they lean over Charles' shoulders and see the plot from

Skerki Bank in the Mediterranean to Matrah Bay in the Persian Gulf. If that doesn't reassure them, a note penciled in around Port Said does: "wire $ Ute-Britt."

"Well, Mademoiselle Fureteureuse, there's a bone for you to chew," Peter says.

But Moira knows who Ute-Britt is. She's the sylph with the impossibly fair hair; what she doesn't know is what she is to Bo. The two conspirators stand in the wheelhouse grinning at each other.

8

"You're going to like the old satan, Bo, I assure you. That's me standing next to him on his right. Major Peter Tomlinson, Artists Rifles, and Sultan Said bin Taimur. We were helping the old scalawag put down some homegrown Reds in Dhofar. The photo's a bit scruffy, but you get the idea I wasn't always as soft as I am now."

"He looks like a court physician in a Persian miniature," Bo says, sharing a corner of the photo.

"Quite, yes, but he's from the Abu Saidi family, Bedouin all. But you're right, he lacks the hawkish face of the artist Hogarth's Auda Abu Tayi or of you, my friend. Your people, the Maghrebi, of course think the other Arabs are all impostors."

"They may be right." Bo studies the bewildering squall of saccades crossing Peter's face as his gaze darts around the room. They've dropped anchor where the Matrah port captain designated and are preparing *Morgaine's* cockboat to go ashore to salute the tyrant. Peter is having his way about all this, so why should his eyes resemble two-second flashers in the twilight? Bo feels wary. "Do you remember the Anglican hymn where men make strange, Peter?"

"Yes. Startling phrase, isn't it?"

"Why are you making strange?"

"It's that feeling of something-must-happenness I sometimes get. Sort of a mistral angst. Then, on a mundane level, I have some very fast talking to do to his highness, who's a proper paranoid. That's where you come in. I want you with me. We must not offend the court by bringing Moira, whom his highness would regard as a contaminant."

~

Bo eases the cockboat alongside the port captain's twin-screw pilot boat. *"Salaam aleykum,"* Peter says, saluting with his right hand, heart to mouth to forehead.

"Wa aleykum salaam, Major," the captain replies. They climb over gunwales to the pilot boat and then up onto the dock. Silently they're shown to a black stretch Mercedes whose menacing driver, without saying a word, drives them through Muscat to Said bin Taimur's palace overlooking Matrah Bay.

"Look," Peter says before long, "we're in the walled market, Sur al-Lawatiyah. It's run by khojas originally from Sind." He's pumped up, eager for his reunion with the sultan. It's December, the second of Oman's five temperate coastal belt months. Peter wears a light SAS field jacket stripped of insignia. Bo wears a white shirt with merchant marine epaulets and twill slacks.

Said bin Taimur, wearing a turban, not the kaffiyeh and agal of most peninsular Arabs, embraces Peter ritually but his gaze glues itself to Bo. As he exchanges a few sentences with Peter in Arabic the sultan studies Bo rudely.

"Your friend has told me who you are," he says at length, in English. "I told him I do not think so."

He takes the measure of Bo's discomfort. "Allah only knows." The sultan smiles. He enjoys his own humor; will he enjoy anyone else's?

"We speak English for you, but it is criminal you do not speak your native tongue."

"I speak my native tongue, your highness."

"That is?"

"German."

Said bin Taimur, rascality notwithstanding, enjoys humor in others. He smiles wickedly. "A serviceable language, I'm told. It's like Arabic, one hawks it up." He fakes a few coughs and looks around for approbation. "I do not like its script, however. It's quite sinister, don't you think?"

Peter, hoping to divert Bo from the conclusion that the old devil has seen too many Allied propaganda movies using blood-dripping Gothic lettering, puts in helpfully, "His highness is an aficionado of calligraphy. He owns one of the world's finest collections, including many Celtic illuminations."

Bo's mind is a bit more subtle than that: Gothic script invites him to think of the 1929 vampire film *Nosferatu*.

As he watches the sultan he sees disapproval. "I would prefer the word connoisseur," the old man says, "because my only devotion is to Allah." The cunning of his words amuses Bo, who now breaks into a rash grin. "Ha, see! Our friend knows exactly what I mean. I shall show you my manuscripts, yes, I shall. We shall not allow the major to come with us—the British are very covetous, you see, they cannot keep their fingers off anything that belongs to subspecies. We offend them. They regard our good fortune as unlucky for them. It's a personal affront."

Poor Tomlinson is indeed offended. Stricken. He has never seen the sultan's fabled collection. Bo regards him, concerned. Seeing this, the sultan leaves off his tack. "The Algerians are famous soldiers, major, did you know that? They served many Muslim princes as mercenaries, the Turks, the Mamluks, the Kurds, even the Mongols. Most of them are descended from a savage tribe, the Banu Hilal." He pauses, cocks his head as if listening to a bird call, then says to Bo, "Are you a mercenary?"

"I am a simple merchant seaman."

"Beware the man who is a simple anything. Nothing is simple."

A soldier armed to his teeth pours tea from a height into glasses half-filled with sugar. They sip silently, the sultan in a low field chair, Peter and Bo sitting cross-legged on the floor before him. Then the meeting ends so abruptly that Bo can't tell how or who ends it. On their way back to the boat he asks Peter what happened.

"He's like you, Bo. When he has nothing to say he just stops talking. When that happens it's rude to go on. Besides, it's clear he wants to think about you."

~

Their next meeting with the sultan is to the point. "As you know, your highness, his excellency Achmed Ziyad bin Harbi has informed me that an untold number of ancient shipwrecks were uncovered by a violent storm at Suhar earlier this year. It's possible, if they've lain in rich sediment since they sank, that there has been insufficient oxygen to support the toredo worms and other sea animals that eat ships. You know my intent has been to research the Pearl Route from Oman to the Mughal Court in the country which the magnificent Achmed ibn Madjid, the navigator, called Sind. I have also wished to write about the ancient trade route between Sur and Calicat in India."

Bo marvels at Peter's ornate rhetoric. He understands that he is paying tribute to the hyperbole of classical Arabic in deference to their host, who clearly savors it.

"If these wrecks were pearl ships they might yield many secrets."

The sultan erases words in the air. "They would be no different from the baghalas we use today. You may still see these pearl ships here, in Dubai and in Bahrein."

"One supposes, highness, but one cannot be sure, and there is the question of artifacts. Your highness knows I do not pilfer or even disturb. I am assiduous, even to the point of putting ballast stones back where I find them after I see what's under them. But I have changed my mind, your highness. I have another idea which I pray you will find wondrous."

"When the British have another idea, and they always do," the sultan remarks to Bo, "it is Barings Bank that finds it wondrous."

Peter keeps his equanimity. "Wondrous, highness, I assure you."

"All Allah does is wondrous," the old potentate says. "Is that not so, my Algerian friend?"

Peter deems it unseemly to turn to see how Bo reacts to this aside, but whatever his reaction it pleases the tyrant.

"So, major, be so presumptuous as to reveal Allah's latest wonder to us."

Bo keeps a straight face—he will not be the sultan's straight man—and the sultan approves of this loyalty to Major Tomlinson. It means that Bo can be trusted, as indeed the sultan trusts Tomlinson, for all he delights in baiting him. It's an old game and Tomlinson is used to it. If Bo indulged Taimur it would spoil the balance of the thing and sour the occasion. Bedouin are adept at such tests, as are all cultures that keep their campfires lit.

"Do you know why the foreigners speak of alchemy, your highness?"

"Of course. They wish to paint us as Luddites and associate us with deviltry."

"That is so, but there is a semantic reason that sheds much light on what I beg to do with your tolerance."

The old man snorts. Referring to himself with his forefinger, he says, "Tolerant?"

"The foreigners do not know that al-Kimya is merely the Arabic word with its article for chemistry. Their ignorance is even greater than that, for they do not know your magnificent forebears drew no distinction between the study of chemistry and the study of metaphysics. Chemistry and alchemy were one and the same. The foreigners are unable to this day to appreciate the holistic spirit of Arab thinking. By the end of the century the history of science will have shown their Platonic orientation to be preferable to the Aristotelian."

"Yes, we perhaps should never have given Aristotle to the Franks," the sultan sighs mockingly. The Arabs used to call all Westerners Franks, and the old sultan enjoys this archaism.

Peter is undeterred. "Therefore, highness, I propose to bring this omission to the world's attention by recovering such alchemical artifacts as may be found."

"Bottles?" the sultan asks. "I should think, major, your researches were better done in books than in mud. Isn't that where the alchemists themselves sought the fabled arcanum? By the way, if you should happen to discover how to turn base metals into silver and gold, Oman's share will be ninety-nine point nine percent. That will be sufficient to make you all rich." He winks at Bo.

"I must reprove your highness, really I must. Only the basest alchemists seized on the Greek idea that all base metal is on its way to becoming precious and it merely requires a little help from men to hurry the process."

"So then what did the precious alchemists think?"

"They thought, highness, that all chemistry celebrates the mystery of Allah, who wishes always to turn base into precious."

Bo notices this last remark distresses the sultan. Said bin Taimur waves off his guards. He turns his back to his guests, a gesture beyond any Bedouin's pale, and looks up contemplatively at the four-hundred-year-old Portuguese forts of Mirani and Jalali. When he finally turns to face his guests, his face is blasted like a Flamenco dancer's.

"The alchemists did not know Allah as rulers do. Did he make the Franks less base that they refrained from slaughtering the Jews?"

Peter and Bo stare at each other nonplussed.

"The Franks have much to answer for, highness," Peter says gamely.

The sultan is satisfied. He grins at Bo like a victorious prize fighter. Far from quitting his notion that the old man is a mystic, Bo is even more confirmed in that view because he sees that the sultan is determined to see the face of God. Nor does he finally kiss off this view when he reads in 1970, a year later, that Said bin Taimur, having been deposed by his son Qaboos with British connivance, has taken up residence in the Dorchester Hotel in London, where he will die, a hostage of the infidels.

The potentate gestures to Peter to get on with it.

Peter is getting nowhere. He's squandered his opportunity, not that the sultan is more sympathetic to his writing about pearls, but that the alchemy between them is wrong. Bo, taking his cue from the sultan's trip to his window, walks about in ever-widening circles examining manuscripts, which hang or lie open on book stands. The sultan's eyes follow him. This commitment to the illumination of scholarly and literary works suggests an opening to Peter.

"Your highness," he begins softly, "since the Arabs made no real distinction between alchemy and chemistry in a technological sense, it offers an opportunity to take Arab science out of the books and put it on the table, to actually show how it looked . . ." He means to go on, but he realizes he's talking to a man who banned sunglasses and bicycles, who allows no more than six miles of paved roadway. This is a fool's errand. This man would have exiled Jabir, al-Razi, Ibn Sina and al-Kindi, those great Arab scientists, or worse.

Or would he have? After all, it's the past he's intent on saving.

"A people, in order to be proud of their past, they must be acquainted with it." He is set to squeeze off another bon mot when he sees he's hit his mark. Shrewdly he lets his words sink in. "Without Jabir and al-Razi the industrial chemistry of the Franks would be impossible and yet what do the Arabs of Oman know of Jabir and al-Razi?"

"What do I know of them?" The sultan is not smiling.

"Scientific chemistry was born about two hundred and eighty years after the Hejira," Peter says. "I hope that some artifacts may be recovered at Suhar to celebrate Arab science."

"Pots, bottles?" the sultan says.

This time Peter is ready. "Ask your chamberlain, highness, if you do not have manuscripts by al-Razi, particularly his *Al Kitab as Sirr,* his *Book of Secrets."*

Sultan Said bin Taimur knows exactly what he owns. When he'd asked what he knew of al-Razi he'd meant it. "Is this a book I should have?"

"It is a book you cannot be without!" Peter exults. He knows of course that the word secrets titillates the old man who is above all a collector of them.

"Tell me about it, major."

This is better than the biggest, dumbest trout in all the lakes of Scotland.

"In his *Kitab al-Asrar* al-Razi gives us a complete list of alchemical equipment, and it's more marvelous than all the pearls ever shipped to the Mughal lords. There would be, first of all, the hearth, Kur. Then the bellows, Minfakh—we can't hope to recover them. Then the crucible, Butaqah, and the descensory, But-bar-but, the ladle, Mighrafah, the tongs, Kalbatan, the shears, Muqatti, the pestle, Mukassir, the file, Mibrad, the mould, Misbakah. Those are just the melting and heating objects." He pauses.

"Now we get to the apparatuses used in the processes."

The old man's eyes glow. He loves objects, and the spectacle of a Frank reciting antique Arab objects in good Arabic is irresistible. He invites Bo with his hand to partake of this wonder.

"So many and varied are the instruments, highness, that I must abandon Arabic to recite them in English."

"Why don't you abandon English to recite them in Arabic since they are so marvelous," the sultan quips. Bo grunts with glee and rubs it in by nodding vigorously in Peter's face. But Peter is more than equal to the moment. He's on a roll. He decides he will merely reverse the order: Arabic first, then English. And he gets right down to it.

"Qar, the curcurbit or retort for distillations. Amibiq, the alembic, the head of a still. Uthal, the closed vessel in which reactions occur. Aqdah, beaker. Kizan, glass cup. Qannani, flask. Qawarir, phial. Ma'wardiyah, rosewater phials. Barani, jars for heating. Mirjal, cauldron. Qudur, earthen pots. Tannur, oven. Mustauqad, stove. Atun, kiln. Tabashdan, brazier. Nafikhu nafsih, firebucket. Mihras, mortar. Durj, firebox. Qim, glass funnel. Qanadil, lamps. Shall I go on?"

"You have proven that you could," the sultan says.

"I am especially interested in the Uthal," Peter says, "because drawings suggest that there were many kinds. They are called aludels by the Franks and have incarnated in modern laboratories. I am also interested in the so-called Moor's head used for distilling herbs and flowers in medicine. Did you know, sir, that we owe the concept of antisepsis to the Andalusian Arabs?"

"We owe more than that to them. We owe the cowardly loss of Granada and an example for all time of weak knees."

Bo is growing fond of this old reprobate.

"Peter Tomlinson," the sultan begins again, "I have the *Kitab nukhbat al-dahr* by al-Damashqi. You are familiar with it?"

What a game, Bo thinks. God help Tomlinson if he can't top this.

"It is exactly the kind of thing I'm talking about, highness, a steam oven for distilling flowers to make rosewater is described and illustrated in your book."

"You impress me, Tomlinson. What is our friend here going to do?"

"He is an experienced seaman and diver, highness. He is going to help us find some of these instruments. Then I am going to write a book or perhaps two or three books. The artifacts are of course yours."

"What makes you think these clever Arabs exported their laboratories, Tomlinson?"

"They were in the process of establishing great mercantile empires. What better way to persuade the samuri of Calicat that the Arabs possessed great power than to perform these mysterious transmutations?"

This is an argument bound to endear any sultan of Oman, because Oman single-handedly opened the Indian Ocean to Arab trade and battled the Portuguese for supremacy. Peter successfully guessed that so much did Said bin Taimur live in the past that it replays itself to him like an endless tape.

"That stupid bastard Achmed ibn Madjid, didn't I hear you mention him? Do you know what he did? He showed the filthy flea-bitten Portuguese the way from Zanzibar to Sind. May Allah damn him forever! I know that he roasts in hell. Can you find a hotter oven for him in your researches?"

Bo turns away so as not to laugh out loud. But Peter is on top of the situation. "I will try," he says.

"You're a navigator, Algerian," the sultan turns to Bo. "But are you as stupid as Ibn Madjid?"

"There are no such great secrets any more," Bo says.

"You've lived with the Franks too long, or maybe it's that German mother. That is a British answer, Algerian, a very British answer. The British do not believe in giving away the time of day. Fortunately for the Arabs we do not need it. We taught them how to count."

"Your highness, if we may put aside the stupid bastard Ibn Madjid for a moment, there is the matter of permits."

"You have your No Objection Certificates. That means we suffer you."

"I think your sufferances need to be more specific."

"You want me to say you have permission to muck around Suhar for old bottles, is that it?"

"Something like that."

"How do I know this hasn't got something to do with the British Navy?"

"You don't, highness, but as you already know, if Suhar were any good as a modern port, you wouldn't be so dependent on Matrah and Sur. It's simply too shallow."

"I enjoy vexing the British," the sultan tells Bo. "They are the ideal straight men. They are so intent on getting what they want that they restate the obvious as if it were a revelation just so the rest of us don't feel half so stupid. It's really rather charming, don't you think. But you must never underestimate them. They are very dangerous people. What did the maggoty Vasco do with the fool's gift the bastard Ibn Madjid handed him? Very little, I assure you, compared with what the British would have done. The British are among the world's most deadly people. Oh yes, ask the Scots or the Irish. But who are the British? They don't know. That is why they were able to conquer so many people who know who they are. They have an insatiable thirst for identity."

"That is a very mystical formula, highness," Peter says with the hauteur one would expect of the British envoy next-door.

"What makes you think these bottles and gimcracks will be found, and why at Suhar? Just because the sea has puked up some hulks? What if you find nothing?"

"Curse the infidel in his blindness!"

"He curses the infidel well for an infidel," the sultan says to Bo. Bo feels his turquoise and silver cross burn on his chest.

"The UNESCO papers I have been reading, highness, mention that there were chemical laboratories along the Omani coast, particularly at Suhar . . . "

"I'm glad they do something worthy of the Saidi money they've been collecting. You remind me of Lawrence, Tomlinson, hot to tell us of our glories."

"There will be no Versailles at which I betray you, highness."

"Come now, that is too harsh and, I think, more than a little disingenuous, major. The man loved the Bedu. He was betrayed at Versailles, in spite of the story thugs like Nasser like to concoct. His own people broke his heart. Do not overstep your diplomacy. You and I are old comrades—surely you do not take me for a demagogue's dupe. Does he, Algerian?"

"His heart is pure, highness."

"Yes, Sindbad, I know that," the sultan says. The sultan has had his fun and is ready to revise the requisite permits.

9

When *Morgaine* snugs up to the abrupt cliffs of Matrah Bay, Oman is a veiled, leery kingdom. This sultan, like his antecedents, has at best a prickly peace with the Ibadis of the interior. But Said bin Taimur's hand has been strengthened by the British protectorate with its elite soldiery and diesel muscle.

Oman's gardens depend on elaborate irrigation systems first designed by the Persians. They're much older than the waterworks of the Arabs in Spain, Al-Andalus as they called it. But they're similar, which is not surprising, because some of the more important Maghreb dynasties were related to the Omanis.

In six days they weigh anchor. Their progress up to Suhar is languid. An Omani patrol boat lopes alongside like a playful dolphin. They watch pearling baghalas out of Bahrein, their high poops and long burgees making them look sinister to Bo. Japan's cultured pearls are killing off the great pearl marts of Dubai and Bahrein.

"Just as well," Peter says. "The divers are both underfed and underpaid. They're given no lemons against scurvy, no fresh water for their sores, and no safety measures whatsoever, and yet a more cheerful lot you'll never meet."

Oman began exporting oil in the year Bo sailed on the *Delos*. The exploitation of Arab oil holds an exquisite irony, for it was the Arab alchemists who first identified the many practical properties of petroleum. Indeed, the incendiary called Greek fire, the atom bomb of its time, was used by Muslims against the Crusaders. Naffatun, incendiary troops wearing fireproof clothing, would hurl and catapult pots of Naft, petroleum. They also used gunpowder grenades. Cannons first appeared in the Maghreb, and the West inherited that technology from the Arabs in Spain after being hurt by it.

As *Morgaine* passes a string of fishing villages—the Omanis catch sardine, mackerel, shark, tuna and marlin—she picks up a squadron of magzarooks, the fastest of the merchantmen, which collectively the Arabs call dhows. The elegant zarooks, like the ungainly baghalas, carry Omani dates, limes and pomegranates. Bo stands for hours on *Morgaine*'s starboard weather deck sketching dhows, particularly baghalas. Once, when Peter peeks over his shoulder, he says, "Have you noticed she's no good at all in a following sea? That flat stern will get her pushed around mercilessly."

"She doesn't look especially Arab to me."

"She's not. That's astute, Peter. The baghala's essentially a caravel. Rigged differently, but a caravel nonetheless, like *Nina* and *Pinta*. Prince Henry the Navigator and the ship-builders of Genoa and Venice rigged her to beat to windward. That's why the caravel was so handy. She got where she was going faster."

"You're quite a student of naval architecture then?"

"No, but I like to draw ships. I like the detail. I like all detail —I have a sketchbook full of cracks in walls."

~

At Suhar they raft up with their zarook escort and exchange foodstuffs. The Omanis bang drums, sing, dance, mime and otherwise engage Peter and his crew in high jinks. Bo doesn't notice because he speaks no Arabic, but Peter begins right away to mine information. The nakhodas (ships' masters) know the local waters. Their divers see many wrecks and debris fields. They snag their anchors and nets on them.

Morgaine needs charts. The Admiralty and HO charts are general and outdated and don't reflect the work of recent storms. This is so in part because Suhar is no longer strategic to the great navies and merchant fleets. Here Bo's deft body language helps. The zarook seamen begin showing him what's what. He lowers the Dunlop inflatable dinghy, clamps her gasoline outboard to her stern board and takes them for endless crisscrosses. They show him where they lost an anchor, where there are reefs, where sandbars lurk under the chop, where there are wrecks, where the British dropped big petrol drums, where the littoral has changed. He sketches everything.

But he does something else that wins the Arab sailors to *Morgaine*'s purpose. He makes comic charts for them. His largess extends to the lowliest sailor. He draws an Omani red-legged chukor partridge bombing Charles Arnot with an oyster. He puts hyenas to work with shovels on the beach. He sends a camel to sea in the cockboat. He commissions a cheetah on its hind legs, wearing a turban, to tug the dinghy ashore. He condemns poor Peter to dive from a zarook tied to an anchor. He empowers a roc-like Muscat bee-eater to kidnap Dieter Benedikt. He bids the foxes and wolves of Oman to dress and pay court to Moira. He hands out these charts with abandon.

The Arabs see in them their own good information. The caricatures endear *Morgaine* and her crew to these illiterate seamen. Even more fruitfully, the Arabs outdo themselves to encourage Bo to add more detail, and some of that detail is exactly what *Morgaine* needs.

The Arabs don't know what they know, and they don't know its value, but they want to see it shown in Bo's charts. That he's willing to rip off page after page and give them away is marvelous to them. Of course he's all the while at work, with his dividers, parallel rules and protractor, making a master chart incorporating all that he's learning.

"I think we should present the sultan with our final chart," he tells Peter one day.

"Yes," Peter says, "be sure to show me walking the plank tied to an anchor—he'll treasure that."

Bo has already envisioned this gift-chart. The rukkh or roc—the legendary bird of prey known to carry off palaces and ships, to say nothing of wicked Hollywood viziers in the mold of Conrad Veidt—will emblazon the chart. Perhaps the rukkh will clutch a Portuguese man-o'-war.

Bo has been at work in the dinghy for more than six weeks, the Arab sailors coming and going as their work requires, when Peter signals him back to *Morgaine* one morning.

"Look, Bo!" he shouts as they hoist the dinghy up into her davits. Muhammad abu Zaidi, one of the nakhodas, trails Peter back aft. In his hand is a dark wooden strut of some kind.

"Look at this, Bo. Do you know what it means?" Bo takes the strut from Abu Zaidi and examines it. He can make nothing of it and shakes his head.

"Tell him, Muhammad!"

"No. . ." the nakhoda bites the air rapidly.

"Worms! No worms!" Peter shouts.

"Looks like a rib. It could be a recent wreck. They're still making dhows down at Sur."

"No, Bo. Muhammad was born before the turn of the century. He comes from here. This is old, very old. He didn't even know about it until the last storm. This piece of wood should be worm-eaten. The fact that it's not means the storm has given up debris from oxygen-free sediment. There are no fastener marks, so it's Arab. See here, there are grooves where lashings probably gnawed into the wood." He pauses. "What I'm going to do, Bo, is hire some of these men to dive. We'll let them skin-dive. They know these bottoms. When they find something we'll teach them how to use our gear if they want to. We'll even leave some of our gear for them."

Only Moira at this point recognizes how lucky they are, not in what they found but in what they've not found, coral. *Morgaine* is freighted with pick hammers, crowbars, sledge hammers and drills to deal with coral encrustation, but they haven't encountered any and that's too much to hope.

They set to work next day diving on the site where Abu Zaidi found the rib. The choppy waters yield several similar ribs. But after poking around for several more days they decide this is not the original wreck site. The wreck had probably lain elsewhere, but it had drifted relatively intact and lain here for a long time until the storm ripped open the sea bed. Peter theorizes that the ship sank in deeper water and was thrown up here in the shallows. Within two weeks, tearing away sea grass, they expose enough debris to discern something of the ship's size and design. They're disappointed to find no ballast stones, but not finding them tends to bear up Peter's theory that she foundered somewhere else and lost her ballast there. The Arab divers, untutored but fiercely curious, begin to lay out the debris on the bottom as if it were the original wreck site. By the time they surface the site is abloom with orange buoys marking their finds. Bo, on his second dive, sees that the ship was a big double-ender, perhaps a boom. He makes a series of dives, each time coming back up to immediately draw what he saw and what he guessed. In a few days he's able to give Peter a drawing of what their wreck might have looked like. It's pure conjecture, but it encourages them.

"Let's say she displaced two hundred tons," Bo says. "Maybe she had a crew of as many as forty men. From what's left of her keel, I'd say she had two masts. The foremast might have sloped forward. I've seen them that way. She'd have been lateen-rigged, of course, with huge sails. Probably three of them. They'd be sewn together in long strips. The jib would fly off the bowsprit, which would be pointed up sharply like the shoes of the djinn. Maybe she'd make eight or nine knots in a good wind and could point about forty-five degrees off the wind. That's handy for a chubby merchantman of her time. We know she was sewn, not fastened. They probably slopped her down with fat and lime to protect her from shipworm. The coconut stitching that held her together was probably swabbed with vegetable oils to keep it pliant. Being double-ended, she had nothing to fear from following seas. Being fore-and-aft rigged, she sailed close to the wind and withstood monsoon winds. From July to October the outward-bound Arabs would ride southwest monsoons to India. From November to March they'd return on the northeast monsoons. The southwest passage would have been rough. It still is. Nowadays the Arabs run south to East Africa down the lee of the Hadramawt, falling away before the northeast monsoon wind. They come home just before southeast monsoons kick up." He pencils in the finishing touches on his boom as he speaks. He crews her with Lilliputians and puts her on a starboard tack so that her big-bellied sails don't conceal her deck layout. When he starts only Peter is there. By the time he finishes, Moira, Colin Semmes, Dieter Benedikt, Charles Arnot and a pod of Arabs are gathered round the chart table. Their rapt attention inspires detail—a boom crutch behind the mizzenmast, blocks and tackle, a lazarette before the helm, a brazier before the foremast, an elegant longboat lashed through the scuppers to the starboard gunwale.

"You said she was handy for her time, Bo, what time might that have been?" Peter says.

"I don't know. The Arabs are still building booms. I've seen them off the East Africa coast. We know she's a boom, or at least something like a boom. She has no sterncastle, so she's not a baghala or ghanjah. The Arabs probably didn't build baghalas until the Portuguese showed up in their caravels, and they probably didn't know the Portuguese had designed the caravels after the Arab ships they'd seen around Ceuta. But even after they started building them they were still building booms. So that tells us nothing. I'd hate to sail a baghala before a gathering seaway, but they do it all the time. Another possibility is that the caravel is adapted from the baghala. The consensus is that it's the other way around, but the verdict's not in. I'm sorry, Peter, I just don't know."

"Well, I do, or, that is, I can. It's in its infancy, but there's something called radiocarbon dating. It was developed at the University of Chicago. I'm going to get on the phone as soon as I can, call Dr. Willard Libby, and find out how to preserve some of this wood—I think you have to soak it in polyethylene glycol (PEG)—and then cajole him into carbon-dating it. What he looks for, if I understand what I've read, is Carbon-14. It's an isotope. Its radioactivity decreases by decay and that's how they date a sample."

"Sounds expensive. You think the sultan will spring for it?"

"Of course not."

10

That night, as the ship's generator massages their cognac-stung organs, Peter tells Moira, "It's hard to believe our good fortune in finding Bo. His knowledge of Arab shipbuilding is a great boon. I don't know if he knows this stuff in an expert way, but it hardly matters. It sends us in the right direction. We'll get expert opinion later."

She sets her empty snifter to singing with her finger tip.

"It is fortunate, isn't it, Moira?"

"For whom? I have the feeling we're raping him. The man, with his secrets, his dourness, is a whole, a piece of work. We're breaking him up, like salvagers."

"That's nonsense, surely. He's having a wonderful time. You see that. I'm paying him well. We're his latest adventure. It will be all right, Moira, I assure you."

"I have never questioned your ethics, Peter. You know that. But love can make us amoral. We take what is not ours and we don't care how we take it. We beguile people into thinking they're freely giving it. When we're gone they're impoverished and it takes them a long time to figure it out."

"We, Moira? The human species or you and me?"

"As you like it, Peter."

"It is too bad he doesn't know you better, Moira."

"So you say, but I say his first instincts about us were correct. For all his talents and skills and invisible baggage, the man is a primitive—that's his salvation."

"How do you know this about him?"

"You and I walk into a café in La Spezia and we're aswarm with faces we can't take our eyes off. We have to put our lines out and keep jiggling them. He walks in, looks around, and that's that, he's through, he doesn't need them, the faces, the lines, the bait, the lot of it. He can live without them. We have to see who we attract. What if, thanks to us, he can't live without them any more? Without us."

For the first time Moira's cunning insight fails in its job of stirring his blood. Rather, it sends it scuttling into the darkest rookeries of his sources. He puts down his glass and leaves.

~

Abu Zaidi's wreck yields no artifacts, but ten days after Bo sketches the boom she might have been, Benedikt, diving some hundred yards northeast from the wreck, finds a ballast trail that seems to point towards it. Peter by this time has been down to Qasabayat Yal Burayk to call Doctor Libby, take notes on how to ship wood samples to Chicago, and order PEG and vats. When Benedikt finds the ballast, Peter leaves again to call a Welsh classmate who has become an eminent scientist at the Geological Institute of Cardiff. He hopes that Adam Rhys-Morgan and his petrographers will be able to say where the stones came from. Likely sources are the Arab peninsula, India, and East Africa, but Iberia, Italy, North Africa and many other places are candidates. The Arabs engaged in a lively and sophisticated trade of spices, silks, pearls, opium, ivory, porcelain, textiles, rice, copper, tin, iron, salt, weaponry and horses, perhaps even camels. Opium and rice suggest voyages to Southeast Asia. Arab horses were in demand for cavalry. While he's pleased with Benedikt's find, it doesn't suggest anything he can use in his book.

While Peter traverses the hard Batinah coast, Moira is at work photographing the wreck site and trying to delineate a scatter site, if there is one. She uses one of *Morgaine*'s cabins as a darkroom and shuts herself away in it for hours at a time. Only occasionally does she notice Bo. First, he is disassembling and overhauling *Morgaine*'s thrusters. He's found them unreliable at dynamic positioning—what ships do when they must hold a position under power against current and wind. Then he elaborates on the master chart of Suhar and environs.

She doesn't notice that he spends a lot of time with Uthman al-Biruni, the surliest and meanest-looking of their pick-up crew, one of those tall, hawkish Arabs so severe of countenance one wouldn't think of chatting him up. At first he just eyes Bo—some would call it the evil eye—then he anticipates Bo's moves and readies the dinghy or fetches his binoculars from the chartroom. After a while the two of them can be seen out in the dinghy, Bo working on his charts, Uthman manning the tiller and small mushroom anchor. Then one day they stow ten gallons of petrol aboard the dinghy, some sandwiches and water, mount a tiny British naval ensign on the stern, head northwest coastwise and motor out of sight. They're gone two days.

Uthman doesn't give a rat's ass for the rest of them, but he likes Bo. He thinks they're kindred souls, and perhaps they are, for they not only share a certain resemblance but also a demeanor. Uthman knows the coast better than Muhammad abu Zaidi or any of the others for a particularly evil reason. He has been part of the Dhofari insurgency that Major Tomlinson and his SAS and BATT colleagues came earlier to suppress. Born just north of Suhar and a sailor since childhood, he has participated in numerous seaborne raids. He knows English because he was held prisoner by a BATT unit on the island of Jazirat Masirah for sixteen months.

Only with Bo does he allow he speaks English and then he chooses his own comedic moment. Bo is setting his charts down and hand-signaling Uthman to go first this way and then that way when Uthman asks, "Do you get tired doing all that?"—he makes fluttering motions with his hands. Bo looks at him sternly. Neither of them cracks a smile. After a long while Bo says, "I often work under foreign flag, so I'm used to it."

"You speak only English?"

"German," Bo says. Uthman nods.

Then he tells Bo how he learned to speak English with a Yorkshire accent.

"So are we wasting our time here, Uthman?"

"That is what English do."

"I'm not English."

Uthman again nods. He regards Bo as one of The People whose misfortune is to have become detached from them. He nods, but says nothing. He yanks the engine's starter cord and points the dinghy slightly northeast towards Jask in Iran, going slowly, staring into the water. He looks both for color changes and for bottom.

He picks his way along for some forty minutes, adjusting his course from time to time.

"Here!" he says finally, chucking the ten-pound anchor over the side. The light hundred-foot anchor rode, three-strand hemp, has fathom tags roved through its strands. When Uthman pulls it taut it shows they're in fifty-five feet of water. Uthman shuffles through his pantaloons for something. He finds it and hands it to Bo. It's a Portuguese gold ducat. Bo has seen similar coins in a Lisbon museum.

"There are many of these. It is very cold there. I could not stay without equipment."

"These are valuable, Uthman. How many do you have?"

"Only this."

Bo has known such men. He is one himself. But if Uthman al-Biruni has wisdom, Bo Cavalieri wants to hear it. All his life he has acquired knowledge and skill from men like al-Biruni, not men like Peter Tomlinson. He stares at Uthman until the Arab is moved to speak.

"When I was young I thought that Allah wanted the old sultan dead. After I killed many men I knew Allah doesn't want anybody dead. Until their time. I also knew I didn't care if Allah wanted anybody dead. When I saw the wreck down there and all the coins and plates and cannon shot I thought Allah was making a trap for me, like I make for the English, so I take nothing. You understand this, Bo?"

"More than I can tell you, Uthman. We will dive on this wreck. But first we must fetch equipment. Wet suits for the cold. I'll show you how." Uthman nods.

"Do we need explosives, Uthman?"

"Maybe. I know how to use"—Uthman's lips caress the words —"pentaerythritol tetranitrate." He looks to Bo as if he's just rammed the plunger on some explosives. Bo sputters into laughter. Uthman has seen Bo's tattoo. There is no one he admires more than an explosives expert. "You have latex?"

"We'll use 0-Four if we have to, Uthman. You've used it before?"

"On the British." Uthman's eyes glow.

~

By the third week at the Suhar wreck site the bloom is off the lily. Peter comes back from Qasabayat Yal Burayk the day Bo and Uthman head north. A managerial man would feel his authority challenged. Peter is merely amused by Bo's choice of companions.

The Arab divers working with Semmes and Benedikt have brought up shards, none of which can be pieced into a discernible object. Then, the day after Peter's return to *Morgaine,* Semmes surfaces from about twenty feet with a glass vessel. It's tear-shaped with some kind of lip about an inch down from its mouth. Moira spends two days cleaning it with gingerly care. She should have argued with Peter about this, because glass vessels wrested from the sea are known to explode into dust and sand when they dry out. No matter how much you know about archaeology, marine archaeology is a specialized science. Moira knows just enough about it to know how much none of them knows. Peter combs his voluminous file of illustrations.

Four days after Semmes found the vessel Peter announces, "It's a sublimation and distillation jar." He's elated. He, Moira, Semmes and Benedikt now use brass probes, like the ullage rods used on tankers to measure cargo, to define the depth and outline of the wreck. They're working a large rectangular tract from where Benedikt picked up the debris trail to the point where wood was found. Their dhow—they can't be sure it was a boom or any other specific ship—apparently began breaking up on impact and then at some later time cast up closer to shore. They're refining this speculation when Semmes helpfully brings up a beautiful glass bottle blown in two pieces. Its tall, left-angled architectural Kufic script suggests it's Persian or at least made by Shi'ites. The divers keep asking the value of what they're recovering. Then Charles Arnot, who understands better than Semmes and Benedikt what they're looking for, finds a glass retort. They're back on track.

Judging by where they found the retort, they're able to draw the rudiments of a scatter site—the trail of debris a mortally wounded ship might make. To do this they must calculate how she might have been headed, how broadly her structural parts and cargo scattered.

Five days after finding the distillation jar they're at work on rope grids over the structural debris and the scatter site. Peter assigns Charles to bring up ballast, cautioning him to distinguish by color, formation and surfaces so that he'll have a good cross-section to send to Rhys-Morgan at Cardiff.

He hardly notices that Bo and Uthman have been busy on the poop deck laying out and testing diving gear.

"Here's the plan," he tells Moira, Charles and Bo over coffee in the pilothouse. "Charles's ballast goes to Cardiff. We have to know where the stones came from. Colin's jar, the retort and like paraphernalia go to the Marine Archaeology Foundation at Toulon where my friend Georges Archambault will soak and clean them. I've spoken with him and gotten ample instructions on shipping them. You, Moira, will be gratified to know he was appalled that we brought them to surface without knowing how to care for them. He wants them all kept in sea water. We can shoot them underwater. Bo, you can draw them. But we're going to have to wait to get definitive pictures until Georges uses electrolysis and wax emersion, which could take months, even years. Of course I must hotfoot it down to Muscat to get the old scalawag's permission to move so much as a grain of sand. I need you for that, Bo. Don't ask why. He likes you. He will not want to be seen as cantankerous in front of you."

Moira shakes her head. Bo frowns. It's an invitation and she takes it. "Why should you do that, Bo? The old gentleman is entitled to like you without being importuned."

Bo uncharacteristically decides that Moira has handed him a bargaining chip and he pockets it. He turns to Peter and says, "I'd like to take Uthman up north with some diving gear. I think we've found something."

If he truly feels he needs Bo at Muscat, Peter can hardly refuse him. "Well, when you get back, we'll be ready to report to the old man just what sort of thing we want to ship to Toulon. As he has pronounced prejudices about many things, I wish I knew how he felt about the French."

Bo says, "Well, generically, you're all Franks as far as the

Arabs are concerned."

"And you," says Peter, joining in the fun, "are half-Frank."

"Oh I think he's all frank!" Moira chips in. "Isn't that right, Bo?"

"I'm a seaman."

She shoves him playfully.

~

Peter grew up thinking that he needed more time than life begrudged to make even ordinary decisions, but he learned in Dhofar that he thinks fast on his feet. He felt that if Bo had something on his mind, something he thinks worth bargaining over, he'd be more useful in dealing with Said bin Taimur if Peter indulges him. There's plenty to do in Muscat without playing word chess with the old man. The day after Peter hitches a ride down to Muscat in an Omani coastal patrol boat, Charles finds a second trail of stones and a line of lead shot. Bo orders a third grid. The lead shot intrigues him. It suggests a wreck long after the Umayyad caliphate at Damascus or the Abbasid caliphate at Baghdad, or even the Mamluk caliphate at Fustat, now Cairo. Bo dives on the site to recover shot. Then he asks Moira to shoot it up close, to magnify its indentures and encrustations. He and Moira work swiftly and silently. What he lacks in scholarship he makes up for in common sense.

"You could salvage fire pots and grenades from the period Peter is interested in, but not lead shot," he tells her. "I think it best to concentrate where Colin found the bottle."

"To tell you God's truth I don't know what period Peter is interested in, do you?"

"I think so. After the Mongols sacked Baghdad and razed the Abbasid caliphate in 1258 the Arabs were no longer really in charge of their own destiny, so anything they accomplished in the

East—remember they still ruled in the West—was also a Mongol or Seljuk or Mamluk or Ottoman accomplishment. So we're talking before 1258. I think we're really looking at our own ninth, tenth and eleventh centuries. The Arabs thought the Crusaders gnats compared to the Mongols."

She likes Bo's Arabism, breezy and anecdotal where Peter's is at once romantic and Aristotelian.

"The Portuguese conducted a few bargain-basement Crusades on their own. They attacked Ceuta off the Moroccan coast. In fact the young Prince Henry the Navigator took part in that. Then they fought the Omanis for centuries off the East African coast and here in the gulf. I think we're scooping up pieces of that war. They held a good part of the Omani coast for about a hundred and fifty years, pretty much what the sultan holds now. But finally the Omanis kicked their asses pretty good. The books you and I read all talk about great Portuguese seaman. They don't tell you that wherever the Portuguese went they found Arabs under sail, including China and Japan."

"Are you proud of that, Bo?"

"It's a fact."

"So you think these later wrecks are uninteresting?"

"I didn't say that, but if they're not Arab we will not find alchemical apparatus."

He is thinking of Uthman's gold ducat. He makes a crucial connection. When Uthman made his first dive between Suhar and Shinas Bo scanned the coastline and noticed a ruined battlement with a crenelated tower. It reminded him of Jilali, the Portuguese fort at Matrah Bay. The Portuguese held Suhar once. Wreckage found along this coast could be theirs.

The compulsion to drive on gives Bo a purpose that can't let go.

Peter is back and forth making his arrangements with the

famed and far away.

Moira dives and shoots with Zen concentration. Semmes, a man with an uncharacteristic awe in a cockney for whatever order he can make out, makes most of the helmeted dives. Benedikt, a German with an anomalous lust for disorder, pursues his career of staying out of Bo's way. But as they wrest Islamic crockery from the torn seabed the amiable chemistry they formulated over Skerki Bank breaks down. It's Moira who shakes the distillation minutes after Semmes sends up a blown-glass mosque lamp in a wooden crate.

"Goddammit, Peter, you can pilfer all the crockery you want, but do you know what can happen to glass in the air?"

"I believe you've mentioned it."

"It can dry out and explode into sand and dust unless you know its composition. And wood? Have you any idea how fast it will disintegrate? What have you been reading, science fiction? We're at least decades away from being able to preserve this stuff properly. Radiomagnetic carbon dating is in its infancy. Don't you care? Have you explained any of this to the old man? Or are you just trying to impress your new buddy Bo?"

"Are you finished?"

"No, you sonofabitch, I'm a scientist, not an ornament. I care. You've exceeded yourself. You're just a writer, not a marine archaeologist. Now you're a damned pirate."

Bo is on the sterncastle when she begins talking. He waves off crewmen when he sees Moira thrust herself onto the starboard weather deck and gesticulate exasperatedly to the sea god Poseidon. Now he heads for the chartroom.

"Pilfer? Did I hear you say the word pilfer, Moira? I have never pilfered a thing in my life." Peter is warming to one of their exquisite exchanges when she slugs down some San Pellegrino water and spurts it into his face. Then she heads for the galley.

There she pours herself a mug of freshly brewed coffee and sits down at the long table with its rim fiddled to prevent things from sliding off in a seaway. When she looks up out of the mug Bo is standing in the hatchway. She knows he overheard them, but she doesn't know how much he heard.

"I didn't mean you, you know."

"Bullshit."

He's being had. He feels an urge to grab her cunt and squeeze. She senses it. And smiles.

"What if we were born smart and dumbed down?" he says. "What if that's what growing up's about? Dumbing down and denying it so adults feel comfortable."

"Then I'd say we need to smarten up, to recover from the trauma, to take an accounting before we die so at least we don't die like sharks out of water with silly grins on our dead faces. You're a shark, aren't you, Bo?"

"Don't forget it."

~

Nothing is as good as a little clash to free the bound soul. He rows the dinghy directly to the zarook *Bayzid* anchored nearby, where Uthman is employed. He finds the falcon-faced Arab sitting on a barrel on the poop splicing line. Although he's picking up some Omani Arabic and Uthman has his Yorkshire English, he simply motions to his friend with his head. They climb aboard the dinghy and head back to *Morgaine.* There, with Moira skulking about from hatchway to hatchway observing them, they stow gear aboard the dinghy. Bo prefers *Morgaine*'s cockboat with its larger hold, but he doesn't wish to impose on Peter's tolerance.

He and Uthman begin on-loading Aqua Lung equipment. The Aqua Lung, first called the Scaphandre-autonome, was invented by Jacques Cousteau in 1943. Then a young French naval officer, he smuggled it out of France to keep it out of German hands. Its revolutionary achievement is that it gives a swimmer complete freedom under water for several hours at depths well beyond a hundred and forty feet. It's ideal for the sort of diving they propose to do up towards Shinas. The dread bends, nitrogen narcosis, doesn't threaten in less than a hundred and eighty feet, so in some ways they'll work in ideal circumstances. The real problem is that, unless sediment wrung out oxygen, they can't hope to find much intact. The recent cycle of violent storms gives them their window of opportunity, because it tore away the geological veil.

Oman is waiting to start pumping out the vast oil reserves that will earn billions in rials for its population of fewer than two million souls. Port Qaboos, named for the old sultan's son, Qaboos bin Said al-Said, has not yet been built in Matrah Harbor. For this reason, its thirteen-hundred-mile coast and waters are relatively unsullied. On a calm day, with nothing to roil the waters, Uthman and Bo see much of the sea bed through their masks.

They sleep on the beach under the invaders' ruined fort that first night. Uthman roasts an oily mackerel over a driftwood fire in a sand pit. Bo forgoes his beloved Calvados in deference to his companion's Muslim austerities, but they share some of Bo's Cuban cigars before they fall asleep.

Uthman shakes him awake at dawn. "Light is good now," he says. His gestures suggest that the light knifing from over Iran down into the water must illuminate the bottom helpfully. They ship the outboard engine up out of its running position and row out to the site they marked with orange cork floats on their first visit.

Bo throws out the mushroom anchor, rows against its rode to bury its flange and then pays out a short scope to keep the dinghy near the dive site. There are only two of them and they intend to dive together, although that's not prescribed.

They're down a total of six hours that first day. Once again they see plates, ducats, lead shot, and several objects they can't identify, but their goal is to mark off a rope grid.

At dusk on the second day Uthman begins his ablutions with sea water. He beckons Bo to join him. Slowly he performs the ritual, waiting for Bo to follow suit. Then he kneels facing northwest towards Mecca and begins, "Bismillah ar-Rahman ar-Rahim"—he waits for Bo to repeat it and continues until the majestic shahadah spoken five times a day by the world's second most populous religion is done. He smiles at Bo for the first time —sweetly like a child—and says, "Now you are a Muslim." Then they smoke in silence and fall asleep under a panoply of stars.

With dawn a pale aura out on the gulf, Bo sits up wondering how to proceed. They've seen a long spar of some kind, about fifteen feet long. He'll start with that. He gets to it on his first dive and finds it heavy for a spar. On the surface, after some brushing, he decides it's a crude musket, perhaps the kind that was used on a crutch. In due time it will be identified by Moira as a bronze culverin. To be restored it will need a pneumatic chisel and chemical baths. Culverins were used in the fifteenth and sixteenth centuries. He regards the recovery of this musket as an auspicious start.

That same day Uthman brings up a gold plate. The crust falls away readily when brushed. Bo gasps as he turns the plate in the sun. Clearly etched into the flat center is the outline of a caravel. Inscribed on a riband beneath the caravel are the words *Sao Tiago*. Can this wreck be the caravel *Sao Tiago*? He studies the plate harder to see if she has the castles of a carrack, the forerunner of the galleon and successor to the caravel. Her deck line is lower. She was meant for speed and distance, not hauling and fighting. She is a caravel.

Uthman, who has been watching his friend intently, reaches

over and puts the palm of his hand on Bo's chest to see if his heart is pounding. "What does this mean, my friend?"

"Uthman, see this vessel? It's called a caravel."

"Qurqur." Uthman speaks the Arabic word for ship of burden.

"No, that's just the point, Uthman. It's not a qurqur. There are pictures of them, but nobody has ever found a caravel. If that wreck down there is the *Sao Tiago*, this is important, Uthman. It's a great discovery—and you made it!"

Uthman takes the ducat out of his pocket and studies it.

11

An Arab who wanders the Nafud desert dreaming of hockey must be capable of a good laugh. A half-Arab who sits on an Omani beach thinking of a violent brand of hockey must be capable of some damned thing or another—not a bad account of Bo Cavalieri's life.

He sits there wondering: which came first, the gush of adrenalin or his memories of the butcher's hockey in which he excelled back in Cairnhall, that embittering and indelible boarding school where he lived from his fifth to fifteenth year. In any case, he always has the adrenalin he needs.

Uthman, in spite of his illustrious name—Abu'l-Rayhan Muhammad al-Biruni was a pioneer explorer of other cultures—has never inspired generosity in anybody, not even his mother. Bo's eerie gift is to name such beneficiaries. All he knows about urgency is how perilous it is to veto it; that's all a combat swimmer needs to know. When he thinks of ice hockey he knows something's up.

He's not, like Peter Tomlinson, a storyteller. Well, yes he is, if he has his sketchbook with him. And it can't be said that Uthman looks to be in need of a story. No, he looks, to Bo at least, apologetic. Like any good sufi. Sufis are somewhat embarrassed to be alive. Their lives intrude on God's mathematical purity. They think themselves an affront and long to return to the abstract equation. This would be news to Uthman. Nobody ever bothered to invite him to be a dervish, but then the finest, truest adepts are usually the uninitiated.

"Look, Uthman," he begins.

Uthman's English is not quite up to this. Bo gets out his sketchbook. Uthman loves drawings. Then he realizes he doesn't know whether Uthman knows anything about geography. The man had been born near Shinas, fought in Dhofar and sailed with various nakhodas up and down the gulf, to East Africa and maybe even to Iran and Pakistan. But that doesn't mean he's ever seen a map or chart of these places. Some Arabs use charts, some don't, and they always trust local knowledge and folkways, as do all good sailors.

Bo has an inspiration. Wherever the Ottoman Turks or the Arabs or the Mamluks ruled, he draws a crescent moon. Wherever the Christians ruled he draws a cross. Uthman nods.

Bo ends up with a kind of Muslim platter filled with Christian crosses. He limns in Portugal and in the ocean just west of Portugal he draws a caravel.

Then he draws the musket and the plate they'd found and connects them to the caravel with arrows. He stops then to see if Uthman understands. Uthman points to the caravel and then to the dive site. He's ahead of Bo.

Next Bo draws a tidy little Maltese cross on the lateen sail of the caravel. That's something of a fib. Maybe there were Maltese caravels commissioned from Genoa, Venice or Lagos in Portugal, but a Portuguese would have borne the Cross of Christ.

Nobody has ever paid as much attention to Bo, not even Dieter Benedikt. He draws Muslim ships Uthman can recognize—booms, ghanjahs, zarooks, xebecs, the sort of ships the Barbary corsairs used. He orchestrates a little naval engagement between a galleon and a squadron of booms off Sicily.

Then he draws an oversized Uthman throwing a fire pot at the galleon.

Uthman grunts his approval.

"Nobody has ever seen a real caravel, Uthman." He waves his palms sideways to signify nobody. "Pictures, yes. Like this plate. That's all."

Uthman holds up his hand in the universal stop sign. "Bo, I know how the Ruwallah tribe talks, I know how the Harasis speak. Uthman's ear is very good. The major does not come from Yorkshire, I can hear that. You speak, I will hear you."

"I'm sorry, my friend. I want you to understand this, but . . . "

"Your heart is pure, Bo, so I will understand you."

He is indeed a dervish. Reassured, Bo continues.

"All the Franks had were these big ships with square sails." He points to the galleon. "They were pigs. They couldn't sail into the wind." His words prove choice. Uthman, loathing pig meat like all Muslims, is delighted at the thought of a Frankish ship as a seagoing pig. In fact he enjoys the word so much that Bo draws a huge square-sailed pig infested with Franks lumbering off Sardinia. Uthman rumbles with laughter. Bo tears off the page and gives it to him, then he redrafts what he's drawn on a fresh page so that he can continue his illustrated story.

The more Bo intends to talk, the more he's moved to draw. He finds Sagres at that point where Portugal stabs the 37th Parallel and alongside it he draws charts, an astrolabe or kamal, as the Arabs call it, some rather arabesque dividers, and, for good measure, a compass rose. This takes him some time, but he keeps Uthman's rapt attention. Then he tucks the port of Lagos into Portugal's overhand, just east of Sagres. There he draws the ribs of a ship under construction, a sawhorse, an adze and saw, and a heap of lumber. Sagres, which appeared on *Sao Tiago*'s plate, was a kind of navigational research center over which Henry the Navigator, a hair-shirt ascetic, presided. There were probably a few Arabs at Sagres of the ilk that Said bin Taimur would roast eternally in hell.

At this point he decides he better voyage back to the problem, so he draws a big galleon in the Balearic Sea beating up towards Genoa. On its mainsail he draws a bearded face puking. To make sure Uthman gets it, he draws a pig pointing a hoof at the galleon. Then he contrives by means of the old directional point system to show that this ungainly barca could not sail closer than sixty-seven degrees into the wind. He then jumps over Iberia to show Uthman that the caravel, on the other hand, could sail at fifty-five degrees.

Nowadays, with cup yachts sailing just fifteen degrees off the wind, this difference seems nominal, but in the fifteenth century it was the difference between yesterday and tomorrow. Henry was working on the space shuttle of his day. By the year 1450 there were Venetian square-riggers of six hundred tons or more. But they couldn't sail into the wind. Any time a captain wanted to go exploring his men were likely to conclude they would be sick and old before they returned, if they returned. Henry had seen caravelas—*ela* means little—on the Douro River up north. They were handy little luggers. He admired them.

Then when he went off to besiege Ceuta he probably saw the Arab caravos. This speedy, maneuverable dhow carried slanted, triangular lateen sails and was crewed by as many as thirty men. It could carry as many as seventy horses. Henry probably watched the caravos sail into the wind and pick up speed. Henry was an architect. So he told his shipwrights at Lagos to marry the caravela with the caravos. Hence the *Sao Tiago*, if it turns out that is indeed what she is. She was fastened, not sewn, and that alone, without her debris, signified European design, but she could well be a barca.

Bo decides to push his luck. He draws a pig of a barca sailing down the West African coast towards the Roaring Forties. There he founders her and draws a ship being broken by a devil. For

Uthman's sake he should make the devil a djinn, but he doesn't want to give Uthman the convenient idea that his ancestors caught up with the barca and dispatched her. Then he draws a caravel rounding the horn of Africa borne by angels on her outbound passage. Uthman not only gets it, he gets it so well that he swells his chest to make room for his sense of discovery.

~

Bottom-feeding like carp during their next dive Bo comes across what strikes him as the base of a pedestal, and that proves exactly what it is.

He tugs and twists it until it reveals twin columns at the end of which is a heavily encrusted sphere of some kind. It reminds him of a modern sculptor whose name slips him—an Italian who creates bronze ovoids and ellipsoids and then eats into them with tools and mordants. He always shudders viewing the man's work, but it fascinates him.

When the object is free he judges by its size and heft that he can bring it up to the dinghy with a line. He motions Uthman to surface and drop a line. He fastens the line to the strange object with a timber and half hitch, then surfaces.

When he clambers back into the dinghy he and Uthman slowly raise the object. If he were he not inclined to study the histories of his skills he wouldn't instantly recognize what he sees in the white Omani sunlight—an intact armillary sphere with its pedestal, an astronomical model developed in the fourteenth century. Its solid rings—circles inside the overall sphere—were used to show how the celestial circles related to each other. The sphere may have adorned a room in the very fort that first caught his eye, or perhaps it was being brought there. It's certainly European. Whatever *Sao Tiago*'s design, this is itself a valuable find.

"Qurqur," Uthman says. Bo nods, for it did seem *Sao Tiago* had been an armed merchantman, but qurqur is also the Arab word that gave the big galleons called carracks their name, so he's done Uthman a disservice that their communication is too primitive to correct.

"Caravel," he says. "A caravel is a qurqur." He can't be sure, but it seems unlikely a ship bearing a clutch of plates showing a caravel would have been something else. Uthman has discovered —it's possible at least—the first known caravel. It's characteristic of Bo that he doesn't think himself the discoverer or even co-discoverer, even though Uthman alone would never have even taken a stab at the mystery. Still, Uthman knew instinctively the wreck had value and that's why he shared it with his friend.

~

As he sits in the dinghy examining the armillary sphere he stalks three people's minds: Gundy whom he quit, Ute-Britt who could not tell which man she missed the most, Lakhdar or Bo, and Moira Sayre. Moira at that very moment is again tossing his cabin, nettled by his intimacy with the evil-looking Uthman. She hadn't taken the time back in the Mediterranean to examine several of his books, so she seeks them out now as if they might shed light on his perversity. Just as he has made an important discovery concerning spheres, now she makes one. She lets her fingertips explore the surface of E.M. Forster's *Howard's End.* Tell me your secrets, her fingertips say. Modern action thrillers' readership, she tells herself, is a measure of how few understand heroism. Cavalieri reads no such books because they can't say, can't come close to saying what he already knows about danger and killing. He thinks Forster's Schlegel sisters more heroic than The Duke or Agent 007. But does he know that he does? His reading habits prove it. He can't abide assholes as heroes. They no more impress him than the Sneaky Pete swillers he's known. Less even. Nothing archaeological can compare to this discovery. Moira is thrilled to her core. And she would be ecstatic to know she has defined exactly how Bo feels about heroics: heroes never live where we look.

Holding Bo's book, Moira Sayre guesses she will never again know anyone so well, and she knows something else, something better and more frightening: true sexuality depends utterly on just such insight and is rarer than anything divers ever find. Everything else is masturbation.

She is crushed by this knowledge, by her intuitive forensics, and yet she knows that she has already found more than Peter will ever find and more perhaps—this wastes her with sorrow—than Bo Cavalieri will find.

She looks out a porthole to the horizon and recognizes the truth within: she knows what she knows and the only other issue that will ever confront her is whether she will act on it. What passes in Bo for courage is despair.

Would it make a difference in their relationship if he knew what she knew? What difference does she wish it to make? He's a bird of passage, theirs is a passage of arms.

She wishes she could set the cabin on fire. She wants to give him a Viking funeral, he who isn't dead or Viking. That would be better than wanting him, better than having him. No, nobody will ever have him; he isn't there. She understands the impulse to strangle one's lover, how dark it is, far darker than chroniclers know. When you strangle your lover your lover is always there, forever yours, and you never have to worry about him again.

Does he want Margaret Schlegel, whom nobody would ever strangle, or Moira Sayre, whom many men, though thankfully not Peter, would strangle? And does he himself want to strangle her and set her to sea in a burning ship? Does she inhabit his mind at

all? She knows she does. She'd stake her life on it, is staking her
life on it.

12

If his hidden harem of vampire wives had been discovered he couldn't get a stranger look from Moira when he and Uthman return to *Morgaine*. Not one to dismiss signal looks, he lets his eyes follow her until she is convinced they would accompany her around corners. She is on hand by the portside davits to greet them, but now she vanishes through the salon to the starboard side. He follows her. She leads him back aft, then spins around to face him. They know all about each other's eyes; it is their mouths they trust, not to speak the truth but to tell. The right side of her mouth turns down and her nose quivers like a rabbit's. He likes the sight so much he bursts out laughing. She is exasperated, but she joins him. His hands come up like a vise, then the impulse gives out and he shakes them in mock excitement when his real excitement is quite another thing. He blurts to her what he'd meant to tell Peter.

"Moira, I think I may . . . I think it's possible I've found a caravel. Uthman found it. Well, that is, he found a wreck and we dived on it and I think it's a caravel. I told Uthman . . . "

"Uthman, you told Uthman . . . "

"Goddammit, Sayre, it doesn't matter who the hell I told. Nobody has ever seen a caravel. We've seen pictures of caravels, that's all. They don't tell you enough. It's very important, Moira. Henry the Navigator couldn't have done what he did without them. He couldn't sail into the wind, all he could do was sail before it. Until the caravel, sailors didn't think they'd ever get home, so they were afraid of long voyages. And the caravel is Arab! It's Arab,

Moira. Think what it means, what it means to Oman, to historians, to archaeologists, to naval architects. She's called the *Sao Tiago*. I have an armillary, plates, coins."

She is furious that he shared all this with Uthman, so furious she doesn't even take time to reflect that he would have told Peter before telling her.

"You've got to persuade Peter that this is more important than what he's doing, much more important. Everybody always thought the world would have to wait until divers could get down into the Black Sea where the poisonous hydrogen sulfides that make it black preserve ships. But we don't even know if there are caravels down there. The old sultan will buy into this, Moira, because the Portuguese almost certainly copied Arab ships to make the caravel."

"Why have I got to persuade Peter? He's just as likely to be persuaded by you, more likely I should think."

She's diving, too. She has to persuade Peter because this is the gift Bo has chosen to give to her. "Well, once I convince him of the magnitude of it you'll have to give him the details. And won't he wonder why you told me first?"

"Peter dreams and writes and arranges things. You dive, you shoot, you identify, and, besides, if you're not into it he won't be either. Dream this dream, Moira, it's a good one."

And you want me to have it, she thinks. "All right, I'll sell it. For you and that dreadful Uthman." She lays her palm against his face exactly as he's always wished Ulrike to do.

~

It isn't difficult. Peter senses Bo's excitement and is waiting to hear what it's about. He understands why Bo befriended the fearsome Uthman. Bo and Uthman are sons of Hagar, their hands uplifted against everyone and everyone's hands uplifted against them. Neither of them is comfortable in this Frankish endeavor.

"Can we anchor *Morgaine* there, Bo?"

"Yes. Peter, I don't mean to tell you your business, but I wonder if the old man should be told. It's a pretty remote spot. He'll get reports and wonder."

"Nobody can tell him the significance of it better than you, Bo. I'll tell him that Sindbad wishes an audience, shall I?"

~

So enthralled is Said bin Taimur by Bo's story that for some inexplicable reason he gestures him over to a kind of mihrab and invites him to join him sitting Arab fashion on cushions as if the occasion must be celebrated by reverting to custom. Sitting cross-legged before the sultan, Bo tells him all that he told Uthman. The sultan's English is Oxford-perfect and so Bo treats him to all the attendant arcana. For example, if it were determined that white oak was used to build *Sao Tiago* it might indicate the caravel was built off the Gulf of Cadiz in Spain and the timber floated down the Quadalquivir River. The Spanish would have sold it to Portugal? the sultan asks. Yes, Bo replies, because after Henry's builders designed the caravel its replicates were built in Spain, Genoa and Venice.

When the story is told and all the speculation laid out, the sultan beckons Peter, whom he had excluded from this tête-à-tête, and tells Bo for Peter's benefit, "You shall have whatever you need, Sindbad."

~

"What is your philosophy, Bo?" Tomlinson asks as they sit in back of one of the sultan's limousines returning to the harbor.

"What happens is better than what might happen."

A man who sketches interactions to order his life has to say that. Tomlinson takes it for depth because he wants to. That would irk Bo if he knew it. This defines them.

What Bo really has in mind, because tomorrow is her birthday, is that when he was almost eighteen and Anne Chapin almost seventeen their mothers in their best interests forbade them to see each other. At the end of a long farewell walk up Fifth Avenue from her apartment at Two Fifth Avenue in Greenwich Village they paused and vowed under the verdigris pigeon-potty of a statue of William Tecumseh Sherman at 59th Street to meet there again on her twenty-first birthday, July tenth. Blessed crapshooter that he is, he would have bet good money that the ballerina had been a no-show.

And he would have lost. A failing Anne Chapin thumbed and fucked and drugged her way from the Haight in San Francisco to keep their date. Far from becoming a dancer, as she'd begun to be under Balanchine's tutelage, she had ditched her ritzy mother after one hair-pull too many and gone west. Under the shadow of Charles Baudelaire's look-alike on her twenty-first birthday she slept and dreamed of men in evening clothes, the sort they wore across 59th Street at The Plaza, staring down at her naked wasted body, and she couldn't decide if she were alive or dead, but that they looked like her father and not Bo she had no doubt.

The muezzins affirm that God is merciful, but to whom? Tomlinson would have liked this story, but Bo believes no one is trustworthy enough to be given it. Suddenly he's not so sure Anne missed their appointment. He feels cold waiting on the wharf for their cockboat. He knows she's dead.

~

Soon after they drop the hook at the new dive site, Semmes and Arnot find two crusty swivel guns five meters northeast of the wreck along the ballast trail. From their next dive they bring up a squared timber with adz marks while Moira and Benedikt begin roping off a grid. While they're still doing this, Bo finds a ringed bombardeta and a breech block. On subsequent dives he begins bringing up conglomerates after spotting a deadeye, ringbolt and spike imbedded in one of them.

These finds, heartening as they are, pale in light of what Bo finds the second day—the hilt of a dagger with a small golden Cross of Christ, exactly what one expects in a Portuguese ship.

On subsequent days the divers recover first a wrought-iron harquebus swivel gun and then a bronze astrolabe.

Bo is distracted. What he wants now is evidence of the ship's design. Eventually the remains will have to be sandbagged and the sandbags covered with sand to protect them until experts arrive. But first they must know if *Sao Tiago* is just another barca or a caravel. He removes himself from the sorting and tagging and begins to probe *Sao Tiago*'s final resting place, ignoring the ballast trail and scatter site. He tells Uthman they must find out what manner of ship she is.

Uthman proves talented. A day after this conversation he finds a handsomely curved stem post. When he shows Bo where he found it Bo clears away some sand and uncovers the brace called a deadwood that sits snugly between the keel and the stem post. He knows then he must fit ribs and futtocks. The two men probe deeper. Exhausting work, but it pays off.

They soon find the keelson, big and heavy. A caravel would have a foremast, a mainmast, mizzen and countermizzen. The two mizzen masts would set into her poop. The mizzen sails would be lateen-rigged fore and aft, giving the ship a distinctly Oriental look. The keelson might show where and how the mast posts were fitted. On *Morgaine*'s quarterdeck the stem post draws Bo. It had been given a great deal of attention by its maker, the adz marks show that. It had been hewn and planed. They agree to return the wood to the sea until experts can be called in, so they give themselves two days to photograph, draw and study the wooden remains. The morning after they raised the stem post Bo comes on deck early with a steaming mug of coffee in hand. He runs his hand along the adz marks, wondering if the caravel had borne a figurehead. Then he notices the script, G. da Vizinho. The builder's name, the owner's, the architect's? He turns the post to the opposite side and there it is—confirmation—the deeply etched and unmistakable silhouette of a caravel. Nobody would have done it unless the stem post belonged to a caravel.

He reaches in his pocket, pulls out the boatswain's pipe he's had since his Navy service and blows an all hands. Only Semmes recognizes the signal and motions the others to assemble.

"Look, G. da Vizinho's caravel! She's a caravel. God-dammit, she's a caravel!" He leaps up from a crouch, grasps Uthman's shoulders and shakes him. Then he reaches into his denim work shirt, draws out the coin bearing Alexander's gloriously demented face which he carries around his neck on a chain and kisses it. Alexander, reputed to give sailors luck, had run true to form. Peter steps over the stem post and embraces him, then Moira. Charles and the others shake his hand, even Benedikt; Uthman's they do not seek. But Moira, seeing the omission, goes over to Uthman and clasps his arm.

Peter, a shameless enthusiast, has much to say because he has studied much since Moira told him of Uthman's find. *Morgaine* has a proper library, roughly twenty percent of Peter's permanent collection, but it's far from offering him what he now wants to say about caravels. His network of privileged and hyper-educated friends has been prodded by telephone and telegram long before he gets around to talking to Bo about Uthman's wreck. He deems this good strategy in any event because he wants to give Bo as much space and time as possible to digest his own findings—Bo is, after all, a friend he intends to keep. Accordingly, by the time he judges it appropriate to engage Bo in talk about caravels he can't keep himself from saying such things as, "Her sails will have borne a version of the Cross Patee, or Cross of Christ, I think." Or, "Shall we find plates bearing the emblem of Saint Vincent of Saragossa—ravens piloting a ship with the saint's relics, do you think?" Or, "Wouldn't it be better if it were Saint Peter Gonzales a.k.a. Saint Elmo, walking on waves with fire in his hand?"

"Better for whom?"

A crestfallen Tomlinson wrongly thinks he's annoyed Bo. Bo's distracted. He noticed Moira touching Uthman's arm and it moves him. He does what he must do. He tells Peter all he knows, all he guesses. He listens as Peter regales him with information. But his mind is on Moira. Wherever she goes that day he knows it. He's so distracted he forgets to tell Peter he recovered a dagger engraved with the Cross Patee.

He sits that night in his fo'c's'l drawing *Sao Tiago* under sail, inventing scenarios that might have brought her to her fate. He doesn't know how rare it is for him to fantasize; he knows only how pleasant it is. But none of his fantasies equal the truth that will be ferreted out years later by Peter after exhaustive researches in Spain and Portugal. *Sao Tiago* had been dispatched to Oman by none other than Pedro da Covilha, John the Second's envoy to the fabled Prester John, the Christian King of Africa whose alliance Portugal so desperately sought as her ships groped their way down the West African coast and finally around the horn. Prester John, it turned out, was Alexander of Ethiopia, Lion of the Tribe of Judah and King of Kings. The wily Covilha, having spent more than five years disguised as a Muslim merchant, had spied out all that he could for his king and now saw no impediment to the Portuguese sailing into the Persian Gulf and thence to Calicat and beyond. This famous explorer, diplomat and spy dispatched *Sao*

Tiago to chart the gulf, and now, south of Shinas, where Uthman found her, she emerged after centuries, with her cargo and failed mission. Probably she had been the first caravel to enter the gulf, some time between 1494 and 1500. But for now his own histories are enough for Bo.

By the time—after 1:00 a.m.—Moira taps on his door he's again resentful of his feelings towards her. He's prescient enough to know that some antagonistic urgencies are converging: his excitement over *Sao Tiago*, his enjoyment of Peter's trust and friendship, his need for it, and his desire for Moira. No matter how he plots the courses of these urgencies they collide, and he has no chance of veering off now.

She stands by the door, backlit by the amber passageway lights and front-lit by his reading lamp. Her long hair falls over her right shoulder. He thinks of Scheherazade as she was depicted in Lane's *A Thousand and One Nights.* Her white peignoir is parted—she has practiced how it would fall—and his gaze is drawn to her outlaw pubic mound, which shows through her white panties plush and astronomically black. He can't hear the ship's generator over the disobedience of his heart.

"I . . . " he can't finish. He tries again. "I've been thinking about you, Moira."

"I liked it better the first time. You know, with the emphasis on have, as if you assumed that I knew you had been thinking of me. Because I do know it, Bo."

He smiles at the distinction. One can't, mustn't duel verbally with the privileged English. They are savage duelists. She's now at the foot of his bed.

"We don't know each other because we don't know each other's fantasies. Do you agree?"

In such a heroic presence fantasies seem puerile.

"Doesn't everybody? How many people do you think there are

alive whose fantasies wouldn't damn their most important relationships?"

He hardly believes he's said it. It's much more articulate than he cares to be and a great dishonor, to boot, to such a show.

But she's more than equal. "Few, I imagine, but the few are the only ones I wish to know. You don't want to answer my question, do you?"

"No. But I'd appreciate it if you'd answer mine."

"Well, I think everybody has fantasies. I do. And if you don't, that makes you a very chilling person, Bo."

"Keep it in mind, Moira."

"Oh what a big bad sailor man you are, Cavalieri!"

He laughs in spite of himself. She isn't as tall as he is, but she keeps her eyes, in which he can't find a hint of earth hue, on his face as she does something down below, and then she brings her panties up slowly before his face and drapes them on his shoulder.

"Essence of Moira, Bo, several essences in fact. You won't sleep well, will you?"

She turns for his answer before she leaves.

"No."

Neither does she, but she stage-managed it and he hadn't and so she will at least rest.

~

In the morning Bo feels as though he's sleep-walking through an unfamiliar museum. If you're spooked in your crib you spend the rest of your life waiting for the other shoe to drop. Because he's always savored the eerie beauty, the tyranny of not knowing what will happen next, Bo draws. You can come to terms with what you draw. He should be at work, briefing divers, conferring with Peter, but he sits in *Morgaine's* chartroom drawing. He should draw *Sao Tiago*, but all he can draw is the austere details of the room on

Kaltenheissestrasser and Lakhdar's ugly noose. He feels the malaise he always feels in museums because he's invaded the artist's privacy. He sits on the navigator's stool and draws as Peter said he drew, as Egyptians once created—what they knew, not what they saw. And when he reflects on what he's doing, which is rare, he remembers that as a child he thought that Cairnhall's grandfather clock had somebody's grandfather in it. Men do make strange, as the Anglican hymn laments, but he has the presence of mind to know he makes no stranger than the rest of them.

At 1300 hours he leaps off the stool and shouts the frogman's "Hoo-yaw!" Peter, out on the port weather wing overlooking the dive site, darts in. "I've never heard the rebel yell before, have you discovered something?"

Bo, the one man of his class least likely to reflect Columbia's humanities and great literature curricula, says, "Well, to try to answer your compound question, Peter, no, it's not the rebel yell—that's Yee-haw—it's the frogman's yell, employed not to mean discovery but to whomp up courage, like the rebel yell. I'm not sure it was meant to scare the enemy, like the rebel yell, at least I never heard it used that way, because we sneak up on the enemy."

Peter grins lopsidedly, in part because he's pleased to know, in part to conceal his recognition of the testiness in Bo's reply. Bo breaks his pencil between his fingers. "I'm sorry, that was . . . "

"Unforgivable? Hardly. One can't control the manner of one's edification. So what was the yell about?"

He would prefer Peter give it up. "You and Moira."

"I shall always remember, Bo, that once we occasioned a frogman's battle cry." He touches Bo's arm as Bo himself often touches his shipmates'. Bo had most certainly intruded upon artists' privacy, but never before had they intruded upon his. He remembers an earlier self, face blackened and vest festooned with fragmentation and smoke grenades.

Peter isn't ready to pursue the matter. He regards it as a decoy of some kind, and he leaves.

~

"I've come to refresh my essences, Bo."

The night wind fails to rise to cool their distillations. They toil in them. He commits to counting the hairs of her body and to taste whatever she concocts to whatever end she pleases. She has the focus and alertness of a wading bird. He craves to know the silk, shantung worsted of her.

Fitfully they sleep, awake, touch and touch again, until the sun barges indecent through the portholes and, as she rests her head on his chest, he sees that the roots of her midnight Arab hair are blond. As blond as Peter's.

~

Navigators magnify. Buoys, stars, squall lines, ships, whatever they need to make out for their calculations. But Bo was well on his way to being a seven-by-fifty wide-horizon man before he ever picked up a pair of Zeiss binoculars. We're not meant to get stuck on people, maybe not facts or events either. When we do we magnify them until the horizon vanishes and then we're drunk on them, we stink of them.

He leaves that day. He tells her, "Every ship has a lightning rod in its rigging and a ground wire that goes to a copper plate attached to her hull. Without that ground the ship herself is a lightning rod. Even if she's not burned up in a storm, electrolysis will eat her metals until she's a heap of scrap. Peter's a lightning rod. You're his ground. I think somehow you know this. It's your job."

"And what about me? What I need, what I want?"

"I dunno. If I knew maybe I could stay. It's sad, I know. That's what I know—that it's sad."

"You bastard!" She slugs him. With a balled fist alongside his jaw. "You're a lightning rod too, you know! Who's your goddam copper plate?" She's bawling by the time she says, "If not me."

His head slams against a bulkhead and he is rubbing it when he says, touching the front of her shoulder reverently, "The thing is, Moira, Peter runs around needing all over the place, so naturally lightning strikes. I don't."

"You mean you don't show it, you bastard! You're not as honest as he is. You know that, don't you?"

"Sounds right. I don't know. I don't know if I don't show it or don't need to. But, for what it's worth, you're right. I'm a lightning rod too. I know it. I just don't look as likely as Peter."

"Likely? Likely! What the hell is that?"

"Peter looks like you could burn him badly. I look like I'd burn you badly."

She starts walking around him in the narrow passageway, her head down and wagging. His last remark savages her. She pushes out a ragged sigh. "Yeah, I know. You do. He does. I got it. Is that what you want to hear? I got it. I hate it, but I got it."

He grabs her hair from behind and brings up her face to his. He kisses her elfinly, so that the hairs around her ears lift and her body turns up like a heliotrope in forlorn hope.

She holds his face. "Are you going for Peter or for yourself? He would share me, you know."

He nods.

"Are you frightened?" she says.

He shakes his head. "You and Peter, I like it. You and me, we would worry about Peter. It just does not work. Nobody is that civilized."

"Or that savage?"

When he chucks his sea bag into the dinghy, she climbs down

the boarding ladder and pulls his head to her mouth with one hand. "Rest in motion, dear heart."

Uthman yanks the whipcord of the dinghy's engine. It coughs up its carbon and catches on. Bo squats, then stands up out on the flat water, his face blasted with loss.

Moira is a squall of beauty hanging on the gangway and he is terrified that he'll never be able to put the moment out of mind. His lips move and he fears what they will say.

"Morgaine."

13

Making his farewells to Uthman along the way, they bum a lift to Sallaleh, the sultan's favorite palace, in a feckless jalopy driven by a Bedouin. There Bo tells the guards the sultan might consent to see him. They doubt it, but they're bemused. Bo is met by a chamberlain, who admits him directly in to Said bin Taimur's presence. He salutes the natty autocrat Arab fashion.

"Ah, my Algerian friend whose native tongue is German! I never did show you my calligraphy."

The chamberlain whispers to him in Arabic that the British representative is waiting to see him. "Tell him that even Her Majesty must wait upon higher authority," the sultan says. The discreet chamberlain will of course relay no such thing. But Bo and the sultan recede through archways to the sultan's fabled collection. In the course of this tour, which takes all of two hours, Bo delivers to the sultan a handful of sketches of *Sao Tiago*, pressing home the import of what *Morgaine's* company has undertaken.

"You are here, why?"

"To ask your highness's permission to travel in the country until I can find work aboard ship. I wish to sail with the Arabs."

"You wish to sail with lice-infested vermin on roach nests? I thought you were an Arab, not a romantic. What have you done, killed the Englishman?"

"We left on the best of terms. He is an excellent man. It was time for me to go. In that I am Arab."

Said bin Taimur smiles.

Potentate or no, he enjoys such a trump. "Well, since I have your word the mad major is intact, I shall give you a safe-conduct. Better, let me write a note for you. Take it to the police station at Sur."

"Thank you, your highness. I have one other thing to say, if you will let me."

The old man nods.

"My friend Uthman al-Biruni. You have a death sentence on him. He discovered *Sao Tiago*. Then he showed me. I ask you to forgive him."

"You ask a lot. He would have taken my head if he could. And why? He is too stupid to know! Why do you make foolish friends?"

"Because I am a foolish man."

The sultan grins. "Al-Biruni will soon enough put his foot in a viper pit. He may live."

Bo does not thank the sultan a second time.

"You do many things well and yet are neither richer nor wiser for it, Algerian. You are a dervish perhaps. They are God's fools."

"I am not so privileged."

The sultan dismisses him with a wave of his hand, but when Bo turns to leave the old man's gaze writes onto Bo's back his fondness and puzzlement. The American possesses the perverse grace which, the sultan fears, contact with foreigners will leach from the Bedouin soul.

~

Sur is imbedded atop the nadir of the Batinah range where the Gulf of Oman opens on the Arabian Sea. It's Oman's traditional ship-building center. Here for the first time Bo sees a Malabar teak-built Kuwaiti boom. He's never seen a more beautiful or mysterious ship. The double-ender flies two huge lateen sails and a foresail. He guesses rightly that she's ticklish for tacking close-in but in a seaway has few equals. The high-prowed Kuwaiti boom—nowadays many of them have auxiliary diesels—has been known to make 280 miles on a good day, a feat the twilight jewel of Western sailing ships would not have disdained.

The dates have been harvested in the valley of the Shatt al-Arab in Iraq. The northeast monsoon winds that follow the ripening of the dates will carry the Arabs' booms and zarooks down to Mukalla and Ash Shihr in the Hadramawt of Yemen, then to Mogadishu, Durdureh, Salale, Lamu and the other ports of Africa. In Africa they will wait for the southwest monsoon winds of April and May to take them home laden with coconuts, cloves, mangrove poles from the Rufiji swamps, fabric and all the saleable goods of Africa they can afford. On any given spring day you can find fifty or more dhows waiting in Mombasa for the monsoons to shift. He pulls his sketchbook out of his white sea bag, sits down cross-legged on a wharf and begins working with pencils, charcoal and chalk. Soon the police find him. They've been told to expect him.

Omanis do not relish foreigners messing about unsupervised. The police have orders to treat him as the sultan's guest. They come up silently behind him, two officers, but are immediately captivated by his work and stand a few paces back watching. After a while he senses them, turns, smiles and holds up his hand asking them to wait. He begins a smaller sketch of one of the booms heading south on a broad port reach. He draws quickly. Satisfied, he tears off the sketch and hands it to one of the policemen. He points at him to make sure the man knows the sketch is his to keep. The Arabs' teeth flash in the midday sun. The man to whom he has given the sketch says, "It is *Sheikh Achmed*, a hundred and fifteen tons. My cousin is the mate."

Bo is relieved to hear English. "How high is her mast?"

"Eighty feet. Her yard is a hundred and thirty feet. Three trees."

Bo has his binoculars out. He's seen men in *Sheikh Achmed's* rigging but sees no ratlines to help them climb. Their agility flabbergasts him. He draws the sultan's safe-conduct from his shirt pocket and hands it to the officer. He would never think of sending men aloft to grease the rigging without safety harnesses and lines.

"Yes, yes, it is all arranged. Come with us."

~

The nakhoda of the zarook *Nejdi,* Khaled bin Aissa al-Maeini, has already spoken with the police about Bo, but he takes Bo's papers and studies them. Al-Maeini is more entrepreneur than sea captain. Now in his forties, he sees change riding in like forty-mile-an-hour war camels and sees no need to arm against it. Said bin Taimur, who has instructed him to hire this foreigner, is a fusty relic and will not survive the coming changes. It's time to think big. Like other Arabs, he sails within sight of land. Crossing the Gulf of Aden to Africa, he's not out of sight of land for more than a day. This requires, in addition to dead reckoning, local knowledge—the lay of the bottom, winds, obstacles, wrecks, the sort of things pilots know—but it does not require charts or celestial navigation. When the police visit him with the sultan's instruction, he thinks not as much of ingratiating himself with the old man as of using the old man's folly to advantage. The police tell him Bo is a sea captain. It's technically untrue, but he certainly has the requisite experience. There are ways, al-Maeini thinks, to make these voyages faster, more direct. In a few years most of my ships will have diesels and only poor Arabs will sail on the monsoons. Why don't I get this foreigner to show us how, to plot courses for us?

What al-Maeini is not prepared for is an Arab face, a Bedouin face. He doesn't recognize Bo as an Arab name, and he recognizes Cavalieri only as European. He stares into the gulf-green eyes of this foreigner searching for an answer, but all he gets is Bo's paltry Arabic, "*Salaam alaykum, ya nakhoda.*"

"And upon you be peace, foreign captain," he says in his more than adequate English. He expects Bo to engage in conversation. But Bo studies him quietly. He does not like the cut of this man's jib. They have said almost nothing and already he feels soiled.

"You wish to see how the Arabs sail? They sail like their ancestors, and since we are not ancestor-worshippers what is our excuse?"

The man's cunning. Bo pays out rope, saying nothing.

"That is where I can use you. If you agree to speak a few words from time to time, that is."

This is extraordinary in a traditional Arab, to make reference to a guest's demeanor, to complain of it however charmingly. It means he's unnerved by Bo's reticence, leaving Bo to wonder what he's hiding.

"Yes, Mr. Bo, you will be *Nejdi's* mate. Teach my men how to navigate out of sight of land. Yes?"

If he turns his back on this man, as he wishes, he'll offend the sultan.

"If that is what you want, captain, you must send up to Muscat for Admiralty or American charts. Your men, I imagine, will not be able to read them, but they will recognize the markings and the way the words look. I can teach them, but I must have charts. My charts are no good here. I will make a list of what I need."

Bo's malaise grows when the Admiralty charts arrive. Al-Maeini doesn't know navigation, but he makes it clear he wishes to follow longitude 60 down the Arabian Sea into the Indian

Ocean and then right angle to Zanzibar. Bo traces his finger along the south Arabian coast to the strait of Bab al-Mandab, then down the Somali coast. "Why not this way."

Al-Maeini's reply is unconvincing. "I must have a crew that feels confident on the open ocean, Captain. You will have plenty of time to teach them."

It means broad and following reaches on the northeast wind instead of starboard tacks. It also means slower going. It's arbitrary. It's doing something just because it can be done, not because it makes sense. The ancient routes along the coast make sense. The way al-Maeini wants to go, beyond the protection of the Hadramawt's lee coast, will get them slapped around and maybe even knocked down. About the only plus Bo can think of is that *Nejdi* is a double-ender.

The night before they leave four chests are lugged aboard. Bo lends a hand. They're dead weight. One of the men, an old man in his seventies, loses his grip and they have to set down one of the chests hard. The lid springs and Bo sees that the chest is filled with silver Maria Theresa thalers, Austrian coinage popular with the gulf Arabs until recently. The old man, seeing that Bo notices, looks into his face and waves his palms at him in a gesture that while not perfectly understood seems to be a friendly warning.

~

Nejdi, in addition to Bo and al-Maeini, has but five seamen. Another mystery. Dhows are work-intensive. She can easily carry forty or fifty souls and a crew of twenty. Similar dhows often carry as many pilgrims on their way to Mecca for their hajj. This is looking like a hard slog. She's carrying dates. Dates and thalers.

By the time they cross the equator, which the Arabs usually do in sight of Giamame in Somalia, Bo has befriended Haitham, the old man, and Kanadish, a young Dubai Arab who is bright and able. Bo is puzzled that al-Maeini shuns his lessons, not even insisting that the other seamen be taught. Bo's two new friends are by now adept at shooting the sun and moon. To his surprise neither of them is daunted by the bare trigonometry needed to calculate a position. Within a few days, before they're out of sight of Oman, both men are using Bo's sextant and referring to the U.S. Naval Oceanographic Office's star finders and reduction tables. Shooting the stars with a sextant on the decks of a zarook is dicey. But Bo conveys to them that at these latitudes they need find only a handful of stars. The men are delighted to find the stars have Arab names.

The spice islands of Zanzibar and Pemba are just north of Dar es Salaam in what is now Tanzania and south of Mombasa in Kenya. There are two cities on the island of Zanzibar, Zanzibar and Fumba. The latter is on a navigable bay. They are now and have been since the ninth century the Arab world's trade link with Africa. In many ways they're Arab cities. When *Nejdi* arrives Zanzibar is the world's major clove producer and prices are high, but its earlier prosperity owed less to cloves and mangroves and more to human misery, the slave trade.

Bo helps to off-load *Nejdi's* dates, but he soon disappears into the narrow streets hoping to find used sextants for Kanadish and Haitham. He gets a few leads that first day, but it isn't until the third day that he finds a couple of Danish sextants in working order. He now sets out in earnest to teach his friends navigation. He shows them how to identify markings on charts—wreck sites, which look like beetles, pilings, shallows, buoys, flashers. He shows them how to mark charts. And he begins a series of day and night sails to try out what he's teaching. They spend every other day working on the ship. Winter passes quickly and by early April he feels the winds turning around. There are flat calms and eerie green evenings. He decides to give himself a little quiet time, for the Arabs are oppressively eager to learn, so he takes a room in a shabby hotel. Seeing Bo gone, al-Maeini takes on cargo for the trip home. Bo has been sleeping in his room for three nights when al-Maeini tells him they're ready to sail home. The winds have shifted. They're blowing steadily from the southwest. *Nejdi's* sails have been patched and resewn, her rigging replaced and tuned. Al-Maeini has even bought a new compass. Bo convinces him that it needs to be swung—calibrated—and he takes *Nejdi* off her hook in Fumba Bay to do it.

Within an hour of clearing the bay for the return trip Bo can tell the cargo is different. It's not dead-weight tonnage. The ship jerks around. She handles grumpily. Many zarooks are open, but *Nejdi's* hold is covered. He decides to do what he should have done before setting sail, make sure the cargo is battened down so that it won't shift or get loose when the ship tacks and heels. He finds the gangway to the hold padlocked. He doesn't make too much of this at first. They all sleep on deck anyway, under an awning when the sun is high or when it rains.

"First we go to Nishtun on the Ghubbat al-Qamar," al-Maeini tells him.

Nishtun is hardly one of Yemen's major ports.

"I'll go up coastwise," Bo says.

"No, out to sea. Remember what I told you, Captain. This is a training voyage."

"My ass," Bo mutters.

Al-Maeini has a small cabin just forward of the navigation station. The gangway to the main hold is further forward. Bo waits till the sun makes the spider logy and he retires to his cabin. Then he goes forward and picks the gangway padlock. Frogmen are adept gunsmiths and locksmiths. He goes down below with his flashlight. The air is close. The first thing he sees is a row of white objects, like pearl buttons. When he shines his light in an arc he sees that they're toenails. Then he makes out the whites of eyes. As his eyes adjust he recognizes twenty or more young women squatting against the strakes of the dhow. He discerns two more things when he draws close: were they not emaciated, they would be pretty, all of them, and they're shackled by their ankles and chained together. He studies their shackles more closely and sees that at intervals they're linked to ringbolts in the hull.

Bo is wearing the red and white checkered kaffiyeh of a Gulf Arab with a black agal, head rope. For this reason he does not readily understand the young women's demeanor when they look away; they won't look into his eyes. He squats on the keelson, studying them: a tic in the corner of an eye, a quivering lip, a shaking knee, a constricted throat. He takes out some bubble gum and offers little wrapped clumps to them. He unpeels a piece, puts it in his mouth and starts chewing. Some of them now look at him. When it's soft enough he blows a bubble and pops it. Then he smiles and starts picking it off his nose and lips. Some of the women, the youngest, smile. They're all young, disturbingly young. They sit in silence studying each other. Then, as if on signal, they close their palms together in an attitude of Christian prayer—Muslims pray palms up—and roll their spired hands back and forward in supplication. Water? Please give us water? He sees that buckets of water with ladles are placed at intervals between them. Food? They need food. He sees that they have dates and unleavened flat bread. They need to relieve themselves? He doesn't know how long they have been there. The spider could have taken them aboard that first day he went to his hotel. It might be three days. He sees slop buckets up forward. He approaches them. Their odor tells him what they're used for.

"Does anyone speak English?" They answer by supplicating more vigorously. The situation dawns on him. They take him for an Arab, a buyer or a middleman, but his bubble-gum gambit is not signally Arab. An Arab, especially a Yemeni, might chew qat, but he would not explode a pink bubble all over his face and smile at himself. Moreover, they know the sound of Arabic. He takes several ebony, aquiline faces in his hands and nods slowly. He doesn't know what this signifies, nor do they, but they stop their supplications. He sits among them for some while. He thinks of Moira hanging onto the boarding ladder. Then he rises and leaves.

Khaled bin Aissa al-Maeini is waiting for him at the helm. He sees Bo emerge from the hold. In his hand is a short-nosed revolver. Bo looks behind him as if he doesn't know the revolver is for him. This ruse gains him a few seconds and about a yard. Kanadish is backsplicing a new heaving line under the awning by the binnacle. Seeing what's unfolding, he puts the helm hard over causing the tender zarook to fall off and begin to jibe. The men scramble to control her interminable lateen yard. Al-Maeini loses his footing. As he struggles to right it, Bo pivots full around on the ball of his left foot and slams the nakhoda's heart with his right foot. Al-Maeini drops his revolver and collapses into a sitting position. When he gets back up Bo whirls again and crumps al-Maeini's cricoid with the side of his hand. It's not the practiced cricothyroidectomy he twice performed with a garrote as his unit worked to blow up a railroad bridge at Yosu, but it guarantees al-Maeini will never breathe again.

He picks up the revolver, sees that it's an old Iver Johnson 22, spins the barrel, snaps it back into line and tucks it into his belt. He nods at Kanadish. Haitham, the old man, saying nothing, begins trussing al-Maeini. That finished he finds a grapnel in a chest on the poop and bends it to the body on what appears to be a sixty- or seventy-foot line. About fifteen feet from the bitter end he bends a small fisherman's anchor to make sure the grapnel will bite as it drags. Bo had read the charts and taught Haitham and Kanadish how to read them, but the old man knows that sea bottom better than any of them and acts for all the world as if he has done this before. Bo fishes al-Maeini's pockets, finds a ring of keys, six thalers and a wad of Omani currency. Kanadish brings *Nejdi* back onto her outward bound starboard tack. He motions to Haitham to take the tiller. Bo has been watching the other three crewmen. He knows little about them. They might be al-Maeini's kinsmen. They go about their work making no eye contact with each other, a good sign. With Haitham at the helm, Bo and Kanadish heave the nakhoda over the side. Bo wonders if anybody will pray for him when he's tossed over the side. Haitham has surely lived long enough to see slavery. The Europeans who eagerly profited from it, then showily forsook it, never eradicated it. It might be that even Kanadish and the others have seen it, abetted it.

Kanadish returns to his ditty bag—Bo assumes he's looking for his Koran—and draws out the spare white and red flag of Dubai. He hauls Sultan Said bin Taimur's flag down from its long stern staff and raises the flag of the emir of Dubai. Haitham and the others spare not even a shrug. Arabs are not in general as sentimental or superstitious about their ships' names as northern Europeans, nor as loyal to them. *Nejdi* had probably had other names, even sailed under other flags, and it seems she will receive another soon.

Now a communications snafu of heroic proportion looms. It's not just that Haitham and Kanadish speak only the few English terms he taught them; the real problem is what to do with the women, how the crew feels about them, where to put them off, what to do with the ship, what to do about himself. He decides to do what he will have to do in any case, one thing at a time. He takes Al-Maeini's keys and goes below to free the women. Each of them touches his arm or his face as they pass before him through the gangway. On deck, as their eyes adjust to the light, they take in what happened and then they squat together. Bo searches the nakhoda's belongings. He finds a sack full of thalers—more thalers—but has no idea of their worth. He calls Haitham and Kanadish over and motions to one of the others to take the helm. With his hands he signals that he proposes to distribute the money first to them, then some to the crew and the women. Kanadish opens his palms to ask how much to whom. Bo answers by pointing at him to decide. He makes them understand that he will take nothing.

Step by step *Nejdi's* command passes to Kanadish. The others accept. Al-Maeini had never shared anything with them. He distributes the nakhoda's money judiciously. What he gives the young women will help them stay out of the hands of the people who sold them. But they make it clear they do not wish to return to Fumba or Zanzibar.

Kanadish, on the other hand, does not wish to linger on the African coast. He's thinking clearly but not clearly enough. Dhows make only one round trip a year; that trip has to pay. Bo gets across to him that he should take on cargo—mangrove poles, cloves, whatever he can buy with Al-Maeini's money. Into the pot Bo throws a wad of British currency with which Peter had been paying him. He keeps just enough to get to a hiring hall. The Arabs value British money. It obliterates al-Maeini's memory. Bo is sure Kanadish will know how to buy new papers for *Nejdi*. So the communications tangle he dreaded sorts itself nicely.

He breaks out the Admiralty chart for Zanzibar, an area the British hydrographers knew in detail. He points to the women and opens his palm to ask where they should be disembarked. Arabs think nothing of beaching a zarook or even a high-pooped ghanjah, so if they can find soft bottoms they won't necessarily have to use their small boat.

Kanadish sees what Bo can't. He speaks no Swahili or any

other African language, but he sees that the young women bear the aquiline features of the Arab and that must have played a role in their selection. The Arabs' imprimatur cuts deep in Zanzibar, Mombasa and Malindi, but he judges from his travels that it's more likely these women are Somalis. They're frightened, but they have the haughtiness of the Arab. Between gestures and finger-pointing and his charts he has little trouble showing Bo that he intends to leave the women somewhere on the desolate Somali coast between Giamame and Brava. Why not Kismaayo or even Mogadishu?

Kanadish draws his thumb across his throat and shakes his head. Perhaps his decision is best for the women and as generous as he feels he can be, but it's bad for Bo. Dar es Salaam, from which they're not more than forty nautical miles, or Mogadishu are the ports where he's most likely to find a ship, any ship. He doesn't realize that Kanadish thinks he will return to the gulf with them. Haitham understands: he points first to Bo, then eastward to Dar es Salaam. Sorrow streaks the younger Arab's face like a squall line. Bo has been his fortune.

Coming about and taking up a port tack shoreward is easy enough on the steady southwest winds. It's almost dark on the beach south of Dar es Salaam when Bo climbs into *Nejdi's* long boat with Haitham. He bows slightly and gives Kanadish the Muslim salutation, heart, mouth and mind. *Salaam alaykum, ya nakhoda.* A sob in his chest burns and chokes him, and he knows it's for Uthman, and for Peter and Moira and even the old sultan, as much as it's for Kanadish and Haitham. What he does not know is that it's also for himself and the limbo into which he now goes.

Part II

Djelloul Marbrook

14

He walks around Dar es Salaam licking ices, waiting for a decent thought to pop into his head. When one does he almost smiles— C.P. Cavafy, the Greek poet. Okay, what to do about Cavafy? He lived most of his life in Alexandria, a good port for catching a ship. Maybe even a ship heading for the British Isles, and he has enough money to get there.

Vestris sailed by another name when she was owned by the Mercedes Great Circle Line—the *Kill van Kull*.

He hates seeing a wallowing pig flying an American flag. She's the kind of asthmatic crock that makes a bosun feel like a silly bastard. He contemplates her with distaste and wanders off. But that evening in a nearby taverna he hears she's bound for Valetta on Malta, then Lisbon and Liverpool. Next morning he looks up the captain and is told that *Vestris* needs a navigator. The captain is delighted to find one and signs Bo on.

Merchant crews, knowing he'd been a Navy chief boatswain and frogman, used to wait snake-eyed and surly for him to do something chickenshit. But by the time he made it from able seaman to bosun, as his Navy experience qualified him to do, rebs were calling him bubba, a better reward than his Silver Star because it covers him with the anonymity he craves.

Vestris almost cooks her black gang in the Irish Sea when her boiler blows. She obliges Bo by skipping Liverpool and limping into Port Glasgow for parts and repairs. By the time she makes port her engine room needs every fitting imaginable, and it takes six weeks to get and install them. Her exhausted metals make repair a matter of imagination rather than know-how. Scotland gives him an inspiration.

~

"Rose MacQuarrie?"

"Yes."

"My name is Amir Cavalieri. I'm Ben Aissa's son."

He tries to watch the snow vanishing on the firth, but he finds himself counting the seconds on his watch—fourteen of them before she speaks again.

"Maybe you are, maybe you aren't. Where are you?"

"In Edinburgh. I'd like to see you."

Not driven to fill others' silences, he waits again.

She likes that. "I'm thinking."

"I'm sure there's a lot to think about."

Rose MacQuarrie laughs, high and clear. "Well, a Yank given to understatement is something to think about."

The snow sallows as the street lights come on. He grins in the red call box. She'd been only the second of four R. MacQuarries in the directory. If that kind of luck holds she'll prize loose some of the knots by which Ulrike binds him.

By then it's not a young man fogging the kiosk—with his pea-coat collar turned up, watch cap pushed back—he is a merchant mariner working on a lifelong penchant for tramp steaming over circle runs.

"I wouldna call this much of a city," a stevedore said upstream in a Glasgow pub the second night, "but Edinburgh o' t'other end o' the canal, now that's a city."

Not Liverpool or the Irish Sea or even the Firth of Clyde had conjured Rose.

But looking into the blear face of that refrigerator-shaped Scot with a purple bulb-nose Bo recalled a Rose MacQuarrie whose ward his father had been, a Scotswoman from Edinburgh, somehow his father's guardian.

"You'll want instructions then?" she asks, breaking into his thoughts.

"No. Thank you. I've bought a city map and rented a car."

"Come ahead then."

A wog ward to a Scotswoman is just the sort of Pickwickian notion Ulrike would concoct out of whole cloth. He liked it, of course, the way one likes *Beau Geste* without believing a word of it.

He can't believe the British built the spluttering Morris for their winter or anybody's. Nor is he prepared for Number 11 Cairngorm Road. It is a five-story Georgian brick townhouse. Its Ionic pilasters and white marble steps, perhaps a dozen of them wrapped around a columnar juniper, rise importantly above the slate sidewalk. The second and third floor windows are Palladian. The topmost windows are gimbaled bull's eyes, ajar to spite the weather.

Rose is tall. Almost as tall as he is. Her fine white hair falls in a braid down the front of her left shoulder while wisps quarrel in the snow around her temples. She waves him over slowly, like a conductor listening. As he starts up the stairs he notices that she wears a light blue woolen skirt cut to a Bolshoi dancer's calves. The clerical collar of her washed silk taupe blouse emphasizes her long neck. A matching cashmere sweater is clasped over her shoulders by a cameo.

Hello. Thank you for seeing me. No, don't say anything tweety like that.

He watches her eyes. Startlingly long. Faerie eyes, like his own, steady, unblinking. He can't tell if it's the cold that makes him shiver.

"You take your time sizing a person up."

He tries to say something, grins as if he will, then gives up, rubbing his brow.

"Well, I do myself. It's the wont of an old soul looking for lost companions," she says.

A thin smile pulses along lips carved like a Mongol bow. She gauges the effect of her words and he stands for it out of what feels like ancient respect. He wears a white turtleneck sweater, brown corduroys and oiled work boots. He feels caught in her eyes.

"You're a sailor?"

"Merchant marine, yes. My ship blew her boiler and put into Port Glasgow for repairs."

She opens the door wider and motions him in with a nod. The foyer is bare, its black and white marble tiles bathed in rose-water light from the fireplace in the room to the left. She leads him there. Two conjoined walls of this room hold books ceiling to floor—leatherbound, clothbound, paperback. Each wall has a tracking ladder. Not the sort of establishment one can keep up alone.

He sets his backpack down by a chair, stuffs his gloves in his coat pockets and is holding his left hand in his right hand when he becomes aware that he's leaning towards her as if warming his hands at a depot stove.

"I think you'll find the logs warmer than me."

Rattled, he steps quickly to the fire, but, facing it, he glances over his shoulder to see Rose MacQuarrie studying him wryly.

"I'm used to the cold."

"A son of Ulrike Theiss would be."

He turns his back to the fire to face her, clasping his left wrist behind him. She does the same. They stand some four feet from each other.

"My heart is beating very fast."

She purses her lips long before she makes any sound.

"I see you think I'm the Elf queen, and so for all you know I am, so you must still yourself while I decide."

"Decide what?"

"Precisely."

He turns and makes a point of studying the vertical painting over the mantel. But he sees nothing at first, except the after-image of her gaze. He feels as imperiled as when he got rubber-drunk and two Cuban whores tied him up naked and stroked him with a straight razor.

His father's guardian? How can that be? She's no older than he'd've been had he lived. What do I know? Really know? That's why you're here, stupid. He looks up at the painting. He thinks of Gilbert Stuart's *The Skater*. Rose is skating with her hands in a gray Persian lamb muff, on a port tack, her right foot lifted and pointed down, red hair streaming like afterburn, her eyes looking as if they'd swallowed the pale sun, a dusty blue coat lapping those heartbreaking calves.

He says, "Where's the claymore?" He thinks of fallen Brits at Culloden, or a lover who betrayed her.

She raises her left hand and holds it by her shoulder like a Greek goddess considering—he sees her left-handedness—then gestures, forefinger down, thumb up, to her navel, or so he would realize later. At the moment a stray thought reddens his ears.

"You know something of the Scot if you know what a claymore is."

"My idea of fright is to meet a highlander with a bloody claymore in his hand on a moor at dusk."

Rose feels heat between her youthful portrait and her Saracen intruder.

"In the south of France their idea of fright was to meet one of your ancestors riding white as a ghoul in the gloaming."

"I'm also German."

"Prussian, yes."

"God, what a combination! Better to be one thing or another."

"Well, I'm one thing who'd rather be another."

"What other?"

"Other than one who knew Ulrike."

"That's what I came to talk about."

"Of course."

"I didn't expect from what I'd heard that you'd be glad to see me."

Her lower lip thrusts forward as she considers him. "I'm not sorry." She moves close. "Let me see your face." She holds it in warm hands. "Well, you're not the Swedish count's. He was dark for a Swede."

"How do you know?"

"Four blue eyes canna brown eyes make. I see flecks of green, brave little rhizomes in the sand. I don't know, I don't know whose you are."

"You don't!"

"No, I don't."

"You're my only hope."

"Of the truth? The truth's in you. Or it's not. Let me see."

She holds his face again. Then, left-handedly, she brushes his hair back.

"Yes, it's in you. It will have to do. All I can do is increase your confusion."

"How do you know I'm confused?"

She laughs. "You're here! Besides, no son of that witch could escape it. How did you come by your Italian name?"

"Sandro Cavalieri. My stepfather."

"Poor devil."

15

He disorders the bowels of the place.

He sees that Rose MacQuarrie is a formidable matron, had been a warrior girl, and yet in his presence, she blushes. To whatever it is that recalls her to girlishness he too responds.

"Shall I make you tea in the style of your ancestors?"

Her invitation itches. He turns from her portrait—which is more compelling, the portrait or Rose?—the pink of the girl's cheeks playing in his eyes, and answers her with the gravity of a marabout.

"It would be an honor, Rose MacQuarrie."

She tilts her head back to let her pale eyes fall to the level of his gaze.

"You could be his."

"Were you?"

She breaks into a berserking Celtic smile. The brightness of her gums and disposition of her teeth give her stare a burn.

"You are far more observant than most men your age."

"A sailor's life depends on it."

"Perhaps. Or perhaps the odds favor our never finding the few people or things that can drive us mad, and you have beaten the odds."

She turns and vanishes into a pantry.

He returns to her portrait.

"Are you falling in love with her?"

She's holding a large beaten copper tray, a magnificent silver and copper teapot and two tall glasses.

"Did he?"

"Why yes, he did. He called her a princess of Jerusalem whom he stole upon her wedding day, cutting down her templars with his scimitar and riding off into the desert with her."

Her smile is gone. She's not the sort of woman to trifle with memories.

"I've had historical fantasies myself."

"But surely your princess was not a Scots highlander?"

"French, I think."

"Ah, too bad."

"Well, in fantasies one can revise at will."

"I think I shall like a young man who can flirt with an old woman out of utter need."

"Yes, I need a very great deal from you."

He likes her too much to point out she initiated the game. Not his style anyway.

"And I've not decided what, besides tea, to give you."

"Do women ever?"

"No," she says. "It's a much greater power than brawn, don't you think?"

She pours tea from a standing position into glasses filled a quarter with sugar so that their mint leaves spin in the froth. Handing him a hot glass wrapped in a magenta napkin, she says, "What did Ulrike tell you?"

"That Ben Aissa, my father"—he examines her closely—"was your ward. His family had been wiped out by tuberculosis. You were middle-aged, which clearly you couldn't have been. That he was shot accidentally in both legs by a cousin while hunting gazelle, developed gangrene, refused to let the doctors amputate and died in agony."

Staring up at her own portrait. Rose sits youthfully, one leg straight out, leaning backwards. She hikes up her teal skirt.

Djelloul Marbrook

"I'm seeing if I can distract you from studying my face. Old women are unaccustomed to younger men examining their faces. You are of course looking for the bar sinister, but I am unfortunately for you not an heraldic device. Or if I am, I'm unaware of it."

He's confused, she can see. He'd followed her as far as her distraction, to her calves, but there she lost him.

"The bar sinister in heraldry is a hint or even a proof of bastardy."

They slump like back-stabbed warriors. All the containment drains from his face. A frightened child looks out.

"For the love of God!" she says, almost to herself, "you thought I was your mother, that somehow . . . "

He leans toward her, his glass on his knee.

"I would have preferred it."

He gets up and turns around to her portrait. He hears her rise.

At first she merely puts both hands on his shoulders from behind.

"I would have liked it, Amir," she whispers. "Ward? What an odd word!" She breaks away and returns to her chair. "Ignorant bitch!"

He turns to her.

"You don't mind my denigrating Ulrike, do you?"

"Do I have a choice?"

"No, not if you wish even a fleck of the truth."

"I would like all of it. You seem forthright."

"Oh I was! Forthright with a vengeance, that young Rose MacQuarrie was."

"Was?"

"With age comes cunning, and now it seems the gods unaccountably have given me the means to pay back Ulrike for some of the harm she did me."

"How?"

"Wha' a calm ye keep for one being badly used!"

"I'm used to diving in black water."

"How, you ask. Well, I can lie to you or I can withhold so much of the truth as to guarantee that her lying tongue will earn her the hatred of her son."

He takes his glass for a walk around the room trying to focus in this shape-shifting twilight. "I had hoped it would turn out you were my mother."

"You canna' win me over saying such a bittersweet thing."

This resort to burr and lilt unsettles him. He shakes his shoulders and stares out the bow window into the lamp-lit snow, grateful to be angry.

"How could you know it would be bittersweet to me? How could I not know almost anybody would be preferable to Ulrike?"

He decides to set down his glass, put on his coat and go. He knows how to do that. Although he's been deprived of knowledge needed to live, he'll damned well not be diddled to gain it. He's dealt with netherfolk before. He thinks of Moira. He'd been born of one, hadn't he? This fey witch might well know the truth. And she can shove it.

To leave and not face her would be a cancerous defeat. Of all the things he doesn't know he knows that one thing: you have got to look at what you're leaving or you haven't left it. He takes two deep breaths—diving's good for a troubled man—and turns around fast. Fellow changelings know him by his eyes.

Grief crazes her porcelain composure. She knows what he's set to do.

"I never thought to cope with Ulrike's lost boy, I . . . "

"I never thought a faerie could be overrun by her feelings," he says.

Rose splutters into laughter.

"Well, now you know! That should be worth something. Are you not often overrun by your own?"

"Yes, but I'm a poor sprite if a good sailor. When does your burr come and when does it go?"

"Ah, well, it comes to the rescue and goes when I've recovered my usual icy demeanor."

"Which is natural to the Scot?"

"Lord no! Stoic, yes, but icy, a Scot? Bloody at times. Look, we canna' flirt in the guise of our ancestors, you know."

"Flirt?"

"Don't be dense. We're not, either of us, two freeze-dried Brits having tea by the window studying genealogy or telling tales of the Raj."

His turn to laugh. Not so much at her humor as at her manner: a proud girl telling a dicey truth the only way she can, in a tantrum. How many people had risked such real communication with him?

Nobody except one little girl long ago.

They laugh together until he, figuring out what to do first, irons his face and stares into her eyes. She follows suit, waiting.

"Was I his?"

"I don't know. Amir was the name of a fifteen-year-old boy who carried Ulrike's paints. Her paint boy, she called him, like a bloody *pied noir.*"

She walks past him, retrieves his glass from a window bench and returns to the low table in front of the fire where she pours more tea. When she speaks again her voice is low and gritty.

"When you see someone you love besotted by an obsession with someone else, spoiled, turned inside out, blinded and reeking of her, you're never who you were again. You send away the child in you and never trust her again. It's worse than rape. How can you trust a god who did this to you, much less a human being?"

Coming up at her right, he addresses her portrait. "I'm sorry this happened to you, Rose."

"Yes, it happened. Everything she felt she felt so fiercely. She wasn't meant to be second, you see, to nurse a betrayed heart. I have to keep her here. Partly, I think, because my father painted her—he was gifted—and that's how he saw her and gave her that way to me, but mostly because it's all I'm able to feel about her."

"Yes, I can see that. I need to know who did that to her."

She motions him to sit. "Swedes live near magnetic north, except their feet. They have a grand compulsion to shed their clothes. Such somber exhibitionists. Count Soren von Melen had spent some time in Tuscany. He told me he'd concluded the Italians thought the void to be a woman which naturally they had to stuff, but the Arabs felt quite at home in their inability to stuff anything, so he'd stayed in Algeria. He was a great heron, standing quite still for minutes as herons do. I liked him very much. He invited me to dinner at his villa when I first came to el -Kantara.

"I told him of my father Torquil's fascination with *al-khidr*, the emerald light that illumines the soul's quest in metaphysical or sufic Islam. Torquil was a chemist. Actually he inherited chemical laboratories from his mother's father and they made him quite rich during The Great War. "He'd run across the notion, which to this day is not well understood, that *al-kimya* is simply the Arab word with its article for chemistry and the Arabs never made any distinction between alchemy and chemistry. Soren was thrilled by this idea. I suppose I became interesting to him for my voracious reading. I had the idea the Arabs could abide the synergy between alchemy and chemistry because Islam, before fanatics unhorsed it, was the engine that drove their scientific glory wagon. Sufism was Soren's passion, as it was mine, but the poor man squawked Arabic even more wretchedly than he snuffled French. He had no language facility at all.

"Our conversations became frequent and after a while he led me to the southeast quarter of his villa and I just more or less stayed, with my own little garden and kitchen. Days passed sometimes without our ever seeing each other. He was not unlike my father, a bit distracted, kind but not skilled about people, and devoted to something, in his case horticulture.

"The Arabs and the settlers came to him from great distances bringing strange flora and asking him to diagnose diseased specimens. He helped them improve their date groves.

"Soren was at least thirty years my elder, but having grown up among the elderly I'd never distanced myself from them. I was inclined to think the elderly more trustworthy than the young. I knew he was drawn to me, he knew I was drawn to him. Nothing kept us from being lovers except contentment with our friendship. I'd been living at the villa, except for excursions, for maybe two years. A dust storm blew in off the desert and slashed up Soren's garden in seconds. I was scuttling about securing shutters when I spied him huddled against a garden wall weeping in the wreckage of his work. I came and put my arm around him and he wept like a child. It was a long time before I understood that he was weeping for the inappropriateness of loving me.

"I didn't need money. I'd not only my father's—he died while I was at Cambridge—but I'd inherited a trust from my maternal grandmother. The family business had been ships' chandleries.

"Ben Aissa ben Bou Djemaa, the man we'll have to call your putative father, became something of Soren's protégé, then mine. It wasn't his gift as a date arborist that caught my attention, it was his language facility. I noticed right off that he spoke French a bit —you could say—resentfully. That was characteristic of some Arab aristocrats. Their French is sullen.

"So I deliberately engaged him in Arabic and was astonished to hear a kind of flutey literary Arabic. It's found among very few

Maghribis. But it stopped in adolescence, I mean it sounded as if he'd stopped hearing it while still a boy. His family, it turned out, had been wiped out by tuberculosis.

"We'd been sitting in Soren's garden, the three of us, and Ben Aissa got up and left in that spooky way Bedouins come and go. Soren reflected awhile, then turned to me and said, 'He's an angel, you know that, don't you?' I remember combing the German language—we spoke in German—trying to feel out the spirit of Soren's words when he spoke again. 'I mean it, Rose, the man is an angel. He has no guile. He doesn't see the way we do.'

"I said, 'He sees *al khidr* perhaps.'

"Soren said, 'Perhaps.' But he wasn't sure I got it. 'Listen to me carefully about this, Rose, the man is an angel.'

"I stared at him. Then, to make sure, he said, 'He's not one of us.'

"Well, of course Soren was licensing me to love this Arab boy. Yes, I think I can say that. After all, a man must be half angel himself to recognize one. And after that it was never a question between the three of us. I mean Ben Aissa I'm sure knew I slept with Soren from time to time. But it didn't matter. We three were friends. If it hadn't been that way I wouldn't have, I couldn't have loved Ben Aissa. But I was too young to recognize that. And he was even younger than I was. We never really knew, but I suspect he was no more than nineteen.

"He would come and go, never saying much. We didn't learn that he was a *bash agha* for many months. That's a Turkish title, really. It doesn't have the prestige of a *caid* or *marabout,* certainly not of emir, but the Turks cultivated Arabs who by family or accomplishment could help them handle their unruly co-religionists. A *bash agha* is a kind of fixer. A *consiglieri.* I suspect —well, it had to be, really—Ben Aissa's title must have been hereditary. He wore it lightly, and it was only later in England that

I realized how lightly, because most of the *bash aghas* were henchmen to the French, but Ben Aissa, while he harbored no ill will for them, hated them in the abstract.

"He would come and go, leaving behind a kind of warmth Soren and I basked in. We looked forward to our young Bedouin's visits, which were peculiar now I think of it, because we always felt he had some overt reason for these errands. What, we couldn't have said. We just brightened and beamed at each other at his approach, which was always announced by the sound of his black horse on the paving stones.

16

"I don't know how long we'd known Ben Aissa when Soren said to me one evening, 'Why don't you educate our angel, Rose?' I knew perfectly well he didn't mean anything sexual. I don't think either of us thought of Ben Aissa as a virgin if we thought of it at all. I didn't really know what Soren meant but I did know it was life-threatening. So here were these two blue-eyed *roumis* talking about someone else's life as if we had a perfect right to muck about in it.

" 'You're bored, Count Von Melen?'

" 'Seriously, Rose, why don't you take the boy in hand?'

" 'Deliver him from his unseemly wogdom?'

"I was panicky. I knew Soren very well. Anything he said more quietly than usual was bound to be dangerous. 'Well, I should miss you terribly, dear, but I thought perhaps you might take him to Edinburgh. Or Cambridge. Educate him, dear. You have money.'

" 'He's not an orphan, you know. He's not an urchin. He's proud. It would offend him. This old Scots bag . . . Really, Soren, you're naive.'

"He didn't like my pretending to be matronly. He lifted up my skirt. 'Are these the legs of an old Scots bag or any other kind of bag, my girl? You are a beautiful and distinguished young Druid who is acting like a priss because your friend has proposed an earnest, serious undertaking. We do not—I repeat, do not—often if ever encounter angels in exile here and we are obligated, those of us who see a thing or two, to do something fine when we do.'

"It was funny really, because he was still holding my skirt up. I suppose it was to make me uncomfortable and alert. I blushed. It was so, so possessive, but I couldn't see it that way at all. I was hot and couldn't tell if it was for Soren or Ben Aissa or the idea of the thing or all three.

"Anyway I started walking around in front of Soren. Then I stopped and unbuttoned my skirt and swept it off to the side. I had no undies, so I just presented my familiar long-stemmed rusty rose to Count Von Melen in his garden. Then I offered him my hand and said, 'Let's go talk about this impossibly colonialist idea of yours, Soren.'

"I loved to see his pale eyes darken and grow boyish again when I did something like that. It was in a way my defense against his precipitous wisdom.

"In a month or two Ben Aissa and I were off to Edinburgh, to this very house. Soren engineered it all. I'd hardly said a word to Ben Aissa.

"I had many things to think about when you called, nary a one pleasant, but I fixed on taking off my skirt in front of the count because—I see this now so clearly because of you—it was the start of the most shameful, grievous thing I ever did. No man I have ever known was as generous as Soren—and look at how I treated him. I was never driven by my sex. An interesting sort of organ, I thought when I toyed with it as a child—I can hardly say it was my favorite toy—not half so intriguing as my head or even my eyes for that matter. I was not in love with Ben Aissa. I thought love a sickness, a kind of defeat—a humiliation. I'm not so sure I was ever convinced otherwise. But I abandoned that most decent of men, putting it down to a spiritual adventure. When you're young everything is so damned cosmic. So when you called it was not about Ben Aissa or Ulrike, it was about the fall of Eve. I could have made a good man's life better with very little cost to myself—after all, I liked him immensely—and I didn't have the charity.

"I can tell you very little of what you need to know. Yes, I knew Ben Aissa well, but was he your father? I knew your namesake the paint boy only casually. He could have been your father. So could many another Bedouin. It's not a surprise that any son of hers would be confounded and come searching. How could it be otherwise since her gift is to confound? But I certainly never thought God in heaven would leave it to Ulrike Theiss's son to confront me with the blackest thing I ever did.

"I'm sure someone has warned you to be careful about what you want because you may get it. It's good advice as far as it goes, but I do think we never get exactly what we want, which is a great blessing, don't you think? I mean, you think you want to hear about this young *bash agha* studying in England under my patronage. But really it was all a great potboiler. What was lovely —and what really is all I'm wont to say—is two odd people spending five years together as friends and fellow students, and only at the end as lovers. That is what even now fascinates me. I pursued my studies, befriended Evelyn Underhill, who was making Christian mysticism respectable, and Ben Aissa, for whom we'd planned a career in horticulture, fast became a mathematician. Like his forebears he kenned it.

"At first Ben Aissa wore his blue-gray burnoose, white silk liner and boots. He'd found the French comical and was determined the English should be too. But I think he became fond of their snottiness. He told me it reminded him of the Tuaregs— one must never allow one's admiration of them to devolve into trust, he told me in Arabic.

"The Brits he really liked were the Cockneys. He felt unguarded among them. Eventually he became quite squirely in his dress.

"He was very tall, six-five at least, and he shared the Arabs' great love of falcons. When I first saw him bareheaded his hair was plaited. It amused me to think of him plaiting it. When he abandoned his burnoose he stopped plaiting it and it fell long and black as a Mongol's. I began chopping it, but it was a long time before he would consent to have it as short as an Englishman's. A natural horseman, he thought polo and fox-hunting silly, but he did gather all sorts of medals as a sports rifleman.

"Really, Amir, this is all so much—oh, clishmaclash—whilst I find the few things I want to tell you. Let me sit here and watch the snow a bit . . . "

"We turned heads. I would say he did, but would you trust me if I insisted I did not notice admiring looks? Our liaison itself attracted interest. What in the name of God was it made of? Now of a sudden snowy day in old age I know. Our bond was our indifference to ourselves. I used to watch them—viscountesses and baronesses some of them—disconcerted because they could not keep their eyes away from him nor draw his to them. And not just the women, men as well. If he noticed he never showed it.

"If you accosted him while he was in route to a tutor, or examinations even, he stopped and gave you his full attention as if you unquestionably merited it. Who could you possibly love but a handsome man who did this? For five years a man hung onto my every word and gesture. Could absinthe be half as addictive? But in all these years the recognition that I loved him finally because there wasn't anybody better has been like something I dropped into the sea. A sea of rage. This is not a gentle old lady you've come to see. I've kept that love like reserved sacrament because of how hypnotically it was betrayed. I think it was the betrayal I loved, the betrayal I've kept on loving.

"I wrote to Soren more to keep myself informed than him, insensitive always to what he might be feeling. You'd better watch out when somebody you've hankered for relents; some virus prompts the perverse to acquire us just when they've become bored with us. When they're finished with us they post the banns and wrap us up.

"I'm angry at Algeria, angry over a million sugared teas and a world war, that it gave me no sign, no warning. Damn it to hell, Scotland would have warned me! I would have known if an Ulrike Theiss were afoot—highland, lowland, borderland I would have known, Scotland would have told me.

"We'd decided we were in love. We couldn't think of anyone else to love. So we determined to live here in Edinburgh, but I suppose it felt so threatening that we invented reasons to revisit Algeria to tell old Soren. That was the ostensible reason, but I had grown almost wise enough to want to see Soren simply because I always wanted to see Soren.

"I'm trying to remember how much I understood. I think I'd come to hope some porcelain viscountess would enmesh Ben Aissa. I remember I was always asking him what he thought of this or that creature. My mind by our fourth year in England turned to Soren even in our bed.

"And there was another problem. Ben Aissa's nature. What in God's name would an armed Bedouin angel abandoned in England do? I'd been blessed with the love of two good men who didn't care about my money. My money that had purchased ease and education was for Ben Aissa a gift not from me but from God. He was a true Bedouin. He would happily have done the same. He never mentioned home. Could he stay here, teach mathematics, love someone? I felt obliged to marry him, it was the only idea that would work.

"First I had to see Soren. Soren had orchestrated this entire adventure. He'd done it—we do damned things instead of something else—Soren had done it instead of seeing if I would love him. He foresaw my rebuff and he sent me off with a young man he liked. And damn him if he didn't count on my not growing up anytime soon. I almost bloody did and then like a twit decided to marry and live in my father's house.

"Affianced, as it were, we left for Algeria, me feeling I was going home, Ben Aissa, I think, sad to leave home.

"His son or no, you certainly have his attentiveness. I would think by your face this is the best story you ever heard. Surely it's not. Or are you kind where he was attentive? No, I think not. It wasn't kind of you to come here. Or, if it was, it wasn't your kindness but a queer God's."

16

"Certain faces are occluded, no matter how often or how fast you look, you can't quite get them: they're dark, veiled. Ulrike Theiss had an occluded face. D'ye see it now?"

He shudders as if he'd gulped aquavit. He'd tried, boy and man, to draw that face—he'd drawn hundreds of others—and he couldn't.

The room goes sly, things give up their shapes.

"Some of us see it, see that we can't make out their faces. I don't know what the rest of us see. Now here's the scary part: we can forget it, ignore it, but they never do. They know when we can't see them, and that's how we become the enemy, without even knowing it. Follow?"

He has been staring up at Rose's girlhood portrait. When he breaks away and patrols the edge of this room not trusted to keep its shape, she follows him, determined not to let him off lightly. But he's not trying to shake her off. He frees the hasp of his backpack and pulls out a hefty spiral pad of drawing paper. She hovers behind him so that when he turns with the pad in his hand their faces are inches apart. She steps back with the pad in her hands and begins to leaf through it.

"For why? For why are ye a seaman, Amir? Not a man in millions captures people like this."

"To not be captured. You said it."

"So then you know what I'm talking about." He nods.

"They track us down and. . . well, I was about to say, kill us, but I have learned they're afraid to kill us, so they imprison us.

Our faceless jailers they are. And to deal with them we become shape-changers, go anywhere we wish, see anything and anyone, but we always end up back in the same damned place where we acquired our terrible gifts. The shape-shifter is a globe-trotting prisoner."

"And that's here for you?"

"Here for me. Yes. Here that girl"—she points up to her portrait—"makes her stand, faces them, whoever the hell they are. Knowing she was an innocent girl is my strength. Ulrike, does she know you canna' draw her?"

He smiles at her intent. "She doesn't care. I used to show her my drawings. They disturb her. She never encouraged me."

"I suspect when those eyes of yours clarified in the crib is when your trouble began. She would've looked at them and thought, Oh Christ!"

"Christ'd be an odd thought out there in the Sahara."

"Not for her. Second-most important prophet to the Muslims —but her enemy I'm goddamned sure!"

"Sounds like you had occasion to hold a cross to her face."

"Well, if I hadn't been in so much pain maybe I'd have thought of it. When I first saw her she was wearing a skullcap the color of dry blood. Her tow hair flared out turning her head into a sundog. She'd stuck a bare throwing dagger through a red sash. Blue tunic, white pants, black English riding boots—I gasped like some callow girl seeing a senior class idol in the shower. How men with their funky little faucets can rise to such occasions I'm damned if I know. I guess they run blind on testosterone for a while, then if they canna' hook up their balls to their brains they start wars. She was murderously beautiful standing there talking to the *bash agha,* the backs of her hands splayed on her hips. Once I'd seen her I couldn't shake her out of my head, but I could never picture her face either. Tell you something about that dagger: it was serrated, it had a channel scored into the blade for dry poison. The handle was camel bone aged like amber.

"Her beauty was a contagion. I woke up one morning and sat by my window thinking what to do that day and feeling downright poxy. All I could think about was Ulrike—and I was a woman with plenty to do. *I'm sick of it,* I said. It was interesting I said sick of it, not sick of her. I was sick of her beauty. I got up to see if I could cobble up a useful day when Rose said, *You're sick of it?— we're all sick of it!* Rose was the interlocutor in my head. Still is. Never quite decided who she's talking to. Our dialogue gets quirky at times. For example, I looked into Rose's eyes in my mirror and I said, Ulrike is sick of it.

"I didn't know what I meant, but it is true that there are at least two kinds of great beauties among women. The first, which is the kind I've always liked, says to you, You think I'm beautiful? How nice we agree, thank you very much! And she means it. But the second kind acts as if you've pooped your knickers. She's out to spank you for noticing."

"What does the second kind of woman do if you don't notice her, I mean pretend you don't?" he asked.

"Oh never play that game, it's not fitting for a real human being. Give it up if you play it."

He remembers basking in the sea oats, a suckling of the sun over Great South Bay.

"It's quite clear to me now, after all these years, Rose had something to say to me that morning. If I'd listened it would have kept me safe. But the trouble with my banter back then is that I was a bit of all right myself. Not the kind of drop-dead gorgeous Ulrike was, but a sort of heroic beauty. Come to think of it, neither of us were the kind men like to fuck, not Ulrike because you knew instinctively you might wither, not me because it takes old souls to fuck heroic girls."

Bo has returned from the sea oats but he holds his nose away from her latest words like a wolf sniffing. It can't have been news of his mother's beauty. Rose lets him gather his wits.

"Amir is my interlocutor. I don't know who he's talking to either. But the conversation is the only way I can get through hard times. I talk formally, he's idiomatic . . . "

That feral smile interrupts him, uninhibited, sexual.

"Soon she was wearing Ben Aissa like an amulet, Ulrike was. She persuaded him one day to take her to see the *naib* of the Aissaoua dervish brotherhood. Even when their tambourines were silent the Aissaouas were a presence. Things went into slow motion around the *naib*. Like so many Bedouins, you couldn't tell his age. They just attain a certain look and keep it until they die. Ulrike had seen the *naib* in the marketplace and wanted to paint him. That meant she was serious, if only because she couldn't afford much paint. I can't be sure if he'd seen her sketches. I think he had. They were everywhere.

"In spite of the Koranic proscription against rendering the human figure, the Arabs had become rather inured by all the Orientalist painters romanticizing them. The superstitious among them—that would be the majority—feared that a photograph or sketch made off with the subject's soul. They didn't mention this concern to the French because if the French had souls it might be beneficial for other foreigners to steal them.

"I'll never forget her encounter with the *naib* Si Mahmoud ben Ali, though I'd gladly forget everything about her if I could. She came wearing soft red spahi boots with tassels, white jodhpurs and blue shirt with a black scarf around her waist. She usually walked around with a pack of paints, brushes, charcoals and knives on her back. She had a sort of bravura loping gait, kicking her feet out in front of her. She was poor, so she worked on fiberboard, burlap, wrapping paper, anything she could find, even the backs of old jackets. The children were always bringing her scraps to paint or draw on.

"She sat down cross-legged, Arab fashion, in front of the old man and just looked at him, not smiling but refraining from her usual mocking cocked-head look. He stared into her glittering eyes. He shaded his own with his hand. Then he thrust an open palm at her and she reached over her shoulder and pulled out a board like an Amazon drawing an arrow and started to paint. A gang of Bedouins sat hushed as herons staring at her. She must have worked very fast for well over an hour. Like the Arabs she never brushed off the flies. She just painted holding the board at the top with the bottom balanced above her knees and a brush in her teeth. When she was done she turned to Ben Aissa, who had been squatting next to her, and said she would finish it later. He told her to show it to the marabout.

"When she did Si Mahmoud said, 'Allah has given you a great gift.' She handed the painting to him, gestured Arab-fashion heart to mouth to head and walked off in that heroic gait. I am damned to this day if I know if it was magnanimity I saw or something like flinging a G-string to sailors. I am as distressed now by the gesture as I was then. Something else I noticed. The women idolized her, but I never saw a man who liked her. I saw plenty who were obsessed by her. She wanted to travel with the Ouled Nail, to live with them. Ben Aissa could arrange this. His mother came from this tribe. He was friendly with their caid.

"You'd have to know what kind of woman I was to take this all in without a word. Now that's quite a mouthful, my young sailor, because I didn't know what kind of woman I was. I thought I did.

"No man would ever say, even if he felt his balls shrivel under her stare, that Ulrike was anything but beautiful. Arabs, Bedouins react strangely to blondes. There's some racial lore that they're ghosts, maybe djinn. Redheads they're more comfortable with. Many Berbers are red-haired. It's not unheard of among the Arabs—Crusader's disease. The Arabs took me with a little humor and much good will. Ulrike they took with awe and disquiet. They knew I understood and respected them. I was after all something of a scholar. They felt I had the eyes of a djinn. I was athletic, had done some mountain climbing and skiing and was as able on a horse as any Bedouin. Like them, I could shoot a bird out of the sky one-armed galloping. They admired this. I was, like many Scots, a bit laconic. This, with my three languages, impressed a race easily made drunk on words. Above all things Arabs revere the spoken word. That is the key to understanding their nature. They're like the Celts, creatures of their fables, and they had woven me into their fables.

"Ulrike too was close-mouthed. I think she had the good sense to know she was ignorant. She'd barely outgrown that god-awful stage beautiful girls go through when they're enchanted by their own power to bewitch. We were quite a pair out there on the Sahara, serious Celtic me, cantankerous Teuton her. From the first moment she laid eyes on me I could sense her juices run. The only time I ever saw that glacier melt was when she blushed to see me watch her nipples rise. So this I knew about Ulrike, that no matter what her loony head told her, her body wisdom was toward women. It was not a naughty secret to me. She studied me for signals as only an artist can and when their absence unnerved her she looked as if she were about to reach over and feel my crotch to make sure.

"I felt that if I were a man I'd probably want to fuck her brains out and walk off without a word, and I didn't like that feeling. I think that's where the trouble started. It made her mad. I was the kind of girl—I really wasn't a woman yet, although everybody treated me as if I were entering middle age—who would take a good man to bed out of his need, out of kindness. My mind was simply not blotted out by the notion of love. I didn't know what love is and it didn't bother me. It didn't occur to me that anybody belonged to me or that I belonged to anybody. Soren and I were better friends than either of us ever had. And we were coming to feel that way about Ben Aissa.

"So I suppose Ulrike thought Soren and Ben Aissa belonged to me. I had the allegiance of two serious men who didn't so much want to poke me as enjoy my friendship, and she wanted to fathom that and, if possible, have it.

"Long before we became lovers in England Ben Aissa would play with my hair in the cool night air, he would dip his forehead to mine and look into my eyes until we were dizzy. We would sing to each other, Arab songs and highland songs. He would sit at my feet and play his khyter until I fell asleep. Perhaps we were like brother and sister, or even mother and son, or perhaps it was the sort of love two people conspire not to name lest it flee, I don't know. Some ideas don't like being named. But I knew that Ulrike Theiss was a spoiler, a trifler. I knew she was a thief of invisible treasures, a woman with whom you could not lie down assured she would be there when you woke. I spent a good deal of time, more than was good, rummaging in Ulrike's mind. It was like exploring an Egyptian tomb with wooden matches. I had sexual fantasies that stirred my bowels and I would have staked my life on her having none. A dog you can observe dreaming, a cat no. Maybe a shark's a better analogy—the perfect killing machine. You move, it strikes, a superb, unremitting animal. I saw her like that. Do sharks dream? Can you trust a being who doesn't dream?"

17

"The Sufis say when the student is ready the teacher appears. What blinds us is what we want. I don't know how many teachers appeared the day Ulrike returned from her trek with the Ouled Nail, but I must have wanted a lot because I heard no more than a story.

"Ben Aissa thought he wanted to study horticulture in Edinburgh. That was before calculus in all its splendor ambushed him at Oxford. I don't think he envisioned the future. It's not a Muslim trait. To envision the future is to trespass. As for me, I was more Sufi than Muslim, but I think I believed we would always be together.

"Everything has a harbinger. Few are welcome. I listened to what happened during the Ouled Nail's travels as if it were a bedtime story. A fellow seeker, Si Achmed Arzouan, a Qadiri adept, was the storyteller. Si Achmed looked like a famished falcon. His hope of seeing the emerald light lived in his silence. When Si Achmed spoke one listened. That he paid me the honor of telling me what happened cost him a great deal.

" 'Salaam alaykum, my friend.'

" 'Wa alaykum salaam, lady.'

" 'Something is wrong?'

"Si Achmed violently jerked his thumb in Ulrike's direction. The clans were dismounting in the center of town. Many of their people were semi-nomadic, like Ben Aissa, and had homes to go to. The camels were braying and nipping irritably. Dust hung in the air. He shoved two fingers at my eyes.

" 'It's not news to me, Si Achmed, that the foreign lady has the evil eye.'

"Si Achmed scanned the horizon, as Bedouins do, to get his bearings. Part of his world had flown apart. The psychic ecology of the Bedouins is as fragile as their environment. Their quarrel with the French was not political or even religious. It rested with their perception of the French as disturbers of the peace. And this was now their quarrel with Ulrike.

"One of France's biggest offenses was its desire to count the Bedouins, to conduct a census. This was hardly a mystical objective, since militarily they might very well want to know how many riflemen were out there on the vast Sahara. The Bedouins understood this, but their objection was based on France's trifling with the order of things. They could deal with the theft of children by the Tuaregs, with the perfidy of the Chaamba, with war and catastrophe, but when they perceived evil their equanimity fled and they became disordered. I think they distrusted the French no more than they distrust any townsmen.

"Si Achmed sat on the ground and breathed a melancholy tune into his khyter. He said, 'Allah has put the viper down among us for a reason. Who am I to question the maker of all things? He has not blinded me and so I see at his behest. Perhaps he does not wish me to be made happy by what I see. And if I am unhappy should I complain?'

" 'That is a serious question, Si Achmed, and Allah has not granted me the answer. If you wish to remain silent I am content.'

"He played his flute a while longer. Then he said, 'You are my sister, Rose MacQuarrie. Allah in his compassion has permitted you to be an Arab. I do not wish you to be made ill by this devil.'

"He then handed me a smooth black stone in the shape of a teardrop. It had been worn smooth by thousands of thunderous floods in a wadi and on both sides the hand of Fatima, the

Prophet's daughter, had been etched.

"He said, 'Protect yourself.'

"I have this amulet still. I made prayers with it in my hand. They didn't work. Or if they did work it was not as I wanted them to work. I had one pink and lovely ambition for myself as a sexual person, that my lover, whoever he might be, would be about a pregnant me as a bee about a rose. Ben Aissa would have yearned that way for me. But it was too late. I'd lost him.

"You'd say of seriously alert women we don't miss much. With Ulrike it didn't matter. Whether you were an Ouled Nail, a Targui, a Foreign Legion captain, a shatt, an erg, a wadi or a mud mosque, you were goddamned well going to be whatever she wanted you to be."

Rose's eyes close as she travels inward to recover the sense of it. She throws her hands wide. "I haven't got it, I can't describe what I mean. Take for example Neurath Nachtigal, a German Spahi captain locally famous for what one would have to call his beauty. She charcoaled him as if she'd been on her back with her head between his toes looking up. There he was staring down at his open fly with a riding crop between his fingers. I don't know how it would've looked in black and white, but she'd colored it and it was maniacal. Everybody who saw it guffawed. Then there was the artist Etienne Dinet's tomb in Bou Saada. She plunked it down in Ouargla and painted a lovely Ouled Nail peeing in a garden path.

"She liked to sit cross-legged on rooftops doing street scenes in pencil, ink, charcoal, watercolor and oil. She especially liked to paint groups of people from overhead. I remember one painting of a clique of Arabs gambling cross-legged in a circle. When you looked a second time you saw a middle-aged French strumpet in the circle grinning up at the artist.

"She cracked the solemnity of the Arabs. The women tittered

behind their veils and touched her arm for luck. The men couldn't bring themselves to smile at her so they smiled at each other. She wasn't like boyish little Isabelle Eberhardt, who thought the froggies quite grand but the Arabs grander.

"Ulrike painted alternate realities. No, that's wrong, they were parallel realities. When you looked at them you wondered why you hadn't seen it. One of her most remarkable characteristics was that you always wondered how you could have missed something so obvious."

Amir's smile emboldens her to say, "You're her son, do I exaggerate?"

He opens the palm of his hand to prompt her to get on with it.

"Well, I'm circling the story of the lovesick prefect. It was clear she was teaching herself to paint."

Distress sacks his face. He glances back at her portrait. The girl in that portrait should not have to tell this story.

"She was painting the police prefect's wife in el-Kantara. Lovely child from Provence, but she was wall-eyed. That's how I discovered Ulrike was a banshee. The decent thing to do was to correct this little meanness of chance. Oh, Ulrike claimed that's what she planned to do, that she was just painting the bad eye for perspective and would fix it at the last, but the Arab servants filched the picture and next thing you know they're hoisting it around town on a stick. The prefect, who'd been kind to Ulrike, went bonkers, not because he was embarrassed but because he loved his wife.

"Well, I should tell you, Ulrike had made the girl's face comically lopsided, as if one side had slipped. Well, in fact, a lot of us have lopsided faces, which you see when we smile, but this was a grotesquery, which she called her process. Her process was to make horses' asses of people. I know her claim has some merit in the history of technique, but some little ratchet clicked in my head. Rose, I said, watch out, this is a mean girl.

"Her habit of making ambitious oils of the topography soon played into Monsieur le Prefect's hands. She was sitting cross-legged up on a ridge outside el-Kantara one morning. She'd been painting on the back of a canvas jacket that she'd torn and stretched when she ran out of canvas and she'd stopped to mix paints. She was adept at this. The Arab women were forever bringing her various philters and compounds which they used for potions, foods and dyes, and Ulrike made some of the most gorgeous colors I've ever seen.

"That's what she was doing the morning Jacques Charlet snuck up behind her in the sand and said, 'Sprechen zie Deutsche, fraulein?' She said without turning, 'Javohl, mein herr.' She spoke perfect German, Preusse Deutsche, but bad Arabic and French.

"The prefect said, 'In that case, fraulein, I must ask you to come with me to answer some questions.' 'What for?' she said. 'Suspicion of working for German intelligence,' he said.

"I've only the prefect's wife as a source for this, and according to the wife, Ulrike turned around and said, 'You crazy bastard, I'm an American, I wouldn't know German intelligence from French intelligence and in either case I don't think there is any!' I suspect Charlet was a bit amused.

"But he carted her off to the police station and locked her up, telling her that a Sûreté officer would arrive in a few days to interrogate her in her own language. In the meantime her paintings and drawings were confiscated. She might have demanded to see an American consul but I'm not sure she did. I just don't think it was in her nature to ask anybody for help. Besides, she was disposed to enjoy men making fools of themselves. I don't know if Charlet really called the Sûreté. I doubt it. He was lovesick, not loony. Then too, Ulrike probably made an entertaining guest. Madame Charlet told me that in the second day of her captivity

Ulrike took to speaking only German.

"She would've been raped more than once had the Arabs perceived her as the French did, but her position among the Arabs is what saved her from the dregs of European humanity. Even a French infantryman figured the pleasure of sodomizing the Nazi bitch was hardly worth a shot through the throat from a Bedouin's rifle.

"Ben Aissa and I had been back in el-Kantara for three months or more. I had been unable to tell Soren how our relationship had changed, more because Soren was somehow unavailable than because I found it too painful. We had our usual conversations, far ranging and engaging, but we could not restore the fine-tuning and depth we had enjoyed before I left. He was distracted and struck me to my amazement as a bit foolish.

"This was the situation when Luc d'Ambasle prevailed on poor Charlet and took Ulrike off to the fort.

"Far be it for dear Soren to fathom how boorish the subtle French were with the even subtler Arabs. It never occurred to him that d'Ambasle would take Ulrike under military escort to the fort, just as it didn't occur to d'Ambasle how doing it would look to the Arabs. I can imagine poor Soren remonstrating with his friend, 'My God, Luc, how could you do such a thing? It is better to steal from the Arabs than piss on their rubrics of hospitality.' And I can hear that thick d'Ambasle saying, 'The dirty Arabs, no matter what the hell you do or don't do, they'll do what's perverse!' To which I'm sure Soren must have said, 'Luc, I have told you a hundred times the Chaamba are not the sum total of the Arab race, they are not even Arabs, they are Tuaregs and your stooges.'

"It was an interesting friendship, these two aristocrats. Luc-Antoine d'Ambasle was younger, handsome with the added virtue of seeming unaware of it. He found Soren useful, generous, puzzling. Why in hell would a rich Swedish count choose to live in el-Kantara? I'm sure he thought at first it was sordid, the waifs perhaps. He didn't discover right off—he didn't know then—that Soren was a Muslim. When he realized the older man had the whole of the Maghrib Arabs' history in his head he began to use him.

"What Soren saw in d'Ambasle is more elusive. A good man doing the wrong thing is always fascinating. The Nazis were not very interesting, were they? Vile thugs. But the Prussian and Saxon swells who suffered them were interesting indeed. 'I'm not a damned T.E. Lawrence, you know,' Luc once told Soren in my presence. 'Yes, I do know,' Soren replied, 'that's why I like you. By the way, Colonel Lawrence's friend, R.V.C. Bodley, is in town, did you know?'

"That was so typical of Soren. He always raised the level of information over the din of discord. Luc said, 'Yes, well, you'd better tell the bastard we're not Turks.'

"Soren said, 'Oh, he knows, Luc, he's cut entirely of another cloth, I assure you. I think he's a rather gentle man.' Luc replied, 'If you say so, Soren. Perhaps you would introduce us.' I think—this is the first time I've thought it, really—that what Soren saw in d'Ambasle was a man who wished to grow, and Soren knew how rare that is.

"So it wasn't too surprising that d'Ambasle saw his mistake. He seized on Ben Aissa's reappearance to ask Soren to get the *bash agha* to intercede. 'Soren,' he said, 'perhaps our friend, the *bash agha*, might take Monsieur Charlet's problem blonde to your villa, and for the love of Allah may he do it conspicuously!'

"Corinne Charlet, who was a bit enamored of Ulrike and not the least offended by her painting, confided to me while we were buying produce that Count Soren von Melen had contacted his friend d'Ambasle about Ulrike's predicament. It was then that the cause of Soren's distraction dawned on me. The Arabs presumed

Ulrike was their guest. After all, they'd been the ones to show her hospitality. So when the spahis rode her off to the fort they might as well have raped a marabout's daughter and turned her out naked in the dust.

"Soren von Melen could have remonstrated with Luc-Antoine till their friendship turned sour and could never have convinced him that Ulrike's predicament was France's. The colonel was simply doing his friend a favor. The colonel knew perfectly well that the prefect had been a fathead but he wasn't about to concede that the whole colonial system was at stake. Only an Arab, a certain kind of Arab, could open the colonel's third eye, and, as it turned out, that Arab was Ben Aissa—so at least the surprisingly shrewd d'Ambasle conveyed to Soren, who by then was set up to become anybody's dupe. Ben Aissa obliged Soren, or so I thought, and rode out to the fort.

"The Arabs viewed these forts as ovens where the French baked themselves. Ben Aissa told the colonel that Ulrike for some reason tickled the natives' fancy and it would be proof the French had lost their humor, a quality the Arabs admired, if they were to persist in treating her like a spy.

"Ben Aissa was a charming young man and Luc-Antoine was an aristocrat. Put to him this way, Ben Aissa's point seemed well taken. The problem was saving Charlet's face, hence colonial rule, and Ben Aissa proved more than equal to this task.

" 'Look,' he said, 'my people are childlike, you know that. So it must be put to Monsieur le Prefect and your superiors at the Arab Bureau that, knowing the Arabs, and knowing that the Germans are trying to stir them up, it seemed best to humor them. Particularly because you have the word of Count Soren von Melen and the altogether admirable Mlle. Rose MacQuarrie that the American girl doesn't give a fig for politics.'

"Well, Luc-Antoine knew that Monsieur *le Bash Agha* was

talking down to him. But he was grateful, as well he should have been. And for my part, I saw our wonderful young Arab protégé acting in our own best interests. Really, Amir, I did."

If Amir looks dubious it's because he can't imagine a face lit by such intelligence turning away from so obvious a thing: Ben Aissa was himself taken with the blonde with the crazy eyes.

Neither of them ignore the unruly electricity in the room, but it's only then that Rose fathoms how very much he likes her, and then she feels her bones and tendons part, so that when she continues with her story she senses another story beginning.

"Ben Aissa was always observant about what people wanted. My wanting to know more about the dervishes seemed to him a modest ambition. He was himself an acolyte. So he arranged for me to go to Guemar to meet the marabout Mu'Awiyya ben Khalid, who was said to be descended from the western Umayyads who ruled Al-Andalus.

"Are you up on Arab history, Amir?"

"It was my minor at Columbia."

"Unfortunately it didn't dispel your confusion, did it? I'm sure your professors were charmed by your name."

"Not really. They seemed ill at ease having an Arab studying his own history."

"Of course! They couldn't be as patronizing as they might have been, you see. Now, this marabout, he was a marvelous man. I wanted to see his adepts walk barefoot on coals and pass skewers through their cheeks without leaving a mark. 'Yes, yes, you can see such things,' Ben Khalid told me impatiently, 'but why do you wish to waste your time? They're for ignorant people who thirst for illumination but do not have the eye to find it. We do such things for them. Their thirst must be respected, but it is crude.'

"An interesting thing happened while Ben Khalid talked to me, Amir. He started off in French, because that's how I addressed him, but halfway along he started speaking Arabic. At first I thought it was his way of shutting me out, but then I realized he knew I spoke it. And Ben Aissa hadn't told him! He just knew. In al-Andalus he would have been a scholar, a vizier perhaps, as Ben Aissa would have been a warrior-poet.

"At home Ben Aissa, like all Bedouins, could not be distinguished from his horse or rifle. In his date groves he was in rapt communion with every leaf, every grain of earth. Among a people in concert with their environment he was singularly invisible. And yet he had ferocious curiosity. When I took him shopping, instead of chafing like most men, he'd examine the stitchery of garments, hold their colors up to the light. He was a superb leather worker and jeweler. He couldn't drive, but once in Yorkshire when our little roadster broke down he took it apart and got it running again. He had so many parts laid out on the road that I burst out laughing seeing this *bash agha* in the north country homing in on the problem as if he were sighting his rifle.

"Like many Arabs, he had a natural affinity for numbers. He calculated faster than any cashier and sometimes nonplussed them when he'd laugh and ask them to add up a bill again. He was an excellent man in so many ways.

"The marabout was very old. He didn't know how old. Allah does the counting. The Umayyads were famously red-headed. He liked to touch my red hair. I think he was in love with me. Nothing carnal. We were teacher and disciple, and besides, he was blessedly past all of that silly rigmarole. Goethe and Yeats notwithstanding, Amir, some men do get past the craziness. You will early on, I predict, if you haven't already."

"Have you?"

She sneezes a little smile. "One has relapses."

It's her turn to grope the room, touching things to regain her balance. This spawn of the creature has much of Soren von Melen in him. His directness comes from some impregnable sorrow.

"Ulrike had stirred up blizzards of sketches in places like el-Kantara, where you were conceived, Setif, Ouargla, Bou Saada, wherever her fancy blew her. Her sketches of the Arabs were reverent. What I remember—you've seen them—is the line. She could draw a Bedouin girl nursing a baby with what seemed like one pure line, no shading or hatching. There was a superb elegance to her drawings, rather like the desert itself. Famous artists have been praised for this quality. Picasso, for example. Yet she gave these sketches away as if they were Weimar marks.

"I suppose she earned her bed and board that way. I must say I admired this quality. It was blithe, arrogant. But it was really her sketches of the French everybody loved, even some of the French. They were sly. She had a wonderful eye for that toppled look of the absinthe drinker, especially those women flat on their cushy European tushies in doorways. The dissolute held a special fascination for her. I can't imagine how many sketches she gave to the Legionnaires. They were thrilled. If they had looked closely they would have seen mockery.

"The Arabs collected her sketches of the French and used them like Tarot cards, laughing like gurgling brooks. They weren't half so fond of their own portraits. I don't think any of the French were so dimwitted as to take this for admiration. Ulrike kept up a kind of running in-joke with *les indigenes,* as the froggies called them when they were being proper. If she'd been a flag the Arabs would have raised her. The con was that the Arabs and the French would signal to each other that she was crazy. That way the Arabs could keep on enjoying her antics and the French could dismiss them. But as far as the Arabs were concerned the joke was on the French."

18

"I don't think either of us mentioned Ulrike while we were in England. We had seen her around el-Kantara. Everyone had. I do wonder now if Ben Aissa thought of her. I know I did. I see now I must admit seeing her was an incentive to return. Ben Aissa and I were not lovers when we left for England. I had been playing the lady to his boy, but it was a charade and nobody knew that better than Soren. He had played a kind of trick on himself and he had put at risk his love for me and his genuine friendship for Ben Aissa. I was angry with him. I did owe him a great deal—love, physical pleasure, a grand experience—but I was angry that he had fobbed me off. If these thoughts had any chance of surfacing that was all dampened by the situation when I returned to el-Kantara from the *zawiyya* in Bou Saada.

"La Blonde had fallen ill in the Cockroach Hotel, L'Hotel des Cafards, which is what everyone called La Maison des Artistes. Soren had mustered your namesake, the boy Amir, and gone to fetch Ulrike to his villa. Ulrike was quite ill when we arrived— malaria, dysentery, God knows what else. The French helpfully suggested syphilis. But Monsieur Le Docteur Husserle, a Belgian Huguenot who thought the French melodramatic, prescribed quinidine, rest and decent food. He forbade smoking, which was a great imposition on Ulrike, and alcohol, which was not.

"She was not responding to treatment when Ben Aissa and I reappeared. Soren said, 'I wonder, Rose, if you might nurse the girl.' He felt awkward around Ulrike. The idea of bathing her appealed to me.

"La Blonde seemed grateful that another fair woman had come to nurse her. First I nursed her out of her insistence she'd been poisoned, not because it was unlikely—poison and potions were common—but because Husserle would have known. He'd treated such cases. She was like a child inviting a friend into some secret cubby where the two of them could giggle and share secrets. As sick as she was, puking on the half hour, she put me immediately under her spell. She would play with my hair while I tried to get soup into her. She would smooth my eyebrows and trace my lips with her fingers.

"Months passed. Doctor Husserle visited every few days. Soren paid him each time on the spot. A muezzin in town would start the day. Then Amir would play his khyter as the sun cleared the villa's walls. I would bring in breakfast. In the second month of her illness Ulrike was able to hold tea down. Then Soren would design a floral arrangement and bring it in while I read to Ulrike. She liked *Die Leiden des jungen Werthers (The Sorrows of Young Werther),* morbid crap—it made Goethe famous. I detested it, but I read it bravely in my best chemical German, which amused her.

"The absence of our loved one, Ben Aissa, was the cause of hushed whispering with Soren. Even now I wonder about it. Ben Aissa knew we were caring for Ulrike. He had spoken to her the night before he left with a large hunting party, some of his cousins among them. Soren remarked that the party was more like a harka, a raiding party, and that raised my eyebrow, but no more.

Ben Aissa was apolitical. He was content for somebody's grandchildren to oust the French.

"Ulrike verged on more than recovery. I sensed it because I too verged. Carnal love between women was far from repugnant to me. In the abstract I like the idea very much. It has a sculptural purity. But I wasn't sure it was my dish of tea. Nor was I the sort of woman other women encroach in that way.

"By the time it became clear Ulrike would get well I needed rescue from an impending crisis. I was fairly tingling from her stroking my arm and face. I knew I would have to decide what to do, since she had already decided. In fact I'm not sure she decided such things, she just . . . did them. Luck came from the *marabout* Mu'awiyya ben Khalid. He sent word he wished to see me. I told Soren I thought I should go.

"At his *zawiyya* in Guemar I was ushered into an enormous rectangular room with almost no furnishing. Somewhere *nira*, Arab flutes, and *derbuka*, drums, were being played, probably in an anteroom. Two middle-aged men appeared out of nowhere, took me by the arms and rushed me down the length of the room into a smaller room where they dumped me at the feet of the *marabout,* literally threw me down in front of him. The tempo of the music picked up during this exercise. I was frightened, but I knew enough to bow my head very low before him. He told me in Arabic to sit up. He offered me a candy, which I took. Then he searched my eyes. The music had stopped and we were alone. He leaned over and put both forefingers in my ears. He held them there for maybe ten seconds, then pulled them away explosively.

"Finally he said, 'I will tell you all that you are able to hear. Go home, prepare and come back in a month, Inshallah! First, listen, Red Hair: because you are honorable, too much will be asked.' I bowed again, rose and left. That was the protocol. I knew that much. I had been accepted, I would be initiated and given my *zikhr,* and I thought that his warning meant that the Sufis would ask a very great deal of me. It is not what he meant at all, as I found out when I returned to Bou Saada.

"The villa was empty. It was customarily unlocked, but the outer doors were swung wide and even the gates were open. I went to the garden, calling Soren. His tools were strewn about, dead flowers dried on the walkways. Soren, I called, Count Von

Melen! I heard only my own words exploring the rooms. Amir! Nothing but my own sound. I climbed the little tower Soren had built for his telescope and I noticed Souad, the cook, stomping clothes down in the wadi. Soren had a generator to suck up water from a hundred-and-twenty-foot well, but Souad preferred the old way. I called to her and motioned that I would come down to meet her. Aside from her porcelain skin and beautiful Ouled Nail tattoos, she was remarkable for her lively eyes, but now they were dull as terra cotta.

"I asked, 'Where is everybody?' 'Nasr-ed-Din Soren,' she said, 'has taken rooms in town.' 'What!' She nodded. 'The American woman, where is she?' 'Allah knows.' And he was not talking through Souad. 'Amir?' 'Poof!' she said. 'You look hungry, I will make you supper,' she said. I was hungry. And tired. I nodded and went in.

"I made myself tea and, saucer in hand, inspected the rooms, which were eight-sidedly necklaced around a courtyard and garden. Soren's rooms were untouched. His bed was made. His favorite bush jacket, the one he wore habitually, was draped over a chair. His favorite book, the one he'd read a hundred times, Marcus Aurelius' *Meditations,* lay face down on his table. For all the beauty of Soren's villa, it was spartan, a quality the Bedouin admired. I picked up the *Meditations.* It was open to Book Eight, page 124. Soren had scribbled a star next to this passage: *This disappointment serves you right. You would rather hope for goodness tomorrow than practice it today.*

"I was working in the garden three days later, catching up, when Soren came through the gates. I stood when I heard them creak as he threw their bolts. He approached slowly and when I could see his features I saw that he was smiling like a boy who had been foolish. 'I'll have Souad make us tea,' I said. He nodded. We sat in the garden and I told him about the *marabout* and his warning. 'Yes,' Soren said, 'I'm afraid he's right—when you are honorable too much is asked.'

" 'I don't know if we shall see our young man again, Rose. No, I don't. His cousins have returned and said he went on to Ouargla, Inshallah. Well, that would be where the tribe would be this time of year. Amir is gone too. Ben Aissa thrashed him one morning and he fled. I was too distraught to investigate right.'

" 'You didn't stop him?' I said.

" 'No, Rose, something had happened to upset the balance of everything. I was bringing flowers to the German woman's room and I found them there together in bed.'

"He stared at me until it sank in. It was so strange. My life was sliding off a precipice and all I could think was that Soren was calling her the German woman. Ben Aissa and Ulrike? The man who hadn't glanced twice at some of the most beautiful girls in England when they abandoned their breeding to signal him? The woman I nursed back to health, posed for?

"I got up and walked once around the courtyard. I stopped at the opposite end, stooped and began loosening the earth around some jasmine. Soren sat for a while with his tea in his lap. Then he rose and came to my side, knelt down, and started working too. He bent his head leftwards and low to see my face and said, 'The jasmine are too fabled and full of themselves to enjoy your tears, but the roses would, the white ones, Rose.'

"The year I spent listening to Mu'awiyya ben Khalid healed fresh wounds before they festered. I was free to come and go and spent as much time as I could with Soren. During one of those visits I heard about you, Amir. That is, I heard that Ulrike was hauling her belly around town. You were on the way, Amir.

"Then I received a message from Soren at Guemar: *Ben Aissa interred at Ouled Djellal. Cousins brought him there shot through heart. Shall I make inquiries?*

"Of course we should have made inquiries. But we didn't. I felt I knew what happened. At first I didn't know I knew. The clue was that I had been missing the boy Amir, the way you miss the dog after a divorce. I knew that Amir, fiercely loyal to Soren and me, had found them out—Ulrike and Ben Aissa. Maybe that's why Ben Aissa thrashed him. I think Amir hunted Ben Aissa down and killed him. I think Ben Aissa had taken to the desert in remorse, shame perhaps. Maybe he even knew Amir would kill him. It was useless to try to find the boy. He had no kin. The Bedouins would take him in.

~

"All these events led to the Honey Wagon, Soren's next project. That's what he called the old tank truck he bought from the French army. He knew that diseases of filth prospered in neighborhoods without sanitation, so he decided to hire two young men to pump out latrines. They would drive the honey wagon off into the desert and pump it out where the sun would devour impurities.

"This piece of altruism promptly turned into a very profitable business for Soren's two young men because better-off property owners were soon paying for the service, even for their tenants.

"Metaphorically, trucking the shit out was a healthy thing to do, but I can't say it gave Soren a new lease on life. We worked together in the garden, read the Sufis—Rumi, Ibn Al Arabi, Hafiz, and the others—and eventually Soren pared away a portion of his villa to build a mosque. He turned it over to Mu'awiyya ben Khaled and his Guemari Sufis.

"I was thinking about what had happened, wishing I could see Amir, as I sat next to Soren one day, our backs to the mosque. After a while he leaned his head against my bosom and said, 'Rose, I'm so mortified.' I'd started to speak when I realized he was gone.

"He came to understand, you see, that fobbing me off on Ben Aissa was an impure thing. It soiled us both. As a chemist and horticulturist, he knew all about such things and it offended his soul. He handed me off to a younger man without any regard for my own uniqueness. He just presumed that a younger woman required a younger man. He would not steal my youth—that, I think, is the gentlemanly way of regarding one's contempt for another's individuality. He was concerned how things would look, not how they were. Of course I was attracted to Ben Aissa, as Soren was himself. But it did not mean I would make love to him. I knew exactly how Soren was mortified. But we had those three untroubled years in the end—more than most people have.

"As for me, as I had been bold enough once to market my rusty rose in front of him, I should have been bold enough to say, 'Look here, Count von Melen, I am offended by your nurturing your public image at my expense. The world is full of handsome Arabs, and handsome Scots for that matter, and you must refrain from pimping me out to whoever interests you.'

"Then there was Amir. We both ruined that faithful boy, your namesake. We were both so enamored of the *bash agha*. If I could choose your father for you, I would choose Amir. It was a stupid game we had played, and I sat there in the garden for a long time with the dead count on my breast, thinking that for such an intelligent and grown-up woman I had made a mess of things. But that moment of humility did not move me to forgive Ulrike or even suggest to me I ought to. Of what has she ever repented?"

Bo has more sense than to reply.

~

Bo has the habit when he's ill or confused or both to lie down in some interesting place wherever he is—halfway into a closet, at the foot of a bookcase or window, alongside a wall or, if aboard ship, a bulkhead. Tucking a small window seat cushion under his head, pulling one of Rose's blankets over him, he settles down at the foot of a floor-to-ceiling bookcase near the fireplace.

On cold nights Rose sleeps in a small room off her study to enjoy the radiating warmth of the back of the fireplace. They'd said goodnight an hour earlier. If she had come sooner she would have found him sitting in the bay window watching the snow fall. Now he rests on his right side, his spine lined up against the bottom row of books in her bookcase. She stands over him barefooted in her nightgown for several minutes until he becomes aware of her. When she sees the street light play green in his eyes she thinks of *al khidr*, the Green One of Islamic lore, and of the nights she saw the sufi dervishes sleep on their mats.

She reaches down without kneeling and he puts his hand in hers. She pulls and he rises. She pulls him towards the door to her room and turns to smile at him.

Whether it was the gift in Rose to give or in Amir to take, no woman's loving later is ever as fulfilling.

19

Vestris needs another week before she'll be ready to sail home to Elizabeth. Bo has promised Captain Joe Sturdevant to sail with her. He hitchhikes west across Scotland to Port Glasgow. Out on the highway he tries to whistle *Greensleeves,* but he finds himself compelled to talk to the lorries grinding by. *I have made love to a lovely woman. She poisoned me and now I'm waiting to die, he tells the lorries. Yes, I know the name of the poison. No, there's no antidote. What's its name? The truth.*

He feels relieved. He feels the relief of knowing what's going to happen, what's going to kill him.

I won't think of it now, he tells himself. This elegant poison should be allowed to do its work. I'll get ready. A poisoned man has no constraint. He is fully licensed to do anything. I will do anything.

Vestris should have been turned into razor blades a long time ago. But he's happy to see her. Sturdevant, a fervid storm-lover, takes him to a pub for a drink. "So Bo," he says, "didja get laid or see a ghost, I can't tell which." He can see he won't get an answer.

~

Seamen, Bedouin and homeless people are bound by a common madness. They know that those who can breathe and think inside the shtetl of anything are at bottom untrustworthy. Only mobility is trustworthy. Seamen strive against a greater paradox, being encapsulated in their fo'c's'les and pounding engine rooms in the navel of emptiness. They're wary of touch and prefer in any case to buy it. Holidays are meaningless; seamen forbear them like extraterrestrial observers.

Rest in motion, Moira Sayre whispered to him. An adept of tae kwon do, he had no trouble honoring it. But returning to New York City from limbo at Christmas would daunt a flagellant of any suasion. The city of shadows and light sweats with trade and yammers to itself. People are convinced they know what they're about. Why not Tangier or Alexandria or Malindi or Copenhagen? What difference does it make? He has his papers. He can live anywhere. The difference is that he owns a loft on lower Broadway near Spring Street, subletting it all these years for some damned reason, maybe even no damned reason. Besides, New York is home. He became a fourteen-year-old drunk here and that's more seductive than any parental attachment. Ulrike is a drunk here. Sandro, his stepfather, was a drunk here. Violent and self-righteous, both of them. This is home. The only way in which it's not home is that it hasn't for all its sloppy effort imbued him, like so many drunks, with a fondness for dirt-bag paternalistic bartenders. He's not far gone enough to stomach them.

There's another reason New York is home. This reason he can smell and feel as a navigator but not comprehend. An artist like Edward Hopper, a poet like Hart Crane sensed it, but they too could not comprehend it nor did they need to. You could take your favorite latitude and cross it with your favorite longitude, that would hint at it. New York, Manhattan really, is preadolescent, pre-orgasmic, always verging. He would have died at a table in Chumley's or Minetta's if he had stayed. Maybe worse, maybe in a dumpster or alley. He would return, he'd always known, only if he were half dead so that the city might re-electrify him for a while. Then he would be . . . a what? A golem? He knows about golems because Hettie Warshaw told him about golems. Where is she now? Still alive? He had loved her stupidly. He was a boy then, she was middle-aged, a Holocaust survivor in the survivor capital of the world.

He knows the maps of many cities. None offer the order, the half-dressed possessibility of Manhattan. He knows the line between Spuyten Duyvil and Hell Gate as a starling might know it. He's possessive of the raw, drunk, disorderly East River. The patrician Hudson can be relied on to bank the sun at evening, the winds to flush the streets. Even the West Village doesn't so much conceal as flirt. Manhattan is a city on the edge, a princess whose madness is not yet manifest, whose beauty blinds. Her court is enthralled and silly, even when she goes unwashed and smells a bit ripe. He's tired and nurses a cobalt pain in his side which he covets as the oyster its pearl. If he'd utterly failed to rest in motion he wouldn't be here. Since he is here it won't hurt to see the only thing he owns that he doesn't carry on his shoulder: his useless loft. He feels savage. He takes his pay in Elizabeth, New Jersey, which reminds him how much he loathes power lines, and takes a bus to Manhattan. He catches a cab at the Port Authority. The driver, a Tajik with an attitude, takes him up to 72nd Street, through Central Park and downtown on the wrong side of town. He enjoys the ride. When they get to Spring and Broadway he gets out and stands by the driver's door. The meter says twenty-three dollars and seventy-five cents. "That was a nice ride," he says, "I hope you enjoyed it. Here's ten, keep the change, prick."

"I call the cops. You wan' me call the cops?"

"Yeah, show them your green card," he says, shouldering his white sea bag.

~

The loft smells like Calcutta. Worse, the walls are painted matte black, the floors high-gloss white—an utter disgrace of space. The best one can say for it is that it raises the ceilings, but with the floors seeming to fall away he feels like puking. He thinks he might need glasses. He stands just inside the door and begins to identify the smells—piss, marijuana, butts, beer, and something acrid, biting—unlaundered crotch. He rubs his right side under his ribs, the ribs once shattered in a Korean firefight. Maybe his adhesions are gnawing at him. It dawns on him that when he'd last seen the eleventh floor loft the walls were exposed brick, which he'd painted white. His tenant has pinned up lath and hung drywall, probably damaging the brickwork. He wishes he knew what she looked like so he could hate her better.

"Hey, what're you doin' here, man?"

He turns around to see one of those Jesus look-a-likes who started showing up like swamp gas after the Chianti ran out and before the old men in Washington decided there were too many young men. This young man is bare-chested and wears an Inca vest and black leather pants. Bo intends to answer, tries to, but he can't make the words come. I'm the landlord, he should say, something like that. But he just screws up his face into a stitchy little grin and walks over to the window to consider the east side of Broadway.

VHey, pull your ear plugs, man." He clamps the back of Bo's neck. Bo cracks the side of his face with his elbow, wheels and drop-kicks him, then straightens him out with another kick. He grabs him by the throat. "You live here?"

"Yeah, yeah, man, I pay the chick."

"Pay her what?"

"Stuff, man. Y'know."

"You need a new face. Grab your shit and get the fuck outta here."

~

The east light bangs rudely and wakes him early, but it's the short days and the black walls grinding towards him that wear him down. Deprived of light, deck seamen suffer. His gene pool is ambiguous on the subject—Germans accustomed to heading south like lemmings, hankering to disport themselves nakedly, Arabs adjusted to the prolonged blaze of light and cold thud of night.

The first night he sits propped against the wall by the freight elevator at the back of the loft, listening to the cables slapping and the howling draft, slugging Cutty Sark. He dispenses with the Doberman snarls that usually punctuate his hard drinking. The second night he camps in the middle of the loft in a bedroll. On the third day he starts ripping wallboard with a crowbar and claw hammer, cutting the dust in his throat with liquor and banging his chest like an ape to hammer out the cobalt sob. His side hurts, his face glows sickly orange, and he doesn't feel like smoking cigars.

It takes him four days to remember that the place had no drop ceiling when he left it. But now it does. Adjustable spotlights are recessed in acoustical squares. He finds a ladder and tears the ceiling down. He is astonished that fully three feet of room height have been restored. Good thing the stupid woman left him an illegal subtenant to beat up, even though he's properly miserable about that. The clatter brings a neighbor to the stairway door.

"You Alicia's new tenant?"

"Who's Alicia?"

"The owner."

"No, I'm a workman."

"Want some coffee?"

She's about forty, dyed red hair, finely muscled, definitely not of the attenuated Balanchine school.

"Thanks."

She goes down a floor and soon returns with a pot of coffee and some mugs.

"So what're you doing?"

"I think the owner wants to turn it into a Victorian whore-house. I'm gutting it for the pansies to decorate."

"You're the owner, aren't you? I could run it for you, don't I look the part?"

"No, you don't, you look like you dance so you won't cry."

"And you gut lofts for the same reason."

"It doesn't work."

"I'm Maya Dedekind. You wanna fuck sometime?"

"It would be a great honor, Maya, but I'm afraid I wouldn't rise to the occasion."

"Oh. Well, you could fuck me like a woman. I like women, don't you?"

"Yeah, I never have been able to figure out why they need men."

"There! We see eye to eye already. Don't you feel relieved?"

He does. He is amused, too. Maya Dedekind's a great babe, reminds him of Gerda von Reeperbahn.

"I'd disappoint you. Then you'd act like somebody shit in your hat and we'd both be hurt and we couldn't look each other in the eye and . . . . "

"Why don'' you just lick my cunt. I know all the rest. I'm not like that. Life is much too short. Everything's a gift. Stick out your tongue. Yeah, make it nice and pointy. Oh that will be lovely!"

Maya Dedekind pulls down her panties, hikes up her long hippie skirt and sits on a stool to reveal her pilot light. "You can't do it right if you laugh. Laugh later. See if you can laugh when I'm blowing you."

He's just beginning to enjoy her flavor when she says, "Oh God, I'm coming." She grabs his head and uses it. "I thought I'd have to instruct you, but you're a pro. I am too. Wait and see.""

He nods and smiles.

"You like how I taste? Here, enjoy these while I please you."

She wipes herself with her panties and dangles them in his face while she unbuckles and unzips him. Why is it, he wonders, women insist I'm a panty fetishist. I'm not, am I?

~

Sun storms mistake earth for a bell and ring it. Then rodents scamper crazily, insects learn new dances, epileptics seize. He's seen Saint Elmo's fire and ball lightning. He knows the feeling of change. It was good to have Maya Dedekind massage the gnawing under his sore ribs, reassuring to have sex without performance, but finally scary to think that after so many years in motion he's stopped. He hates the idea, but, camped in an arroyo of broken wallboard, too drunk most of the time to make a plan, hurting, he fights with the idea that whatever is wrong, even if it can't be fixed, ought to be identified.

If the *Vestris,* owned by two Greeks in an empty office in Rockefeller Center, had not picked up wines sold to American brokers in Algeciras he would have never thought of being here, much less would he have thought of it as coming home. But the Greeks needed a navigator, he had the ticket and the pay was good. He'd regretted it the moment she cast off. He planned to catch a pier-head jump to go back out to sea from Elizabeth, but something rang his bell, something made him crazier than usual. That's how he wound up here making sisterly love to Maya. He ought to pile the debris onto the freight elevator and get it hauled off, repair the brick walls, get his pain diagnosed, find some good cigars and Calvados, go to the bank, but his oil is yellow and smells foul, his fuel is full of algae, his cargo has shifted, he's down by the bow . . . hell, he can't even entertain himself thinking like this.

When he finally does get the debris carted off, he doesn't remember the furniture and he can't stand it. Alicia-What's-Her-

Face must have sold his furniture. Maya asks if she can have two chairs. He says no. She understands, but he doesn't. He calls back the hauler and junks it all. Now his Arab has a proper desert.

When he had bought his loft in the five hundred block of Broadway in Hell's Hundred Acres nobody had yet gotten the chichi idea of calling the old shirtwaist and junkyard section of Manhattan after London's Soho. Now it's chic, which is why the spartan Arzberg china and futon he buys would have cost much less on Fourteenth Street. He likes what has happened, the wine bars, galleries, performance spaces, street musicians and jugglers. It's gala, like a perpetual feast of San Gennaro, and, like so much else in Manhattan, paradoxical, because the old cast-iron district is inherently sinister, unlike the leafy West Village, which had always been simply called Greenwich Village.

He'll have to find some paintings, or maybe he'll hang charts everywhere. He feels good for a little while, contemplating this decorative idea. He even buys himself some Miami cigars made in the Cuban style—he'd been to Cuba often under foreign flag—but they make him ill, and he notices that liquor gut-punches him. Thinking maybe he has an ulcer, he buys a quart of milk, sips it patrolling the perimeter of his loft, then hits the futon between two windows.

Face to pillow, top eye shut, he hides under his nose, listening to his heart. Still at it, dear heart, he thinks. He'd never heard the expression until Rose called him that.

It's not really his nose but Auda abu Tayi's, whose entitlement to it had been established in the villa he built of Turkish railroad ties, or so it was reported by T. E. Lawrence. Now he sees Auda's Bedouins, their bolt-action rifles slung rakishly on their shoulders, nudging their camels down the dark side of it, tickling him, and he scratches it. It is his nose. He has simply to earn it differently. True, no Kennington had memorialized it in art, no Lawrence temporized under it, and he's certainly not a shaykh, but it's as fine a Saracen beak as ever darkened Christendom and he will not let Auda, that old thief, have it, a healing thought.

He tries to go back into that alpha state where before waking we are reconciled to ourselves. But the way is barred: what he had understood so perfectly eludes him. He remembers he failed last month to send Ute-Britt money, a crucial ordering element in his life. He washes and sets out for the bank. But on the third to last step to the street—he likes to climb and descend the stairs for exercise—the ground falls away. He clutches his side and lurches down into the cell-like foyer and crumples. Eventually he sits up against the wall, sweating and spasming in excruciating pain. His tongue feels too big to be useful. Maya Dedekind finds him on her way to the grocery. She has little trouble hauling him up and slinging his arm around her shoulder. She lugs him out onto Broadway and hails a cab.

The driver queries her with a look in his rearview mirror, a mannerism that amuses her. "Saint Vincent's? It's your choice, lady. Somebody shoot 'im? Saint Vincent's good at that."

"Good at shooting people?"

Even Bo, hurting, enjoys the repartee. There are, he knows, worse ways to die.

"Saint Vincent's . . . step on it!"

"Y'know, lady, I was wondering just the other day if anybody was ever gonna say that t'me."

"So are you a playwright or something?"

Dog-legging his way up into Greenwich Village as Bo gasps in pain, Cesar Aponte explains his true profession as if he thinks it might heal his beet-faced passenger. What he really does, he says, is to tell stories to children in libraries and foster homes. He's a storyteller. Sometimes they're stories his mother told him back in Puerto Rico, sometimes they're stories he's read, and most of the time they're stories he makes up. "Like this one, lady, I'm gonna tell a story about you and your friend. I dunno what it's gonna be, but I'm gonna make it up. When I get goin' there's no stoppin' me. Kids gotta have stories. Did you know that?"

~

By the time they wheel him shivering into the recovery room, his legs banging the bars of his gurney uncontrollably, Bo has made the acquaintance of Cesar Aponte, Arawak shaman, frightening but somehow beneficent. The shaman stands over the gum-chewing anesthesiologist making sure he earns his money. Now the shaman stands by his gurney shaking rattles violently and conjuring Carib gods. And it's he who arranges for Bo to fall asleep in this acidic place.

Maya walks into his room shaking snow off her coat. It's a long Navy officer's surplus coat that sets off her red hair. "That's quite a bag of marbles they took out of you, Bo. Now you've lost your marbles as well as your gallbladder. Feeling better? You looked like a painted clown. You have acute pancreatitis. Liver shoe-leatheritis. Got any relatives you want me to call?"

"Got a mother over on Beekman Place somewhere."

"Want me to call her?"

"Did you know there are more than eighty snowflake shapes? And it's not true at all that no two flakes are identical; it's just improbable that anybody's going to see two identical flakes. Some of them look like bullets, others like ferns. The shape we always think about at Christmas is a dendritic crystal . . . . "

"And you could go on like this?" This is the instant Maya Dedekind decides Bo is not a serious person. He will never get down to business. He will go to great lengths never to get down to it. She is so overwhelmed by the sadness of her discovery that she flees his room without her coat and he has to bring it home with him a few days later when the hospital discharges him. She had desperately wanted Bo Cavalieri to be a serious person, because he is in so many ways a promising person.

He knocks on her door. Then he hands her the coat with an expression so rueful that she almost glimpses his soul, but instead of holding his eyes and inhabiting the moment she steps back and invites him in for coffee. He steps in and asks for Scotch. When he's thrown back his shot and bared the obligatory snarl, he says evenly, "This doctor said he had a look at my liver and figured it's about to give out. He gave me three to six months unless I stop drinking."

"I see you're taking his advice."

"He didn't offer any. Good man."

Maya isn't going to offer any either. A man has a right to drink himself to death. What he doesn't have is a right to be seductive doing it. Then again, there's a seducer and a seducee. She'd given Cavalieri her best shot. She doesn't intend to sink with him. New York is full of gifted alcoholic murderers; it's up to you to decide whether to be the stand-in victim. She will not stand in for somebody over on Beekman.

What saddens Bo most about this is that he sees that he and Maya Dedekind share the ability to close the gap in an instant between what we perceive and what we do about it. Most people wander all their lives in that debris-filled limbo. He fears he's come back to Manhattan to wallow in the gap, to muck about in the shallows and to wind up poked with sticks on the beach after decades of wisely keeping to the deep.

"Gotta rip up some floor. See ya, babe."

"Sure, Bo."

20

He knows his short-term memory is slipping, but it seems to be replaced by the recovery of things he'd forgotten, and one of these is a remark of Peter Tomlinson's one night on *Morgaine's* bridge. "Are you a religious man?" Peter asked.

"I was raised an Episcopalian, for a time anyway."

"Yes, but are you religious?" Unless on duty, Bo never feels obliged to answer a question and he didn't answer Peter's.

"My religion is this, Bo: there are subatomic relationships that rule everything we do, everything that happens—relationships between people, between animals, between sentient beings and the inanimate—and you might consider this knowledge God."

He wishes he'd pursued this conversation. He'd ask Peter if this is what Giordano Bruno meant when he wrote of star beasts. Is God the fifth element? He'd ask Peter if he thought this is what Mary Baker Eddy meant when she said God is all in all. He would . . . he is overwhelmed by his nostalgia for Moira Sayre and Peter Tomlinson. How, he still wonders, could he ever have made that relationship work? He rubs the sob in his chest that hurts more than his torn gut, more than pancreatitis. He can't remember Maya Dedekind's telephone number, he can't remember his own, but other things rush back to him so vividly he doesn't think he can bear it.

~

He sits on the low stoop in front of his loft building, his sketchpad on his knees. He is sketching nothing. His eyes bombard his brain without mercy. Its filters crumble. Memories of Moira's sea tang, Ute-Britt's Baltic zest, Rose's magnanimity fail to whet his dying will. The stars and planets still populate his navigator's mind, which desperately chucks pieces of his life through its windows to make more room for them. His brain is a ransacked and darkening room. His home is not eleven stories above him, it's Lahkdar's attic where he hangs in the frugal light forever foreign.

Everything—yellow cabs, green buses, artists carrying their canvases, vendors heading home, girls drying their nails in the evening light—is beaded the way a slow-timed camera paints a continuum. There's nothing to sketch. No need for the stars constellated in his mind. No room for memories.

Could you be Amir Cavalieri?

I could try.

~

He has maybe three months before his liver seizes—that's what they told him—and he won't go out cheap. That means Islay's best and the kind of Calvados you have to hunt up in Madison Avenue specialty shops.

He imagines clown makeup running down his neck.

If the sun rises over Brooklyn, making its brick waterfront a kiln, why doesn't it penetrate the East River? Sunlight ricochets, shipworms croak, but down in its bottom his mind toils in the eel nests.

He knows a lot about Manhattan's watery frame. His first marine job when he joined Columbia's notorious legion of drop-outs in his third year had been on a bottom-sucking hopper dredge in Wallabout Bay, an East River elbow that forms part of the Brooklyn Navy Yard. He'd gotten the job by getting white-eyed on boilermakers with a bunch of dredgermen on Tenth Avenue. He remembers their tale of sludge bubbles spitting up human bones. Sometimes in August the sludge seethes and spits up bubbles violently. It used to be Sunday sport to go out on the Gowanus Canal coal and lumber quays to watch the black oily bubbles. But of all the fish that survive mankind's monumental contempt—the cunners, tomcods, sturgeon, shad and so many more—only the male eel thrives in all seasons, like vampires, nocturnal feeders. In the summer they lay up in the port of New York's eight or nine hundred wrecks. They live in a foot of filthy water or ninety feet of clear blue water. The females—they're called roes—live in fresh water streams until they mature. Every fall millions of them run down the Passaic, the Elizabeth, the Rahway, the Hackensack, the Raritan and the Hudson to rest in the harbor before going to sea with the males to spawn.

In his binoculars he sees the stakes up along the shad rows during the Sunday he starts to obsess about the East River. He supposes maybe some of Joe Bonnano's boys fitted canaries and other selectees with cement-bucket shoes on the Brooklyn docks, but in general the East River is not one to pester with such chicken-shit endeavors. It's mean, intolerant and purposeful. He knows that damned well because he used to swim it when he was in high school and college. He never told anybody. Only his dog Fritzy knew, and Fritzy was long dead of Sandro's violent, drunken kicks. Fritzy was the only being he'd ever let himself miss until now. He mourns him. He and Fritzy used to walk along FDR Drive at night. He'd start at Nineteenth Street—Sandro and Ulrike lived on Nineteenth between Second and Third a few doors west of Columbus Hospital—following the river down to the gashouse district. The tugs showed a red eye heading up to the Harlem or the Sound and a green eye going down to the bay. Something in their deep growls and mournful groans and respect for the river got into his bones; he started to long not to work on them but to be like them, and when he watched them shoulder and bully ships out to Amboy Light he knew what to do. He started getting drunk religiously on Tenth Avenue until he made some buddies who got him into the National Maritime Union. By that time he'd run out of the words you needed at Columbia to prosper. He'd run out of the gamesmanship. He fell silent in his third year, cut classes unless they interested him, and finally gave up.

The swims kept him going. When he left the house and Fritzy and took a sour room over on Seventieth Street off West End Avenue he stopped the swims. He needed Fritzy there waiting for him and somehow he knew that if Fritzy wasn't waiting for him he had no need to return.

He had learned to swim in Great South Bay where only with extraordinary luck can a boy, even a klutz, drown. It seemed to him that most of the boys and girls at Cairnhall in West Islip knew how to swim. He assumed it was because most of them were English. They had been sent there to escape the war. He assumed they were superior people and in that little outpost of empire in West Islip they did all they could manage to encourage his assumption. Lottie Donovan, being Irish, did not. She couldn't very well imbue the little eight-year-old wog with the comfort of her Catholicism, but she was convinced Rudyard Kipling's well-worn poem, "If," would serve him better than the impostor Church of England's eucharist and prayer book. Kipling's imperialism substituting for the eucharist was an irony lost on this most compassionate of women. He'd been at Cairnhall almost three years when Lottie arrived. She saw a little green-eyed wog drowning in the midst of English aplomb and took him on as her project, which meant teaching him how to swim. He had no athletic proclivities that anybody had identified, except that he had been known to key Georgie Stankowicz's roller skates onto his shoes on Carroll Street in Brooklyn and go careening suicidally down towards the railroad bridge.

That was the year Ulrike decided he was becoming his grandmother Huldah's son and shipped him off to Cairnhall.

Lottie saw two things about Amir: he was defenseless, and his head was tight and aswarm with tears. But he proved, against all evidence, to be a natural athlete. Just as this bluff and earthy Irish woman was tucking Amir under her wing, Cairnhalls's black cook, Stella Kidwell, Cairnhall, noticed that her youngest boy, Bobby, a scrapper if ever there was one, had taken a shine to Amir and was following him around.

These two women had some things in common. Lottie lived and taught at Cairnhall to provide her daughter Pat with a good education, albeit more British than she would prefer. Stella lived in little more than a shack nearby and accepted poor pay to earn the same education for her two boys, Bobby and Kenny. Lottie called up the pluck in him, but Stella enthralled him with the dignity of the underdog. No one at Cairnhall, no matter how well bred and educated, had her gravitas. She was the mother he would have chosen for himself, and because Bobby and Kenny sensed this they admitted him to a brotherhood of boxing and baseball. They were fellow outlanders. Bobby, who was nine at the time, had a round cherubic face, mischievous and quick. Kenny, twelve, was of another cut, aquiline, dour, immensely reassuring to him. Stella had never told her boys they had different fathers. She let Bobby's ne'er-do-well father take the rap.

The outcome of the attentions of these tolerated women was that Amir became over time an accomplished swimmer, catcher, ice-hockey player and boxer. But he knew nothing about boxing the day Lottie Donovan actually took him in tow, not yet. She became his first boxing coach and only then turned him over to the Kidwells. Her break came on the day he returned from an ice-skating outing with a shiner. It seems some of the local boys started to taunt him and Dacia Wadeleigh about their parentless state. He got into a shoving match with Johnny McKewn, whose father owned the Kozy Korner bar and grille, and Johnny popped him one.

"And what did ye do then, lad?" Lottie asked. He didn't have to answer her. It was obvious he had just started to bawl. "Mind yourself," Lottie said, "it was not a toward thing to do." He broke into an idiotic smile because he loved new words and words used in new ways.

"Toward?"

"Yes, not toward means it bodes no good, lad, it bodes ill. Bodes ill for you. Here, let me tell you what you must do. You go down to that scurrilous place and when Mr. McKewn asks you what you want, you say you want to speak with his miserable Johnny. When Johnny comes out, poke him in the eye. He's not going to like this very much because he's a bully, so there will be a few seconds before he decides what to do. That's when you sock him straight in the belly, like this. If he doesn't bawl—and I think he will—you straighten him up like this"—she showed him an uppercut that was more like a bolo punch.

He marveled at Lottie's instruction. He marveled so much he was halfway to Kozy Korner before he got scared. But he would rather take another pounding from a bully than disappoint Lottie Donovan. He did exactly as she told him, but the bolo proved unnecessary. Johnny McKewn folded up on the floor and retched and bawled out of proportion to the velocity of Amir's punch.

"You filthy little bastard, is that what they teach you in that Limey fen?" said Mr. McKewn.

Lottie Donovan feasted out on this story for months.

"Limey fen, did he say then!" she said with glee, because of course she agreed. He always considered that the chief benefits of this encounter had been to learn the secondary meaning of toward and the primary meaning of fen.

He asked Lottie one day if there could anywhere be an untoward fen.

"Well, I suppose if yer a piggy," she said. He did thereafter, at dire times, regard Cairnhall as an untoward fen.

He regretted years later—and regrets now—that he never sought out Lottie and Stella, Bobby and Kenny, to tell them he had become a frogman.

~

Slowly, as the shad and sturgeon begin to need the Hudson, as certain persons crowd a room, an idea fills his mind, and the idea begins to stalk and kill every other idea: swim the East River at each coordinate. What does at each coordinate mean? He doesn't care. He feels the peace of peasants when their lords break their swords on each other's heads. Like a peasant he goes about his business, which, if he were asked, he would say is to die well. He goes over to Maggiani's chandlery on Dover Street in the fish market district and buys two charts, the Hudson from Sixty-Ninth Street to the Battery and the East River from Tallman Island to Queensboro Bridge.

He isn't sure he can do this without Fritzy. Fritzy, so named because the young Bo saw that he had been born in a black and white SS uniform, was always there guarding his clothes when he got back, looking as if he'd never had the slightest doubt his friend would be back. During all the years he had been a frogman he imagined Fritzy waiting for him. The worst thing he'd ever done was to leave Fritzy on Nineteenth Street with Ulrike and Sandro. Fritzy lived eighteen years and might well have lived longer if Sandro hadn't given him a vicious kick under the table one night in a drunken fit. It was many years before he heard from Ulrike how Fritzy had died. He was grateful not to have heard it sooner or he would have killed Sandro.

His first choice, a two-hundred-and-fifty-yard passage from Forty-Third Street to Belmont Island, a heap of riprap defending a flashing green navigation light, conforms to the methodical way he pursues his profession. Far and away the easiest passage he can make, it has the advantage of giving him the option of swimming back to Manhattan or going some three hundred and fifty yards more to the pier at the foot of Forty-Eighth Avenue in Long Island City. He chooses an outgoing tide to help him reach the island. If he makes it to Long Island City it will suggest he is a still a strong enough swimmer to breast the tide coming back.

Until he stuffs his wetsuit, face mask and boatswain's knife in a gym bag and heads that evening in mid-April to Forty-Third Street to scope out the site and see where he might conceal his clothes and climb up out of the river, he forgets this isn't where he'd crossed the river as a boy. He chooses it because it's logical. When he gets to Forty-Third Street he realizes his boyhood swims started downtown between Twenty-Third and Twenty-Fourth streets.

Standing near Forty-Third Street over iron rungs bolted into the concrete revetment at his feet he recognizes a problem that apparently hadn't bothered him as a boy—tugboats. At this hour, ten-thirty, there aren't many pleasure boats, but he's already seen and heard two growling tugs greeting each other. Probably there were more tugs when he was a boy. New York was no longer as busy a port as it had been.

He jogs around in a loop for about twenty minutes to warm up, nips some brandy and enters the water. He swims slowly but strongly, stretching his muscles and making sure he keeps his line of sight. A two-mile swim in the Navy had been duck soup. He reaches Belmont Island easily and scrambles up to the flasher, which is fouled with guano. He sits long enough to watch a northbound tug make the east passage and then heads for Long

Island City. There he jogs in place a while, shakes himself out and heads back. His left calf cramps during the lap between the island and Manhattan. He resolves to undertake a stretching regimen.

Back at his loft he gets out the chart and a divider. The swim from Twentieth Street just below the sewer outlet to Greenpoint is some eight hundred yards. He whistles in wonder. Nowhere to stop. Kid must've been a hell of a swimmer. He would have had to swim northeast across the Poorhouse Flats Range to a red flasher at the foot of the Greene Street pier. Even if the kid had used an incoming tide to get there he would have had to swim against the tide coming home. Something stuck in his craw. It was that he'd thought of the word home. Living with Ulrike and Sandro in that hellhole of drunken shouting and banging was not a home. Had Cairnhall been home? Had living with his grandmother Huldah over on Carroll Street in Brooklyn been home? Hell no! Home was whichever ship he was on. And now? He sits by the window, the chart weighted down at the corners with books on a coffee table, and rifles his mind desperately for a home.

~

Soon he's making the Belmont and Poorhouse Flats passages regularly. He's made each of them maybe five or six times by the time he adds Corlears Hook in early May. The hook is just south of the Williamsburg Bridge and the fireboat station. He swims the four hundred yards to the pier at the entrance to Wallabout Channel without difficulty, by now using sidestrokes, backstrokes, breaststrokes, crawls and any other stroke he can think of. Not bad for a dying man.

Nothing changes his opinion that New York is wickedly rich in beautiful women, but now he gives up his lifelong habit of sketching in watering holes because each woman who stares at him until he looks at her strikes him as more vacuous than the last, and if not more vacuous then angry behind a mask. He knows a lot about the angry women with Medusa's gaze and nothing about anger in himself. His neighborhood, infested with dives when he bought his loft, is surrounded now by trendy bars crawling with poseurs. He doesn't even know if Chumley's and Minetta's and the White Horse Tavern still exist, and he doesn't bother to find out. Besides, he doesn't belong where people aspire to a break.

But he doesn't seek out dives with genuine whores either. Instead he patrols the waterfronts, swimming, sipping Calvados, smoking cigars.

In short, he is in control, like all drunks think they are. He's doing something perilous every few nights. He owns the secret. It's power. He's in control of his drinking. He's not the sort of controlled drinker who takes pleasure in responding to others' confidences about their drinking problems with, "Well, if you can't handle it . . ." but he nonetheless takes pride in handling it. Everything is going well and nowhere. What is unusual about this is that he has spent his adult life going somewhere. The best testament to his control is that he's forgotten what the doctor at Saint Vincent's said about his liver. Well, not forgotten: he's holding Medusa's head under water, so to speak. She looks too silly that way to turn anybody into stone.

~

Byron swam the Hellespont because Troy looked out over it and he was a romantic. Bo has nothing in common with him except that they both had prepossessing mothers. If you'd asked Bo what they had in common he might have said they both had mothers and let it go at that. But he's as driven to swim Hell Gate as Byron the Hellespont, and Hell Gate is more dangerous. He loves the name. It gave birth to his lifelong obsession with charts. Does it mean that if you're heading north you have to negotiate the gate of hell? What does that say about Harlem, the Bronx, Rikers Island, Connecticut and the Sound? Does it mean that if you're heading south for Manhattan and the Atlantic you have to deal with hell for the privilege? Are you entering hell or leaving?

He sits down with his chart of Tallman Island to Queensboro Bridge and studies. He's looking at five-knot currents and what the hydrographers rather blandly call swirls, mean suckholes fully capable of dragging you down to old wrecks. He wants to swim the eleven hundred yards from Horns Hook at Ninetieth Street to Hog Back on Wards Island. But there are two easier courses: a short lap from Rhinelander Reef off Ninety-Second Street to Mill Rock and then six hundred yards to Hog Back, or a five-hundred-yard swim over to Halletts Point in Astoria and another five hundred yards to Hog Back. The swirls and current would be worst making the eleven-hundred-yard run east of Mill Rock. He isn't daunted by the dicier course, but he wants to live to gloat. He resumes the nonsense dialogue of his childhood. "So whuddya wanna do? Doo-wah, doo-wah. So whudda we do?"

"Whuddaya wannabe?" He is sniffing Moira's fragrances about the loft like a hound and rubbing the sob in his chest, which can be drowned by drink but is otherwise ineradicable. To a huge awning window he says, "Whuddaya wannabe?" Immediately it strikes him as an adult concern, not something a child would give a damn about, and yet he remembers that he often asks himself just that, and no sooner he remembers than the answer comes, creeping into his mind like a frogman with a knife in his teeth and a grenade in his hand: he wants to be Moira's fragrances. All of them. Not just her saline sweat, her ammoniac pee, her acid lubricity. What an ambition. He approves it so much he laughs and fetches a cigar and some Calvados.

When he's ensconced in the roomy window sill, launching smoke dirigibles toward New Jersey, only then he savors that he's never once wondered where Moira is. His clock stopped in a cabin one night aboard Morgaine.

"So whudda we do?" He launches another dirigible and knows. This is a great endeavor, he thinks. I have something to do. I know this isn't home. I know where home is. It brings things here and takes things away, and yet what I have to do I have to do here. But what is it? What the hell is it? He falls asleep in his clothes asking the question.

"If you don't get it it's because it's not time for you to get it. Don't worry. I'm gonna explain it to you another way. If you still don't get it, I'm gonna explain it again because I like you. But if I don't like you, you're fucked."

"What if I don't like you?"

"You're fucked."

It was one of his favorite conversations. He had it years ago with Stamos Vafiadi, the vagrant Greek seaman who taught him navigation. Each mind is so quirky that it accepts a thing in certain ways and not others, from certain people and not others, at certain moments and not others. Bo's star gate was very narrow and bitterly guarded by his demons, but a guileless man like Vafiadi could pass through it without challenge. He tries to remember how they became friends. It eludes him till morning. He had been drinking in a crowded little hutch on the Bari waterfront when Vafiadi asked if he could sit down at his table.

"You like my cap, Yank?"

"I fuckin' hate it."

"You wanna know how come I know you're a Yank?"

"No."

"I think maybe we're gonna be friends, you and me."

"You know what I hate about Greeks?"

"This is gonna be good, I think."

"They don't know when to shut the fuck up."

"You must be a radio officer."

"I'm not any officer."

That was a lie. He was a third mate, the chief mate's gofer. He was also a damned good cargo officer, having a draftsman's sense of space.

"How you hate my cap?"

"You speak pretty good English for a Greek."

"I sling a lotta hash on Second Avenue. You gonna answer my question or what?"

Vafiadi motioned the waiter to give Bo another drink. He suggested Metaxas, which didn't improve his standing with Bo, who detested Greek brandy. But a man who bought you a drink before payday was entitled to maybe one answer.

He leaned forward to see if he could find anything to like. "There's a certain kind of middle-aged jerk-off with a gray beard, a ferret's face and a tic who haunts every goddamn marina in the States wearing one of those damned things."

Vafiadi looked as if he'd just come down from Delphi with a sacred trust. He stared into Bo's face for some time, leading Bo to think the man didn't have enough English to understand what he'd said.

Then Vafiadi started laughing. Pretty soon he was laughing so hard he was blowing snot out his Olympian nose.

"Jesus Haich Christ, Yank, what a rotten fuck you are—I ain't never gonna be able to wear one of these things again, and m em. Now I gotta get me one of those." He pointed to Bo's watch cap.

"Yeah, well, at least you can keep this on in a blow."

21

The sun bubbles up from Brooklyn. He wakes and undresses. How did this man in his mirror become a clown? He has the melancholy but not the desire to humor or the need to be liked or the concealed impulse to stick it in someone's ear. He's been under sentence all his life. If he'd stayed home listening to the telephone and waiting for the mail he'd be dead already. He goes out to the kitchen area, slugs down the last drops of a fifth of Cutty Sark, then showers.

By then the antennae of east Manhattan are clawing the sun. He pops a Heineken. It tastes like chemical waste. He rubs his side not to assuage pain but to assure it of his friendship. He's found a magnificent friend and must not let him down.

~

Being in control isn't emboldening, it's steadying. He doesn't think he can cheat death. Not even when he swims Hell Gate the long way from Rhinelander Reef to Hog Back east of Mill Rock. A man less accustomed to death might say to himself, You just swam eleven hundred yards across Hell Gate and back, so forget what that dickhead at Saint Vincent's said, but he understands how worthy of respect death is. A man can swim Hell Gate and die soon enough of a shoe-leather liver and not industrial waste, and he knows it. And with pancreatitis the cosmetician is just giving you an advance look at the clownishness of it all. So he swims across Hell Gate three times and back for the hell of it, looking for the suckholes, floating motionlessly when tugs pass so as not to catch anybody's notice. He swims in May, when nothing smells quite as hopeful as wet pavement, when the night clouds reflect infernos and the lights on the bridges look like dandelion seeds. He swims face down, stroking powerfully, rolling over on his back, shouting hoo-yaw and continuing.

The Belmont Island and Poorhouse Flats courses are in their own way as dangerous as Hell Gate. Most shipping shrugs off the continent and veers eastward away from the Rhinelander Reef - Hog Back line, but crossing the muscular East River at Poorhouse Flats means putting yourself in the way of cruise ships, police and fire boats, ocean tugs and their strings of barges.

Still, he likes this passage better because it reminds him of Fritzy and their nocturnal companionability when he had finished his homework and was eager to see life that might be less violent. This was before television. Television might have given him a reprieve from Ulrike and Sandro and their drunken fits.

By the end of May he's as used to scurrying up the rocks on Belmont Island as the possum-sized rats. Actually he does it better. He's amused to see the rats clawing, scraping and cheeping as they slide backwards into the water.

He has perhaps crisscrossed the river at this point a dozen times when he sits one morning before dawn watching Long Island City's horizon line turn faintly green as if a huge emerald sun has perversely set in the east. He is nipping a pint of Cutty and talking to Fritzy as if his old friend sat behind him with his chin resting on Bo's shoulder, as Fritzy often had. Manhattan is for Bo, as for so many others, a fiery end-time engine. The artist George Bellows, hypnotized by Manhattan excavations, intended to scratch hell, but Bo, like Giordano Bruno, the magus burned by the church in 1600, ushering in the modern world, is inclined to think of star beasts lumbering in the vasty universe. Although Manhattan's lume—its uproar of light bouncing off its cloud cover, concealing the stars—prevents contemplating the stars, you know better in Manhattan that they're there. In Manhattan you hear them grunt and paw, sing and mate. But he can't imagine the artist to say so, not even Bosch. So he sits at the tip of Forty-Third Street attending the dawn, wondering what Vermeer would have done about that big Pepsi sign.

On many a dog watch he'd imagined the stars spinning out of their courses. Particularly Sirius, the Dog Star, the Bright Star, the one he had importuned to quit its course—and there had been times when he, like Bruno, knew the stars responded. But he isn't that angry now, he isn't angry enough to manage the heavens.

Because he thinks of beasts, his right shoulder, the one that's the closest to Sandro and Ulrike's place on Nineteenth Street, shudders as he remembers charnel Sunday nights when hung-over hunters brought in their deer and bear carcasses for Sandro to skin. Sandro, who had made a tidy little fortune in real estate with some help from his friends and didn't have to work, persisted in his first profession as a taxidermist. He relished cutting the hides away. That done, he'd salt them, turning them into boards that could be stacked in layers. Then he'd build manikins of excelsior and wire. It was a point of pride never to stock manikins.

"I'm not a manufacturer, I'm an artisan," he'd say. Each manikin had to be different, a foot poised, a head turned, a neck craned. When the manikin was built, the skin would be softened and stretched over it. Mouths and eyelids were waxed and painted. Glass eyes made in Germany were fastened with wires. Hooves were painted. Sandro liked to ridicule the hunters. "Whuddid you use on this guy, a machine gun? Why dincha just throw a grenade at him?"

The hunters took it because Sandro was the best taxidermist in New York and because they knew he didn't give a damn. Besides, he looked like a man who had friends.

Bo, irradiated by the green horizon, stunned by booze and pain, spins and becomes a vortex, pulling in terrible images from Nineteenth Street: bloody carcasses, slabs of venison, stacks of hides, doors banging, mountains of food and opprobrium heaped democratically, everything awash in shouts, Silver Label Kinsey, homemade marsala, zinfandel, naptha, benzine.

His fingers spasm. They're strong because, coming from Cairnhall to live with Sandro and Ulrike when he was fourteen, he'd sewn hides into rugs after school. He used big three-sided needles and drove them through the scar tissue of polar bears by pushing the skin down on the needle and using a three-finger vise to pull the needle through. He worked on huge planks riddled with needle pocks. He learned to cut away worn or discolored surfaces, make patterns of good fur and sew them into the excised areas. He dreamed about polar bears slapping each other across the arctic wastes. Sandro made half-heads and snarling three-quarter heads of papier-mâché for these rugs. The plaster molds in which these heads were made were stacked floor to ceiling in the basement, making it look like a primordial cave. The soaked fur was stretched over the casts and held in place by brads. Purple wax tongues were glued into place. Sandro was famous in the trade for making snarling heads of bears and cats. Besides the bears, others inhabited the four-story building: cougars, pumas, leopards, cheetahs, panthers. But Bo's specialty was to repair hides, baste in batting and cover it with twill or felt linings with a discreet up-and-down stitch. Often, too, he would open these linings with a razor blade so that the hides could be cleaned. They were taken down to the basement, soaked and nailed onto drainboards. Benzine and cornmeal would be rubbed into them and they would be put into a huge drum to shake out the corn meal. Then they would be stretched with nails on the drain board, scrubbed with soap and water, flushed and left to dry.

Sandro was forever recasting the molds to get better snarls. He would rise about six-thirty each morning, stomping into the kitchen wearing only an undershirt, his balls banging his thighs. In the kitchen he'd gargle down three-quarters of a water glass of Kinsey. Then he'd go to a mirror to practice his snarls. When he found one he liked he'd go upstairs to the loft and translate it into a mold. He can't remember Sandro heading first for the toilet. What kidneys!

He throws up suddenly, as he reaches inside his pea coat for a cigar. Then he feels a hand on his shoulder. In the two seconds before he turns he knows he's ill because he doesn't think to wheel around or jab his assailant with an elbow. He simply turns his head and looks up blankly.

"So what're you doin' here?" The cop looks bemused, as New York cops often do.

Bo stares at him. He's still pulling in subatomic particles. The cop studies his face. It isn't belligerent.

"Let's keep it simple. What's your name?"

The cop's demeanor is reassuring. I'll tell him my name, tell him I've had a bit too much to drink, I'm sorry, I'll go home now. But he can't get it out. He sort of burbles, but he can't form words. He waves his hand to beg the cop to give him a few seconds. But it's no use, he can't come up with his name.

"Okay, pal. Don't get upset. You don't know what you're doin' here, you don't know your name, that's fine, I feel that way most of the time myself. I'm just gonna reach into your jacket here and get your wallet. Then we'll see what's what. Okay?"

Bo nods. The cop pats his ribs, then reaches for the single pocket on the right side of his pea coat. Finding nothing, he pats Bo's pants pockets.

"So we got a little problem here. How 'bout I look in your gym bag? That okay with you?"

Bo nods. The cop holds up Bo's wet suit.

"You been swimming in this river? Hope you got a tetanus shot. You got some kinda fancy gear here."

"I went over to Belmont Island. Then I went over to Forty-Eighth Avenue. I came back the same way."

"To Forty-Eighth Avenue?"

"Long Island City."

"You swam over to Long Island City? Where's Belmont Island?"

"That little pile of rocks out there."

"You remember your name now?"

It's on the tip of his tongue. He feels it should be. But it isn't. He begins to rock back and forth in pain and confusion.

The cop has seen this before. "Look, don't sweat it. What happens is you get a little too much on your mind, so your mind throws a few things out. No shit, that's what happens. It's like making a airplane lighter. Trouble is your mind don't tell you what it's throwing out, you gotta find out the hard way. Nice, huh? Why don't you just put on your shoes and we'll take a little ride and sort this out. I gotta tell you, I think it's a crime to swim the river, probably a misdemeanor or something. Just take it easy. Shit happens. I'm gonna help you."

He zips Bo's gym bag with its wet suit, fins and mask. He stretches and readjusts his belt, his revolver, nightstick and handcuffs. When his gaze returns to Bo he sees that Bo is having trouble tying his shoelaces. He has an inspiration.

"Jeez, my watch stopped. What time's it, pal?"

Bo looks at his watch. Then he stares at it. Finally he takes it off, turns it around and tries to read it that way.

"Lemme see, five-thirty. Whuddya say we go get ourselves a cup of coffee and then we'll talk to a guy I know who's a whole lot smarter 'n me."

Bo likes this cop. He's kind, the sort of professional Bo is. But what kind of professional is he? This chiseled Italian face before him belongs to a cop. Who does his own face belong to? The toxic river, that flood of solvents, has eaten his identity, his savvy. What's left? He does feel lighter, that's true. What's left feels lighter. He feels better. But the idea of coffee makes him retch. Maybe he's done what he came to Manhattan to do. Maybe it's over. Fine, he chucks his watch, his treasured Navy watch, into the river.

"Aw, jeez, didja hafta do somethin' like that? Ya need to know what time it is. This is nuthin', you're gonna get over it."

I am over it. It's over. But what's over? He feels as if he has nothing else to do. Wherever he goes with this amiable cop, whatever happens now, he doesn't need to swim the river again. And he doesn't need his watch. He doesn't need time. He doesn't need to look for coordinates or vanishing points. All that's over.

"Jan Vermeer!" Bo blurts out the name.

"Thas your name?"

Bo shakes his head.

"Too bad. Nice name. Who's he?"

"Dutch artist."

"You know 'bout art?"

Bo shakes his head.

The coffee tastes good. They chat about this and that all the way to Bellevue.

"I'm gonna leave you here with my friends," the cop says. "You're in good hands. They're gonna help you. You take it easy now." The cop pats his shoulder and starts down the corridor. He turns to one of the nurses and says, "Swam the damned East River back and forth, can you believe it? Nobody swims the East River. Oh yeah, his name might be John Vameer, couldja tell the doc that?"

22

Amos Perchuk, the young psychiatrist assigned to John Vameer, looks as if it's a mistake to look like Amos Perchuk. This intrigues Bo more than excavations captivated Bellows and for the same reason—it conveys an anomalous hell. Not that there is anything wrong with the way Perchuk looks. He's handsome, his vigorous black hair cascading down on a face full of chisel cuts. He comes from an exceedingly tactile family. His father, Simon, is a fabric merchant, always singing the praises of some new fabric, like velveteen. His wily mother, Ida, inherited a garment-making business and runs it ruthlessly. Perhaps Amos Perchuk's look of not quite inhabiting himself is a side effect of trying to escape the oppressive tactility of his father, always fingering, and his mother, always shaping and tucking. Something else Bo notices. Perchuk is a big man. He reminds Bo of cows he's seen up the Hudson in Echo Tarn twitching off flies in a pasture.

He begins to sketch Amos Perchuk after their sessions, first on napkins, later on paper Perchuk brings to him. Consternation is Amos's response to the first sketch. Then, on reflection, he feels rather guilty he doesn't find it funny—Bo has drawn Peter Rabbit with the face of a Mongol khan.

Amos asks him, "What does this mean to you?" Bo cocks his finger and draws a khan wearing Peter's face and brandishing a bunch of carrots. Bo asks, "What does this mean to you?" Amos says, "Putting the therapist on is SOP for not dealing with your own demons. It's called denial. I don't need to know why you swim an open sewer in the middle of the night with an oh-point-fourteen blood alcohol level, but you need to know. Maybe you could draw yourself a picture. Draw the swimmer, see what he's up to."

Perchuk chooses the phrase *draw yourself* carefully to underline his patient's need for self-knowledge. He doesn't miss his mark, but he hits it obliquely. Bo takes his remark in an unintended way. He's never drawn himself a picture, although he has drawn himself, albeit rarely. He draws others a picture of how a phantom apprehends them at a particular moment in their lives, and if he pretends to be more than a phantom he can't draw them at all.

His authority comes from his intent to elude its consequences. No wonder he became a frogman, a marauder. His sketches are raids, precise, surgical, elusive. He does not intend to be caught and more often than not he gives the sketch to his subject.

While Bo considers, Perchuk decides he's wrong to be so confrontative. Bo, he now sees, isn't withdrawn, he just prefers to communicate by drawing. If he wants to draw Amos Perchuk, what's the harm? He might ultimately say something that he, Bo, needs to know. He might even say something Perchuk needs to know. But who the hell is he? He gave his address but said he had no phone. Asked if he's married, if he has a family, he says he doesn't know. He can't remember his Social Security number.

Given time, Perchuk can make a military records check. Bo's tattoos suggest Navy service, especially the one that says Death Before Dishonor.

He finds Bo on the third morning leaning on a window frame, sweating profusely. His eyes look like egg yolks frying in fat. He shakes. "I had a bad dream. It felt like a dream, but I think I was already up. There were these big long turds with shiny tin wings. They were clicking across the ceiling single file. Shit birds. Honest to God shit birds."

"D.T.'s" Perchuk says. "Honest to God D.T.'s. They always seem like the most real, the most vivid dream you ever had. They are real. Delirium tremens—you're lucky it was only shit birds, coulda been pterodactyls picking at your liver." He drapes a blanket over Bo's shoulders. It's clear the man suffers from pancreatitis. Perchuk asks him, "Know why you drink?"

"I'd like to."

"Well, I think you drink to anesthetize pain. Yeah, you're an unlicensed anesthesiologist. I think you try to drown your demons in it. Demons are memories. That's their real name, generically. You're holding their heads down in booze, and I think you're getting tired. And even if you don't know you're getting tired, your body is telling you so. In fact, it's giving you a deadline."

"Yeah, I heard that before."

"That's where you got that fresh gall bladder scar, right? The doctor told you, you're killing yourself. They always look at the liver when they do a gall bladder. You've been sober for four days, how's it feel?"

"Like shit."

"Right. It's gonna get worse. Because if you stay sober it'll dawn on you that you're a child, a scared little child. I'd say you were a teen-ager when you became a drunk. When you get sober you're emotionally the age you were when you became a drunk. You don't do any growing up as a drunk. Can you picture it?"

"Well, not easily, Doc, I'm not an abstractionist. I don't do squares and doodahs."

"You don't like squares and doodahs?"

"I love them, they're what I do for a living, but I'm not talented that way."

"You do squares and doodahs for a living? Tell me about it."

Bo grabs a piece of paper, draws straight lines along the edge of another folded paper and triangulates them.

But he can't dredge up the meaning.

"You're an architect? A draftsman?"

"Doesn't feel right."

"Well, nothing does, which is why you drink. Drunks are not afraid to die, they're afraid to live. They're also very fucking angry, did you know that? Mean as horned vipers, every damned one of them, including the most waggish, charming rummy at the Algonquin. Keep that firmly in mind—drunks are mad as vipers poked with a stick. No matter what their shtick is, it's just that, a shtick. Drunks cannot be trusted. They cannot trust themselves."

Perchuk takes more time than he has with Bo. Filing people in Bellevue for thirty days' observation is only a street-cleaning operation. Perchuk is more interested in why he's interested in Bo than he is in Bo. He discovers the reason readily when he sees staffers showing each other the sketches Bo has made of them. They prize these sketches because each offers a pleasant surprise about its subject. Bo's hand unerringly finds a quality his subjects hide from themselves. This acuity, so well masked by Bo's taciturnity, draws Amos Perchuk.

He sets out on one more stratagem, non-electric shock. "I know why you swim in sewers," he announces on day nineteen. "You're practicing to die in your own shit. Tell ya how it works. The liver shuts down quietly. It's painless. It stops processing ammonia and mercaptans—so you die in the kind of crap a skunk sprays you with. Nice, huh? But there's a plus. When the liver fails the benzodiazepine in your gut goes straight to your brain and knocks you out. God is merciful."

Perchuk does notice for the remaining days of Bo's detention that his patient's eyes follow him.

The day of Bo's discharge Perchuk tells him, "If you're a veteran—I think you are—go to the VA hospital. You're in a lot of trouble."

Then Bo, a certified member of the immense tribe of John Doe, touches his arm, nods and leaves.

Outside the sun pops windows and cars with short white blasts. Everything looks too hot to touch. The people look as if they'll fall into heaps of ash if you approach them. He walks about a hundred yards away from the old hospital's entrance, turns around, and says, "Cavalieri, my name is Bo Cavalieri, what's it to ya?"

~

Some men and women are beset by the notion that a place or a time or both is lost to them, they can't inhabit it, because it belongs to someone with whom they've fallen out, someone who betrayed them. No matter how much they might love a place, they're outlanders, Ishmaelites, because of someone's prior claim. They stagger under the weight of this fixed idea. Bo knows about inherent vice. It's what seamen think of as each cargo's potential for disaster: each cargo carries with it a disposition towards a particular misfortune. But seamen also know how to lose themselves. They know the limitations of vision, the illusions to which distance is subject, the distortions to which space is subject, the size of a place. And so, mercifully or pitilessly, it doesn't occur to Bo that Manhattan belongs to Ulrike Theiss in her new penthouse on Beekman Place or Weybrandt Gundersen over in Weehawken. Manhattan is not verboten. No place is, not even Hamburg. Perhaps this is why the rash of graffiti afflicting New York now puzzles him. He understands political graffiti, slogans, but he doesn't understand graffiti as territorial dog piss. When it's artful he stops to admire it, but when it's spiteful, it strikes him as mindless and frightening. It's something new and yet familiar. He starts to wrestle with it. Or rather he's seduced into wrestling with it by his walking, brandy-guzzling tours.

He sticks a small sketchbook behind him under his belt and when he finds some cornice, some brick basketwork, some melée of roof angles, he stops and draws them. This exposes him to more girlfriends' names than he'd prefer, more expletives and vulgarities. He is, he realizes, walking into another dimension. Everything but not everyone takes on a sense of déja vu.

On the day of his release he thinks he might just follow the graffiti. Somewhere. It doesn't occur to him he doesn't know how to go home, doesn't know where home is. But Manhattan feels like home.

"So where to, Fritz?" he says. He begins to turn quickly to catch someone shadowing him, not in paranoia or fear but in hope. Finally he recognizes that Fritzy is supposed to be there, his tail curled up over his back, panting with the daft smile of the border collie, keeping up, always game. And by the time he realizes Fritzy ought to be there, leading him towards home, his legs give out and he sinks to the ground among the other drunks in Stuyvesant Park, knowing how much akin is the mindlessness of the aerosol scribblers to his own drinking, which began here, a few blocks away, so many years ago.

"Are you ready for the truth?"

Bo is sitting in the northeast corner of the park where he and Fritzy always sat. He looks his questioner hard in the face.

"No."

"It was a rhetorical question. I know you're ready."

"Will it help me tie my shoelaces?"

The derelict, whom Bo imagines wearing a White Russian cavalry officer's uniform, walks away. He walks maybe twenty yards, then he hurries back.

"Angels are subatomic events traveling light waves. I know that much, but from whence do they emanate?"

"Sirius A, Canis Minor."

He regards Bo gratefully. "I can't bear for them to see what we do."

Bo nods.

Alf Lindstrom, who it turns out taught mathematics at the Friends School facing the park until he was seduced by chaos theory, spends the night with Bo shuffling around Stuyvesant Park, wondering why Bo knows so much about the heavens.

23

He wakes under an Alba Superba magnolia's lemony spritz. Its lambent white blossoms yawn in the prematurely warm spring. He struggles to order his thoughts. That too proves premature, since he has none to order. The stoic Emperor Marcus Aurelius comes unbidden: "The good of a being is to follow its own nature." He sighs. Well, then, let's see if this being can remember how to tie his shoes. He can. He looks around and sees Alf Lindstrom still asleep under the south side of the tree. He still can't remember where home is.

He sits with his back against the tree and closes his eyes. Behind their lids he sees baboons, werewolves, moray eels and finally, like the moon passing through its phases, he sees himself, transfixed. And then distinctly he hears the words, *I am going to open up a way.*

Lindstrom wakes. They stretch, put themselves together and set out for coffee on Fourteenth Street. They stroll from Second to Third Avenue and part company. Both of them have things to do, although Bo can't remember what.

He passes the RKO and Academy movie houses—he remembers the last of the vaudeville shows—Luchow's, where the hard-living architect Stanford White wined and dined showgirl Evelyn Nesbitt and bought newspapers from a fourteen-year-old Sandro. He passes pinball arcades and hot-dog stands and comes to Union Square Park. He isn't that far from his loft, he recognizes these places, but his brain persists in mislaying his address. He turns north and passes the S. Klein bargain zoo. Already it brims

Djelloul Marbrook

with women elbowing and poking each other. He dog-legs over to Gramercy Park, passes the impresario Lincoln Kirstein's home on the park's east end, very near to where he lived with Ulrike and Sandro, and picks up Park Avenue. By now he has company: the swift Manhattans. First he construes them to be nineteen-twenties or nineteen-thirties phantasms, men slouching in fedoras, women wearing berets or ornithological Lilly Daché millinery and Hattie Carnegie simplicities. Dissatisfied with this, he makes them pre-Columbian inhabitants of Manhattan Island with clearer eyes, better ideas.

As he walks up Park he spies the severe Manhattan natives reconnoitering aloof knockouts walking their Salukis, or is it aloof Salukis walking their knockouts? He doesn't miss those smoky blondes; he foresees a race of androgynes. What those Salukis are good for, if anything, isn't licking muggers and rapists. In any event he has to rub them out; they belong to the late nineteen-forties or early fifties. He rubs them off the surface of his mind because he likes it that this feckless tribe of blonde hoity-toities with their Salukis has been supplanted by the drop-dead calves and pectorals of don't fuck-with-me babes walking down Second Avenue like Bruce Lee, supplanted too by dark-haired women whom he chooses to think of as Manhattan Arrabiata, spicy, punctuated by black olives.

The trouble with Hell Gate, he muses—he's using it now as a metaphor for all of Manhattan—is its disorderly lingerie. But that's a young man's plight, he thinks, seen by an older man; an old man's view might be hydrostatic. He thinks nine knots stately enough and safe. Fools dawdle. Hell Gate is uptown over in the right brain area. There! That feels better, he's getting his bearings. He feels Ulrike's terraced apartment where the river halts the grand march of Fifty-Second Street as a right-brain turbulence. He doesn't look.

The trouble with Hell Gate, he muses—musing to make sure it's in the past, behind him—is that it's a right-brain feature and can't be logicked out. He doesn't know what he's doing. His mind is staggering like a wounded animal, thrashing in underbrush, making cracking reports and thuds. Still the navigator, he veers hard over to port and starts walking west on Fifty-Third Street.

Soon enough the sinister cave mouth of the Museum of Modern Art, imploding behind the abbreviated Gothic Saint Thomas Church, comes into view. He rubs his pancreas out of habit, but it no longer hurts. He's thirsty but will settle for ginger ale. The trouble is his marrow; it has been replaced with lead. He's having trouble hauling his bones. Food, I need some food. But the idea sickens him. The usual sob in his chest is pumping itself up and gagging him.

The museum opens at ten. I'll grab a coffee and wait. Wait? Fuck art! I'm going down without a pump.

He and Fritzy often watched the grave Saint Thomas ushers in their dove-gray morning coats on Sunday mornings, just as they watched the swish toppers of Saint Bartholomew's on Park Avenue roll out royal blue carpets for wedding parties. These scenes never struck him as ostentatious but rather throwbacks to genteel times. The poor Anglican offices observed at Cairnhall seemed coal-mine fare compared to this proprietary pomp. But Bo is not in the best of times judgmental. The rich do not offend him for being rich, nor the poor for being poor.

You in there, God? Getta grip, you're beginning to think like sailors talk, through their assholes. It escapes him that he has stumbled on a piece of his identity: sailors.

He goes into Saint Thomas Church, stuffing his watch cap in his peacoat pocket. Guess you better wait for me outside, Fritzy. He sits down about four pews up from the narthex, a mile or two from the altar. He pulls out a kneeler to pray. He starts to pray but realizes he has nothing to ask for. Not personally anyway. If some of his memory has gone south, so what? World peace, yes, pray for that. He pushes the kneeler under the pew in front of him and sits back. A young man in a gray tweed jacket with leather elbow patches bustles about the altar, smoothing altar cloths, snuffing candles. He is blond and wears a clerical collar. Bo watches him with something like longing, because the young man has a something to do. Purpose is enviable. If he had his binoculars he'd use them. Bo watches him with something like hope as well as longing. Then he falls in on himself. He lowers his head, not to pray, but to drown. Tears plop on his knees. He pokes a teardrop with a forefinger as he might blood. His tears seem curious. Can they be his? When has he cried? Not in the Navy, not . . . since he cowered in his room off the kitchen listening to Sandro rage at everything and everyone—the cripple Communist Roosevelt, the crooks (by which he meant the government, not the Mafia), the goddam Irish and their corrupt mayor. His tears keep coming, stately, quiet.

The young priest leaves the altar and comes briskly down the center aisle to the narthex. Bo tries to smile or at least nod; he can't. His pants are soppy with tears. He can't find a handkerchief, so he takes out his cap and wipes his face. The young priest passes, stops, comes back and slips into the pew beside him and kneels on the bare floor. He pulls Bo down with him and he puts his arm around Bo's shoulder. He too touches Bo's tears on his pants and holds up his wet fingertips and says, "Lachryma Christi, if they're yours, they're his." Bo looks into the priest's face. It's beautiful, like a mirror that reflects not your body but your soul. He looks into the man's eyes for a long time. He thinks a forlorn, distracting thought: the older he gets the sadder he gets that the young cannot have wisdom. In any event it's not wisdom he sees, but transcendent love.

"Wait for me." The priest gets up. The words shake in red in Bo's mind, like Christ's in the gospels. Christ has told him to wait. When the young man returns he's taken off his collar. "Let's take a walk."

Down Fifth across from Saint Patrick's they buy hot dogs. "I'm Will Hallam. You?"

"Bo Cavalieri. Most people call me Bo."

"Why Beau?"

"Not Beauregard, Bo for bosun. I'm a merchant seaman."

The roulette stops at another piece of his identity, but he doesn't notice.

"Bo, a man in trouble is usually listening to doors close and doesn't hear one open."

"I'll tell you what I heard." Bo stops and leans against a granite building facade on the west side of Fifth Avenue. "I was in Bellevue—guess I'd been swimming the East River drunk and the cops took me there. I slept in a park when I got out yesterday. I remembered something Marcus Aurelius wrote when I woke up: The good of a being is to follow its own nature. Then I closed my eyes and saw baboons and werewolves and eels and the moon going through all its phases in a few seconds, and then I heard this: *I am going to open up a way.* That's what I heard."

Will Hallam smiles. "Yes, Bo, there is a way."

"I am the resurrection and the life?"

"Something like that."

They walk and talk the entire way down Fifth Avenue to Washington Square, through the morning into the afternoon.

At Eighth Street in Greenwich Village Will takes Bo's arm. "You're trying to run a very sophisticated engine on piss and vinegar. It can't be done. It's what's wrong with stoicism. When you grow up unloved from day one you don't have the proper fuel, that is a given. Your carburetion is no good. The more you improvise—using stoicism for fuel, for example—the more you splutter."

"How about booze?"

"Booze is anesthesia. You'd be surprised at how invested society is in keeping people drunk. Getting drunk is what you do instead of what you ought to do."

"Which is?"

"Deal. Take a good look at the hand you are dealt, make certain judgments about it, throw over the table if you like, anything except pretend that it's not disastrous to be unloved."

"Why did you mention stoicism? Marcus Aurelius's *Meditations* is sort of my Bible."

"Marcus, yes, well, I don't disparage him. But I have a name that'll do you more good right now. I know Marcus didn't tell you this, but stoicism is not a poor man's fare." He took out an address book and wrote something on the back of one of his calling cards.

"David Llewellyn?"

"Yes, he's a priest like me, and a psychologist unlike me. Actually in his Welsh heart I think he's a Druid. He's not an analyst—that's good for you, as you are not talkative. I'd like your phone number, I want to stay in touch."

Bo opens his palms in a gesture of helplessness.

"Forgotten? Not a problem. Promise me you'll see Llewellyn. I'll get in touch with you through him."

Now what will he do without this man's lovely face, his measured, engaging English accent, his love? He weeps and hugs Will Hallam for dear life.

~

Grotesques rope-dancing on the catenaries of Williamsburg Bridge wheedle him to drink. Panic scorches like reflux in his throat.

A pretty woman, vividly short of beautiful, smiles at him, cracking the brittle control of his demeanor and sending him on his way to see David Llewellyn. In that decisive, improbable prompting he sees a tangible stupidity lurking in the girl's look and it berserks him, tears at his liver like a ghoul, pounds his pancreas. He's afraid and angry.

It seems to him that all that's wrong in his life has flashed between a cheery stranger and a drunk: has he seen what he thought he saw? Stupidity granted beauty, beauty cursed with the grantor's meanness? Or has he projected and spoiled the spontaneity of her smile? He looks up, around; the street lights come on and he sees that the Williamsburg grotesques have leapfrogged the gashouse and Knish Alley and are squatting on the cornices around him.

By the time he drops a dime and hears David Llewellyn pick up he's ready to pipe a spiel: "Will Hallam gave me your name. I'm trying to stay sober. I'm sick. I'm scared. I don't know where I live. I need help. But if you're going to tell me it's all in my head, don't bother."

The silence at the other end comforts him. "Sounds like somebody's been fucking with your head. We'll see who that is and cancel that hunting license. Come on over, I'll wait. What's your name?"

He had it a few minutes ago, Will Hallam knows it. But it's gone. He fights back tears.

He wants to say guest boy, but "That's a problem," is all that comes out.

"I don't know about that. It's kinda refreshing, don't you think?"